ONCE *Upon a* SUMMER

PRAISE FOR MANJUL BAJAJ

'Bajaj writes with an unbridled candour that takes the reader straight into the rich emotional cauldron of the lives of her characters. And one cannot miss the awareness with which she chooses her words that convey the meaning intended so powerfully.'

—Deccan Herald

'Completely at ease with her material, Bajaj skirts dangerously close to stereotypes, only to spring a little twist that alters, quietly subverts, and in doing so provides a glimpse into human nature's profound ability to be lofty.'

—Outlook

'The unmistakable vernacular spirit—not only of her ancestral Punjab but of much of rural north India—comes to sensual life in the English fiction of Manjul Bajaj [...] The complexity of Bajaj's empathy for the poor and dispossessed prevents [her work] from crumbling into the sugary simplicity of sympathy.'

—Los Angeles Review of Books

'[Bajaj's work] reminds me of the rich literature evident in the writings of the progressive writers [...] She brings English to capture the nuances of the real India. Now only if other writers would venture that far.'

—Asian Age

ONCE *Upon a* SUMMER

MANJUL BAJAJ

HarperCollins *Publishers* India

First published in India by HarperCollins *Publishers* 2025
HarperCollins *Publishers* India, Cyber City,
Building 10-A, Gurugram, Haryana-122002, India
www.harpercollins.co.in

2 4 6 8 10 9 7 5 3 1

P-ISBN: 978-93-6989-497-0
E-ISBN: 978-93-6989-769-8

Typeset in 11/14 Berling LT Std
by HarperCollins *Publishers* India Pvt. Ltd

Printed and bound at
Thomson Press (India) Ltd

MIX
Paper | Supporting responsible forestry
FSC® C010615

This book is produced from independently certified FSC® paper
to ensure responsible forest management.

HarperCollins *Publishers*, Macken House, 39/40 Mayor Street Upper,
Dublin 1, D01 C9W8, Ireland

Dedicated to the memory of my uncle, A.D. Bajaj, and my father, Y.D. Bajaj, and to the many joyous memories of summers spent in Nainital thanks to them.

Thank you for the magic.

'[...] great love is never justified. It's like the little tree that springs up in some inexplicable fashion on the side of a cliff: where are its roots, what does it feed on, what miracle produces those green leaves? But it does exist and it really is green [...]'

—Wisława Szymborska

ALFRED

New York

1959

ALFRED A. ALLYE was finally coming around to acceptance. Nothing remained constant. Values. Priorities. Sensibilities. Tastes. The old order must cede before the new one can express itself freely. He took off his reading glasses and placed them on the desk, the gold-rimmed frame glinting against the dark mahogany wood. It was time for him to retire gracefully. He could see Norman Jr restless to be at the helm of affairs. His older son had been patient long enough, deferring to his parents' vision for their publishing house. With Rose gone, Alfred's own energy and enthusiasm were waning. He should let the next generation usher in the 1960s in their own style.

All around him was the intoxicating aroma of old books—peaty, mossy, redolent of vanilla and woodsmoke. Books, he mused, like flowers, filled the air with fragrance even in their dying. All along the book-lined walls of the alcove in the library where he was seated, he could see the titles that he and Rose had acquired, translated and published over the years.

From the large bay window of the ivy-covered brownstone, he could see the red maples on the sidewalk outside showing the first flashes of yellow and orange. In another month the whole street would be a blaze of red, the maples lined in a declaration of war against urban conformity, challenging the palette of greys and browns, of asphalt, brick and stone that ruled the city. Yet, however glorious the colours of fall, it was nature's rule that winter inevitably followed.

A clarity that had eluded him till yesterday came and sat upon his upturned palm like a butterfly, small but vivid. The time had come to hand over the reins of the publishing empire to his son Norman Jr. The world of publishing had changed rapidly in the years of the Great War. Alfred and Rose had been an integral part of the Council of Books in Wartime, the non-profit group that had spearheaded the notion of books as weapons in the war of ideas. Armed Services Editions, the small, pocket-sized, cheaply produced paperbacks, distributed to the troops between 1943–47 had changed the face of publishing forever. With well over a hundred million copies distributed, it could not have remained a mere ripple in the pond. The very waters were changed. Reading and books were no longer the exclusive preserve of the upper echelons of society. High-brow literature had crashed into the rag-tag world of cheap dime novels, and the turbulence was yet to die down. It was not clear to Alfred where it would settle, but the business of books was larger now and some of its innocence seemed permanently lost. Of late it was as much about lucre as it was about the love of books.

Large conglomerates from the newspaper and radio business were sniffing at the heels of family-owned publishing houses like theirs, eager to invest big money, increase the print runs exponentially, take books with newly designed covers (as garish as sin to his old-fashioned gaze) to the mass market, position them next to magazines, toothpaste and peppermint-flavoured chewing gum in drugstores and supermarkets. Norman Jr's eyes shone with excitement as he discussed the possibilities with Alfred. He had signed a slew of new authors to write romance and detective fiction with an eye towards instant bestseller-dom.

'Rose, I suddenly feel like an ageing horse on a steep incline. Not equal to the climb,' he whispered to the photograph of his wife. Her eyes sparkled from behind the glass of the sterling silver frame on his desk. Her lips were parted in the hint of a smile. A partnership of over fifty years had ended when she breathed her last in his arms, in her hospital bed. He would not have had it the other way around. He would not have wanted her to face the bleak, lonely, partnerless life that was his now.

Alfred was introduced to Rose on the steamship to New York by the captain of their ship, the *SS Alexandria,* over an informal evening gathering on the deck. He bowed to her and was rewarded with a smile, a timorous, momentary twitching of her coral pink lips. She was primly dressed in a high-collared gown, her hair braided and coiled in a firm high knot above her head. A personable young woman deliberately dressed to look older. And plain. There was a vulnerability to her which had piqued his interest.

The next morning, he noticed her alone at the deck, reading quietly. He walked up to where she was seated and bowed to her. She looked up with a guarded expression on her face, the slightest uncertainty playing in her eyes.

'We were introduced yesterday but ...'

Many introductions had been made at the captain's tea party the previous evening. It was perfectly understandable that she could not recall his name.

'Prince Alfred Asghar Ali at your service.'

'I'm Rose Eliot,' she stood up from the blue-and-white striped canvas folding chair she was sitting on and proffered her hand in a sensible handshake.

'You are travelling without a companion?' He had noticed earlier that she seemed unchaperoned. It was unusual for a young woman of her age and class to be travelling alone.

'Neither my mother nor my aunt could be spared as two of my older sisters are expecting to be confined later in the year. I have been offered a very attractive position with an American family in New York. One it would have been foolish to turn down for want of a chaperone. An English nanny is something of a status symbol there, I'm told,' she said. Again, that gentle half-smile transfigured her face. 'May I be so forward as to ask what takes a prince to America? Where are you from?'

'From a small, independent state located inside the north of India. Of course, we are loyal subjects of His Majesty, King Edward.'

'India! An Indian prince! My mother would have been delighted to meet you. My family has had a long association with India. As a matter of fact, I was born in London on the day of Queen Victoria's Golden Jubilee celebration. Mamma was in the spectator gallery watching the queen riding her gilded landau with six cream-coloured horses, escorted by the Indian cavalry. They were wearing unimaginably splendid uniforms. Mamma said she was so entranced by the ceremonial dresses donned by the Indian maharajas that she didn't realize …'

She stopped abruptly and blushed fiercely. She was embarrassed by the direction the conversation was heading in, the start of her mother's labour pains an unsuitable topic of discussion between them.

'Yes, I believe the Indian contingent found much favour with Her Majesty and the British public that year,' he said smoothly, ignoring her awkward pause.

'You must be travelling with a whole entourage of attendants. If there are any magicians and monkeys accompanying you, I would be very excited to see them!' she said, the merest suggestion of a smile lurking in her eyes.

He threw back his head and laughed.

'I'm sorry to disappoint you. I'm something of a prince in exile. Out of favour with my father's court and travelling alone like you.'

She looked at him with an open, interested expression, as if waiting for him to say something more.

'I will be honoured if you will agree to walk a few turns with me on the deck. I'll tell you about the intrigues in my father's state in exchange for the story of your life.'

'My life is not much of a story,' she demurred.

'Every life is a story. In fact, what are our lives but stories we tell ourselves?'

He was keen to know what life she was leaving behind her and what she hoped to find ahead.

She fell in step with him. They walked a discreet distance apart, conscious of the curious gaze of other passengers aboard, suddenly alert to their interaction. A shy young British woman. A personable gentleman, with the merest hint of something exotic about him. Apart, they were of modest interest to anyone. Walking together on the deck, conversing, they attracted a lot of watchful eyes. There were a few disapproving glances and many others just intensely curious.

He told her he was travelling to New York with an idea to set himself up in some business, distant from the intrigues of his father's little fiefdom. His mother was one in a sequence of many beautiful women who had captured the nawab's fancy. She had come to the court to teach ballroom dancing to the royal ladies but had ended up as one of them. Long years of benign neglect from the nawab had followed the initial years of sweet romance. Now his mother was dead, and there was nothing to hold him back in the small, fractious kingdom. His father had agreed to sponsor his passage to America, possibly relieved to have one heir less fighting for his seat.

Rose—he learnt from her—was the fifth daughter of a gentleman with a modest country estate in Sussex; her greatest asset was her education. Brighter prospects lay across the Atlantic for someone in her situation. She looked upon the chance of starting a new life in a new country all by herself as a stroke of marvellous good fortune.

'Better to stay afloat in America than sink to the bottom of the pond in England, as John Milton didn't say!' she laughed. 'See, I'm not even there yet, and I'm already hobnobbing with an Indian prince!'

Their shipboard courtship progressed rapidly, as if they were two kindred souls who knew each other from some other time and place. They shared a passion for books. Also, for printing and calligraphy, for maps and atlases, for old manuscripts and foreign literature.

It culminated in a small wedding on the ship. Rose wore a gown of dawn pink taffeta, graciously pressed upon her by a fellow traveller and altered to fit her by another. She looked certain and trusting as she said, 'I do.' The wedding was officiated by a clergyman who was travelling as a co-passenger. The ship's captain gallantly hosted a lavish lunch for all the passengers. There was a triple layered cake and a band playing music. They could not have wished for a better wedding celebration.

Their first few years in New York were full of challenges. Despite the princely suffix to his name and his light skin, acceptance had been difficult. A mixed-race couple was an anomaly in those times. It had taken them longer than they had hoped to settle in.

However, a few years of dogged perseverance later, Asghar and Rose had succeeded in setting up a small press operating out of a single room in Manhattan. Their first foray into publishing was a series for children called *Stories from Around the World*. It was Rose's idea and inspired by her deep knowledge of tales written in different European languages. To this stock, Asghar contributed his own cache of oriental folktales and myths. The fifty books in their first series were elegantly produced hardcovers, beautifully illustrated with black ink drawings, and translated from different languages.

Over the next few years, Prince Alfred Asghar Ali simply became Alfred A. Allye, Esq. Rose had not asked him or expected him to surrender his eastern heritage, his religion or his language. She had loved him for who he was. He had gone down the path of assimilation of his own volition, of his own desire to belong somewhere unequivocally, to not merely survive but to thrive in their chosen homeland. The change in the spelling of his name was just one more step in a series of big and small steps to start a new life.

From children's classics, the publishing firm had moved onto fiction, philosophy and poetry translated from European languages as well as Persian, Turkish and Arabic. Rose and Alfred carved for themselves a niche in producing high quality, eclectic and elegantly produced books. Fifty years later, they had ten different book imprints, editorial offices in twelve cities across America and Europe, as well as a marketing and distribution network spanning the English-speaking world. It had been a great run. Now it was time to sit still, yield control, go back in time and pay the past its dues.

Alfred walked to the floor-to-ceiling wooden bookshelf by the bay window and picked up the very first book they had published. It had aged with him. It smelt of times past and memories unfurling. A fragrance difficult to describe filled his nostrils. Like tinned tobacco or roasted almonds. Perhaps, like pressed flowers between the leaves of a poetry book. Something organic, feral, doused with associations. He stared at the small black-and-white logo, barely a square inch in size, of two horseback riders on a mountain slope and the epigram at the start of the book: *Life is a story we tell ourselves*.

It was time to revisit his own life, his own story—for Alfred to retrieve Asghar from the folds of his subconscious mind.

It was time to keep his promise to a young boy called Azeem from the princely state of Rannpur.

Fate had brought Asghar and Azeem together in a military camp in Baluchistan. Asghar had learnt of Azeem's love for a young British girl called Madeline and how that had led to his imprisonment and banishment to the military camp in the cold, brutal North-West Frontier. Asghar had wished to help Azeem escape, but his very help had failed Azeem at the end. Asghar remained to tell the story. Azeem was long gone. As if he had never been.

Now, with Rose's passing, there was no one to remind Alfred Asghar Allye of Azeem. It was up to him to honour the trust reposed in him. He would have to stir the dregs of his memory and pull out of the darkness the boy to whose courage and sacrifice he owed his life.

He brought out the dictaphone machine that had been gifted to him four wedding anniversaries ago. It was still to be taken out of its packaging.

The next morning, he sat down at the desk in his study where he had set up the recorder. He poured himself a glass of cognac. He knew, of course, that it was too early to drink. His children would not approve, but there was no need to tell them. To go out in search of lost time, lost lives, he had to blur present time, current people. Alfred placed the bottle of cognac on the top of a bookshelf in case more was needed and slowly pronounced the name aloud. *Azeem*. He repeated it again and again, many times, willing the boy to come to him.

He tried to recall the boy's face. It eluded him completely. He had one last memory of a strapping, handsome, young Azeem—wide shoulders, smooth unblemished skin, dark eyes, dark, wavy hair, a cleft in the chin—stealing out of the military camp in Baluchistan on a bitterly cold, dark morning just before dawn with a stolen horse, stolen money and stolen travel papers. Madeline would be meeting him in Aden, and Azeem was willing to risk everything for her sake and reach there in time.

That single image had stayed with Alfred these fifty years. He needed more if he was to tell Azeem's story. As he sat at his desk, Azeem came to him in dots and dashes, like Morse code from a distant continent. If he caught all the disconnected images, the memories of the smells and sounds that came to him in flashes, would they come together to form a picture of Azeem, of his life up to that moment in a faraway place when Alfred had left Azeem behind forever?

He began to speak. Rose was not present to hear the voice she had been enraptured by, that she had fallen in love with, when they had first met. Rose would never be there again. It was not the same voice in any case. The nasal twang conferred by his natal Urdu had softened, vanished into an American accent long ago. Accents, he had learnt, were the best camouflage available to the human animal to survive in an urban jungle such as New York or London. He had worked on his, perfected it. Urbane. Upper-class. Devoid of history.

He tinkered with the position and angle of the dictaphone and made his peace with speaking into a new-fangled device with its spinning vinyl discs for the purpose of recording Azeem's story. The past came to him sepia-tinted, at first. Still. Slow. Like an eight-armed octopus swimming underwater, trying to surface. He grappled with images flailing about in different directions.

He could see a double-storeyed house, a mansion with burnished red-oxide floors, cool and smooth, and overhanging latticed balconies. It was a house full of people, a hustle and bustle about it, women, men, children, servants. Horses and hounds.

He saw a decaying building with many small rooms around a central courtyard. There was a large guava tree in the courtyard and several caged green parrots uttering profanities and cackling wickedly, their wire cages hung with metal hooks on the tree's branches.

He could see a school for boys. It was in the compound near the mosque. There was another mosque in the same city, a very grand mosque. It had three big domes and four tall minarets with gold pinnacles. Outside that mosque there were bazaars and beyond them, the city spread out to its many majestic gates with large canons atop them. Outside the city there were acres and acres of open farmland, orchards and an unfolding view of high mountains.

There was a library somewhere. A magnificent library, full of Oriental manuscripts in Arabic, Turkish and Persian, in Urdu, Sanskrit, Hindi and Pashto too. Thousands of books lined the walls from floor to ceiling, the whole hall overhung with the woody smell of old books.

Somewhere else there were barracks, and men in uniforms and horses. More horses. A universe of horses and mules. The sound of their neighing and whinnying and breathing heavily. Sighing.

He could see narrow mountain trails and high precipices and sheer cliffs. The vision of a man and a brown stallion galloping at a furious speed came to him. He could hear the hammering of the man's heart as he rode towards the port of Aden to meet the girl who was expecting him to see her there.

AZEEM

Rannpur

1895–1904

A YOUNG BOY stood with one arm draped on the banister, his other arm bent at the elbow, with his chin held in the upturned palm of the hand. His face was turned upwards, his eyes fixed on the worn dark teakwood staircase, as he waited for his father to come down. Azeem was a light-skinned boy, with a fine nose, big almond-shaped eyes, soft pink lips. His dark brown thickly lashed eyes were lined with a dash of antimony. He looked fetching, clad in a dark green silk kurta with silver buttons and wide-bottomed white cotton pajamas.

As he waited for his father, the laughter and shouts of his cousins playing in the grounds outside wafted to his ears. He concluded that he had not been missed. He had stolen away from the game of hide and seek, quickly had a bath and got dressed to go out. His brothers and male cousins, his sisters and girl cousins had not noticed his absence.

There were thirteen of them altogether, eight boys and five girls, the oldest his brother Arif (who was almost thirteen) and the youngest his sister Arzoo (just a few months old), too young yet to join in their games. Arif, Samina, Salman, Azeem, Altaf, Shireen, Shaukat, Akram, Akbar, Amina, Salim, Amir, Arzoo. Their home, Afzal Manzil, was always alive with the sound of these names as they called out to each other while they played in the grounds or stood on the balconies of their rooms talking, their conversations zigzagging across the length and breadth of the front of the building. Their names ruled the air as mothers and aunts called them in to eat or bathe, as fathers and uncles summoned them inside for scolding or disciplining, as servants cajoled them to co-operate. Their games, chatter and horseplay were the substance of Azeem's days. But today, he had more important things on his mind.

His father descended the stairs at last, clad in a black buttoned-down knee-length sherwani coat, his matching velvet Persian cap on his head, his feet in open, tan leather shoes embroidered on the top and curling upwards at their tips. Abba picked up his carved walnut walking stick and turned to go out of the main door, his footsteps measured, his mind deep in thought, a slight frown on his broad forehead. He had not noticed Azeem waiting at the foot of the stairs.

'Wait, Abba!' said Azeem. 'Take me with you to the palace, please.'

He had been lying in wait to catch his father as he left home to go to the nawab's durbar. His father was a high-ranking official of the nawab's treasury and needed to be present in court every day. When he was younger, Azeem often begged to be taken along. There were minions and attendants in his father's office who looked after little Azeem while his father was busy at work. Though Afzal Manzil was grand in its own way, seeing the grandeur of the nawab's magnificent palace excited him enormously. His father indulged him. It pleased him that Azeem was enamoured of the courtly life, eager to walk in his father's steps.

Abba paused, taking in Azeem's appearance. The child was bathed and dressed, his wavy dark hair combed back neatly, so as not to give Abba any reason to turn down his plea. His eyes were shining with hope, large and liquid on his young face, the cheeks flushed pink in excitement, his neck tilted up in fervent appeal.

Outside the house, the voices of his playmates rose high and fell silent alternately, to the rhythm of the game of hide and seek, muted breathing interspersed with shouts of discovery and tumbling laughter.

'You will miss your lessons, Azeem.'

The maulvi would be arriving soon. His siblings and cousins would then abandon their play and sit down for their lessons on dark blue woven durries with a maroon border, the small square mats laid out on the veranda in neat rows. A maulvi sahib came each day to teach them in the covered veranda, its air kept circulating and cool by servants pulling the fans and periodically throwing water on the vetiver grass blinds.

'Please, Abba. I will ask Arif to teach me today's portion later in the evening. I'll catch up, I promise I will. Please let me come with you.'

His father's eyebrows came together to review the situation. Azeem held his breath till he saw the furrows on Abba's forehead relax.

'Very well. Get your cap.'

He rushed upstairs to the room that he shared with his older brother Arif and his cousin Salman and quickly pulled out his white, embroidered muslin cap with tiny mirrors stitched along its front. He put it on his head hurriedly and rushed down to join his father, a whoosh of relief leaving his lips as he bounded down the stairs. Abba had agreed! Now he would get a chance to speak to him alone on the drive to the palace and plead his case uninterrupted by anyone. And later roam the stately palace grounds, fantasizing about how he too would grow up and become an important official in the nawab's court someday.

Father and son sat in the horse-drawn carriage, and his father ordered the coachman to proceed towards the palace—the clippity-clop of the horses' hooves against the road, the occasional squeak of a carriage wheel, the soft swiping sound of the coachman's whip cutting through the air, all music to the boy's ear.

Azeem's father was an important man. Their family was a powerful one. Guns and rifles lined the wall of the main sitting area in Afzal Manzil. Another wall gleamed with Rannpuri daggers, curved with long blades and ornate handles. Heads of antlers, a stuffed cheetah, pelts of leopards were strewn about carelessly in the living room. His father and uncles accompanied the nawab and other nobles for shikar, the hunting parties which ended in grand outdoor feasts and picnics. Apart from horses, the family had its own pack of dogs—large, smooth-haired, crossbred sighthounds—which were special to their state.

Afzal Manzil had more rooms than Azeem could count and more relatives than he could drop in on, on any single day. They pampered him with dried figs, raisins and almonds when he went to their rooms. His father had three wives. Azeem loved his Ammi most for the light in her eyes when she called him to her, but he liked his stepmothers and aunts too. They were all always together in the zenana, the mothers and the aunts, gossiping, cooking, playing cards, chewing betel leaves, singing. His father had two unmarried sisters and two younger brothers with multiple wives of their own. There were two great-aunts and a decrepit old granduncle who played the harmonium and sang classical songs in a quavering voice in the late afternoon. He sat in a golden pool of light streaming in through the open window, signing off each day's riyaaz when the sun set. Azeem always listened from a distance. Up close, the granduncle smelt rancid, his skin emitting an odour like stale curd. To wriggle out of his embrace was tough; it was better to listen from afar.

When Azeem's family sat down to dinner, each night seemed like a feast night. They sat in a large circle on white sheets spread out over thick carpets. There were pilafs, kormas and kebabs prepared by the cooks and served by the bearers. The naan breads were served separately on huge silver salvers with high copper handles. The curries, fragrant with threads of saffron and crushed cardamom, were laid out in huge, broad-bottomed copper vessels, and everyone dipped their bread into them and ate.

The women sat down to eat after the menfolk were through with their meal. Fresh white sheets were laid out over the carpets for them by the servants. There was a selection of sweets and desserts. Sweet saffron rice, cooked with ghee and syrup, topped with finely chopped almonds, was served every night because the cooks knew it was Azeem's favourite. His eyes always shut with pleasure as the first burst of sweetness hit his tongue.

All the children in the family belonged to all the adults collectively and vice versa. Only his Abba stood out, the head of the family. No one asked anything of Abba, everybody only deferred to his wishes. Except Azeem, who was determined to remain his father's favourite and not let his baby sister Arzoo nudge him out of that coveted position, though every time he looked at Arzoo, Azeem felt there could not be a more beautiful creature in all of creation, all of her sweet-scented, warbling cutely in her cot, her podgy legs cycling in the air, her arms stretched up begging to be lifted into his arms.

'Abba,' Azeem said, placing a tentative hand on his father's sleeve.

'Tell me what it is you want,' his father asked, turning around to look into his eyes, a smile playing on his lips. It was not difficult for him to read into the heart of this son who was most like him in nature, worshipping him devoutly, emulating his every gesture and mannerism. It was clear that Azeem was excited and impatient about something.

'I am going to be ten years old soon. Please may I have my own horse as a birthday present?'

'A horse! You have big things on your mind, my little son!' said his father, clearly surprised by his request. 'You know that Arif and Salman got their own horses only when they turned twelve.'

'But Abba, I'm already as tall as them. As strong too. I can ride and control my mount as well as them. You say so yourself so often, Abba.'

'You'll need to wait another two years, Azeem. It's only fair.'

'But according to maulvi sahib, two years is seven hundred and thirty whole days! I asked him again just yesterday at lesson-time! 365 x 2 = 730. It is almost as bad as waiting forever! It doesn't seem fair to me, Abba. Every day that I spend seeing Arif and Salman riding and grooming their own horses—while I share a mount with the little babies of the family—I'll feel wretched and envious. Surely Abba, that much envy and misery cannot be good for me.'

'Azeem, you must learn to control your feelings,' said his father with a frown. Yet something in his voice suggested to Azeem that Abba was not unmoved by his argument. That he might relent still.

'Don't you see if I could simply have a horse of my own, such feelings will not arise at all? Why create them and then tell me to learn to manage them? It is totally in your hands. If you say I am to have a horse this birthday, who will object? Arif and Salman will be happy to have me join them in their rides.'

'You make very big arguments for a little man, *chhote miyan*. Give me some time to think about it.'

'*Ji, bade miyan.*'

Azeem's face broke into a smile. *Chhote miyan, bade miyan.* Little man, big man. As the wheels of the coach rolled on, he knew his mission was as good as accomplished. They were a natural team, his Abba and he, reflections of each other in time's telescope. He settled back into the upholstered seat, thinking of the day ahead. He would spend it watching his father at work and loitering about the palace gardens and stables.

If he was lucky, he would be able to persuade Wasim chacha, his father's clerk, to take him to the bazaar and buy him a kulfi, sinfully sweet, pistachio flavoured, the iced milk lolly on a stick melting upon his tongue as he sucked on it.

TWO DAYS BEFORE his birthday, Azeem rode out with his father's horse groom and a clerk from the office to a breeding farm outside town. The owner of the farm had a snake tattoo along his forearm extending all the way onto the back of his right hand. As he pointed out the horses to them—young, well-groomed, two Arabs, three Kathiawaris, a beautiful brown and white Marwari—thick silver rings with different gemstones on each finger glinted under the sun's rays. The horses ran about free on the farm, tails swishing, manes flowing, eyes lively, hooves pointed and graceful like dancers. Azeem's heart turned cartwheels inside his ribcage at the sight of them. He rode them one by one.

He finally picked an Arabian filly and took her for a round of the farm. She was a beauty, her head slender and haughty, her limbs wiry and strong. Energy and intelligence shone out of her. She was a bit restive, showing just a hint of moodiness, a flaring of her nostrils as Azeem's heels embraced her sides. He would need to bring her around, train her firmly.

'I'll take this one!' he told Wasim chacha, the office clerk. Wasim chacha looked at the horse groom for his opinion. 'She's a bit spirited,' the groom said. 'That one's better for him.' He pointed towards a well-sprung, speckled Kathiawari colt.

'No, this is the one for me, I'm quite sure,' insisted Azeem, his palm stroking the flank of the Arabian filly.

'On the condition that you will not ride out alone with her till I give you permission,' said the groom.

'I agree.'

It was decided that she was the one the groom would recommend to his father. It was the happiest day of Azeem's life.

And then it wasn't.

As they stood discussing the final price for the filly and arrangements for her to be sent to Afzal Manzil the next morning, a lean, distraught-looking man with an ashen face and a shaking frame came hurriedly to where they stood talking to the stud farm's owner and called Wasim chacha away. Azeem watched them from a distance, as Wasim chacha's walking stick began to shake uncontrollably and his face turned colourless. The other man held him, steadied him to prevent him from falling. Wasim chacha's white muslin cap flew off his head and dropped to the ground like an injured dove. He picked it up and placed it on his head again with a vacant gaze and walked towards Azeem.

'We must leave right now!' said Wasim chacha to Azeem. The look in his eyes reminded Azeem of the chickens in the yard in the moment the khansama beheaded them for cooking. A restless flutter, then a recognition in their eyes of the death approaching them. Then stillness. Something cold and wet, a feeling of having been touched by misfortune's clammy paws, or of some unfortunate lost soul's shadow falling upon him, spasmed through Azeem. He followed Wasim chacha and the groom quietly, without asking any questions. There was a sudden stealth in all their footsteps when they walked, as if the very ground beneath their feet was less certain, less theirs than it had been a few minutes ago.

They had barely driven a half mile out when Wasim chacha asked the coachman to stop, in a voice so hollow that it seemed to belong to a ghost. Leaving Azeem and the horse groom seated in the carriage, Wasim chacha and the thin, trembling man from Rannpur who had come with the message, stood a short distance away and conferred with each other in muted voices. After a while, they beckoned the horse groom to join them. Finally, they walked back to the coach.

'Azeem beta. I have some bad news. Some er ... difficulty ... er accident has happened. I need to rush back to er ... your father ... immediately. The groom is going to walk with you to a village nearby. I have relatives there. I am sending instructions to them to take care of you. I will come to get you as soon as it is safe.'

None of what Wasim chacha was saying made any sense to Azeem, but the expression in the eyes of all three men told him that this was no time for questions. Something terrible had happened. His Abba was in some sort of danger. Azeem must do as they said. The coachman took the reins of the carriage and drove away with Wasim chacha and the messenger.

'It's going to be a long walk,' the groom warned him. He nodded back.

It was late in the evening before Azeem and the horse groom reached the home of Wasim chacha's relatives. It was a modest village accommodation, the house of a farmer. The groom said something to the head of the family. After watching another muted, ominous conversation, Azeem found himself and the groom shown into a small, dark room where they could sleep for the night. After some time, the farmer brought them a plate with a few thick rotis and green chillies. He apologized that there was nothing else.

The next morning, the groom left.

'What about me?' Azeem asked him as he was leaving.

'I don't know. Wasim bhai will make some arrangements and come for you.'

'What has happened?'

The groom began to sob, his face a broken, ugly thing held in his bony, knotted fingers, his shoulders curling into his fluttering ribcage.

'I command you to tell me what has happened.'

'I am not allowed to say!'

The groom let out a strangulated cry and beat balled-up fists to his forehead.

'My Abba is dead,' Azeem whispered. An awful knowing had sprung from the pit of his stomach and become this cold certainty.

The groom only nodded and wailed louder.

An icy numbness settled into Azeem's heart. *Abba, Abba-jaan, Abba-huzoor, dear Abba, beloved Abba.* What had happened to his father? And why was he himself hidden away like this in an ordinary hut in this nameless village? Why was he not being taken to Rannpur to be with his family?

For many days, Azeem simply lay in the corner of the room allotted to him, curled in grief and terror that enveloped him from all sides, a darkness without shape or dimension. No words could penetrate that blackness. He lay there, a mute boy inhaling the earth scent of the packed mud floor, his fingernails scratching its surface. The elderly woman of the house brought him his meals. The look in her eyes was not unkind, simply vacant, hollow and devoid of meaning. Nothing in the hut yielded any meaning—the elderly farmer, his two grown-up sons, the bullocks tied outside, the cows, goats, hens, the stacks of hay, the all-pervasive smell of cow dung in the air, the buzzing of flies everywhere. What were these to him, how had they claimed him for their own?

After many days, Wasim chacha came at last. He had shrunk into a very old man, his cheeks sunken, his eyes in gloomy shadows, his body frail. His voice trembled as he spoke to Azeem. 'I must tell you the truth, *chhote huzoor*. I have been unable to find any lies that could cover this calamity, keep it hidden from you. I hope you will be able to forgive me for being the bearer of such evil news.'

While Azeem was at the breeding farm choosing his horse, his life, as he had known it, was coming to a brutal end. His father, his uncles, his whole family, every single member, had been gunned to death and Afzal Manzil set on fire. Wasim chacha had only rumours to offer, no explanations. No one knew what exactly had happened. It was not clear whether dacoits had targeted the family to loot its wealth, or a powerful rival had struck at Azeem's father, or whether he had run afoul of the nawab himself and the nawab had given the orders for the execution.

'You must stay here for a few more weeks. Your father's enemies must never find out you escaped the massacre.'

'Let them come and get me. I don't care!'

'I too will be killed, *chhote huzoor,* and these poor people who agreed to shelter you at my behest,' said Wasim chacha.

'What is to happen to me, Wasim chacha? How long must I hide here?'

'*Chhote huzoor,* I have eaten your father's salt. I must do my best to save your life. Give me time to work something out. I do not have much to give you except my loyalty. I am a poor and powerless man whose chief benefactor has been cruelly snatched away. I will not be able to give you the life you deserve. But Allah Taalah saved you, Allah Taalah must have some plans for you.'

Watching Wasim chacha's abject helplessness, Azeem felt a sharp straightening of his own spine. He was the only reminder left of his noble father, of his entire bloodline, on the face of this earth. How he lived, wherever he lived, he would live with his pride intact. No one would ever beggar him of that.

Extracting a promise from Azeem that he would not reveal his identity to his host family, for no details had been given to them, only some money to pay for his food and lodging, Wasim chacha left. No one called him *chhote huzoor* again, not even Wasim chacha the next time he came to visit. He would nevermore live the life of a 'little master'. His tenth birthday celebration, his beautiful Arabian mare all belonged in a future that had been wiped out forever. It would remain forever suspended out of time, out of reach, on the fringes of his memory.

The next morning, Azeem woke up early and took a bath. Wasim chacha had left a small bundle of clothes for him. He picked out a singlet and a pair of cotton pajamas to wear. He walked to where his host's son was chopping firewood for the day, sweat streaming down from his brow.

'What can I do to help?' Azeem asked him.

The older boy, some twenty or so years old, appraised him slowly as he wiped the sweat off his own face. He was clearly discomforted by the question.

'What do you know how to do?' he asked, at last.

Studying, playing, hunting, feasting. Azeem hesitated. 'Nothing of use here. But I will learn if you teach me,' he finally muttered.

A rooster with its neck held high walked into the yard, sniffed and poked about the bundle of wood, flapped its wings grandly and flew back towards the chicken coop.

'Today, let me just take you to our fields, show you a bit of the village. Then we'll see later how you can help.'

The boy walked inside the hut and called to his mother.

'I'm taking the yateem with me to the fields. Pack some extra food.'

Whatever else Wasim chacha had kept from his host's family, his parentless status was clearly no secret here.

Yateem. Orphan. That was his reality now. He was an object of pity. By giving succour to him, others could rise in Allah's esteem.

Yateem was not a new word in his vocabulary. He had lived at the other side of it once, coming out with uncles and cousins on feast days to give alms to cripples, beggars and orphans outside the big mosque in Rannpur. How grandly they had all bent down to serve the indigent, how safe they had felt in their pious humility.

Over the next few weeks, as he walked through the village and learnt to tell one crop from another, learnt to tell useful plants from weeds and pull out the latter, learnt to water the animals, to milk a cow, to sweep the chicken coop, the word yateem followed him. It stretched out its arms to claim him. He remained firm in his resolve to elude its grasp.

At night, before he slept, he recalled the names of his siblings and cousins, repeating them in his mind like counting beads on a rosary. Arif, Samina, Salman, Azeem, Altaf, Shireen, Shaukat, Akram, Akbar, Amina, Salim, Amir, Arzoo. Arif, Samina, Salman, Azeem, Altaf, Shireen, Shaukat, Akram, Akbar, Amina, Salim, Amir, Arzoo. Arif, Samina, Salman, Azeem, Altaf, Shireen, Shaukat, Akram, Akbar, Amina, Salim, Amir, Arzoo. Arif, Samina, Salman, Azeem, Altaf, Shireen, Shaukat, Akram, Akbar, Amina, Salim, Amir, Arzoo. Arif, Samina, Salman, Azeem, Altaf, Shireen, Shaukat, Akram, Akbar, Amina, Salim, Amir, Arzoo. Arif, Samina, Salman,

Azeem … Azeem … Azeem. This was the natural order of things, the order he was born inside. This was his place in the world, whatever anyone else thought or said about him. He would not let the other world, with its other words, claim him.

Inside of him he would remain Azeem. The greatest. The favoured one. Always Azeem.

Never yateem.

AZEEM FELT INVISIBLE as he walked down an unnamed lane in Rannpur wearing a mud-coloured kurta pajama set. The expression in his dark eyes was bleak, emptied of expectations, no longer on talking terms with hope. The lower lids were also no longer lined with surma to ward off the evil-eye. There was nothing left in his life to attract anyone's envy. The long shirt hung too loosely on him. The wide-bottomed cotton trousers were fraying at the bottom. A small cloth bag hung from his shoulder. Walking beside him was Wasim chacha, his aged face careworn. There was a nervous energy in the old man's footsteps, a muttered prayer on his lips.

Boy and man walked down an endless labyrinth of streets. The small houses on either side were so close to each other that it felt as if they were walking inside a tunnel. The smell of cooking collided with the smell of open drains. Flies abounded. And a jumbled mix of sounds spilled out into the streets from the tiny windows and small doorways—of children laughing and crying, hens crowing, dogs barking, goats bleating and cooking vessels clanking against each other. Past the warren of houses there was a small clearing, and in the clearing stood a mosque. Behind the mosque was a large, shabby-looking structure with roughly plastered walls and tin roofing. It had a central courtyard open to the sky with rooms arranged along its four sides.

Wasim chacha finally had come for him and was now escorting him to a residential school for poor boys in Rannpur. That was the best he had been able to arrange for Azeem after many months of trying. His relatives in the village were becoming restive, they could not keep the boy forever, even though they had come to like the lad. A village was a small place to hide such a big tragedy. Questions were being asked, rumours had begun floating about the boy's identity. Sooner or later, there would be trouble for them if Azeem stayed on.

The old clerk introduced Azeem to the teacher in-charge of the establishment as a relative from his village whose education he wished to sponsor, to earn merit in the eyes of Allah. Azeem's wavy hair had been trimmed to within an inch of his scalp, and he had on a white lace skullcap. The clothes Azeem was wearing and another set in his bag belonged to the farmer's two sons, much older than him. Wasim chacha had bought new clothes for them in exchange for these. It was important to drive home to the maulvi the humbleness of Azeem's circumstances. New, well-fitting clothes, even inexpensive ones, risked betraying Azeem's comfortable past.

It was only after he returned to Rannpur that Azeem recognized the village he had sheltered in as the haven it had been. The gruff but kindly farmer, his taciturn but watchful wife, his hardworking sons, their humble, toiling life had provided just the refuge he needed then. The village with its vast fields, mud paths, domesticated animals, unfiltered sunshine and star-filled nights was a world so different from Rannpur that no comparisons with his earlier life had tormented him there. It was another reality. Its stoic skies offered him space to grow the spine and muscle that he needed to face his bleak future.

The full measure of his dislocation only hit home in this boarding school for poor boys. It was a small establishment, wholly spartan and functional in design. Forty-eight boys of different ages lived in the eight rooms that lined the courtyard—each, a small cell-like structure with just enough space for six mattresses on the floor and with six hooks on the wall on which the boys' clothes were hung. The remaining rooms were used as storerooms, a kitchen and classrooms. Day-students from the neighbourhood also attended classes there. The school—a flat, single-storey structure—had off-white walls, with uneven patches and stain marks. It held a few tiny square windows with iron bars and creaky rough-hewn wooden doors. In certain places like the study hall and the corridor, its roof leaked shallow puddles the colour of dog piss, and the faint odour of dispossession saturated its every crevice and corner.

At night, when Azeem lay down to sleep, he shut his eyes and summoned the names and faces of his siblings and cousins for comfort and a reminder of his place in the order of things. They refused to come to him with ease.

They tugged out of his mind's reach and ran away to the safety of Afzal Manzil. He could not follow them there. The hard floor of his hostel room held him down, the thin, lumpy mattress its accomplice, the clothes hanging on the wall fluttering like headless ghouls. Even the image of the granduncle with sour breath whose embrace he had cruelly shied away from refused to come to him, to this place without music, or dainty latticed windows, or golden afternoon light streaming in.

Dispossession, he discovered, had a limited vocabulary. Riches had many words in the lexicon to be described and felt; poverty was very often abrupt and angry. In this school for destitute boys, dispossession spoke in punches, jibes, pokes, an occasional kick in the shins, or by tripping someone in the dark. Laughter had lost its open, good nature, and now most often came in slyly, following someone's humiliation. The boys were organized in gangs. The rival groups competed in being mean to a newcomer like Azeem. His torment was their triumph. He kept to himself, tried not to attract notice, lost in his thoughts of Afzal Manzil and his longing for his family. But new entrants were always an object of attention, especially for the older boys and the hostel bullies.

One evening, the casual mistreatment, the jibes and insults, the orders to fetch and carry for senior boys grew to the point where they became intolerable. Azeem's insides screamed at him to retaliate, to mark a boundary around himself that no one dared transgress. He forgot his circumstances. He forgot that he was an orphan, and that too one who had been instructed by Wasim chacha to not attract any notice to himself. He got into a scuffle with a sniggering, oily, ill-mannered bully among the seniors. A boy named Salman. A boy everyone secretly hated for his nasty sneering tongue and his abusive language. A boy Azeem himself hated because he was called Salman. He had wrested away the memory of a beloved cousin and instated his unctuous face in its stead. The outcome of his ugly fight with Salman was unexpected. Suddenly, inexplicably, Azeem was regarded as one of them, welcome in their circle. His life became easier, for he had spoken in a language they understood only too well. Resentment. Rage.

Azeem became used to the place gradually. The faces of his childhood companions faded one by one; their names got lost in the noises of his new environment, some stolen away by other more immediate companions, others drowned in the din of lessons learnt by rote and recited out aloud, and everyday games. He strove to do well in his studies. He had a head start over the others there, many of them entirely unlettered when they were first admitted, their fingers clumsy and taut as they attempted to learn the basic alphabet, their eyes frightened of the maulvi's shadow, their egos bristling with the indignity of having been left out first and then included suddenly in the folds of literacy. Azeem tried to help them out when he could. It was a solace to still have something to give, intangible and undervalued as learning was here.

In the centre of the paved, roofless courtyard of the school building was a guava tree, its fruit hard to bite into and tart to the tongue. Boys and parrots competed for the guavas in the fruiting season. The boys used them as ammunition to hit each other. It was a wholly original team sport they had devised. They divided into two teams—the same two each evening—and clambered on to the tree and pelted members of the opposite team with guavas. There were no clear winners or losers, just the thrill of the melee, the taking aim, the shouting, the running.

The parrots' cages hung from the branches of the tree. As the game grew more riotous, the parrots flapped their wings in agitation against the bars and hurled obscenities at the boys. The cuss words recited by the parrots had been picked up from the boys. At some point in the tumult of the evening's play, the maulvi rushed into the courtyard. He raised his arms to the sky and sternly said, '*Lahaul-vila-quwwat.*' There is no force but god. The parrots squawked *Lahaul-vila-quwwat Lahaulvilaquwwat Lahaulvilaquwwat* after him.

The boys were shooed away from the courtyard and the maulvi let out the parrots from their cages. Their wings were clipped. They could not fly out of the compound. They squawked wildly, attacked the fruit, attacked each other, attacked any boy who might still be standing around in the courtyard.

Long after Azeem had forgotten everything about the school he stayed in for five years—the indifferent taste of the watered-down lentil curry, the under-cooked potatoes and the dry bread served at each meal; the indifferent education imparted on black slates with one cheaply printed textbook rotated between all the students studying in the same grade; the shared six boys to a room accommodation that was too hot in the summer, too damp in the monsoon, too cold in the winter, uncomfortable in every season, its walls and ceilings alive with the alternating slow movements and rushed fornication of beady-eyed geckos—the image of the courtyard stayed with Azeem—the guava tree, its fruit tart and unpalatable, the boys with their cruel game designed only to give hurt and dodge hurt, and the caged parrots with their clipped wings, singing out 'There is no force but god' after the maulvi.

The parrots loved the maulvi for letting them out in the evenings, not knowing that he was the one who had caged and mutilated them in the first place. It seemed to Azeem like a metaphor for life in Rannpur with its grand court, its sparring nobles, and its suffering common people.

IF AZEEM'S EARLY weeks in the school had passed like long years, the last years sped by like mere weeks. When his time at the school was over, Wasim chacha sought the help of the maulvi in finding him some suitable employment. Wasim chacha, while he could not do much for Azeem, still did all he could, never reneging on his loyalty to his benefactor's family. As a result of the joint efforts of the maulvi and Wasim chacha, Azeem was given the job of an apprentice—he'd be one among many other boys like himself—in the royal library.

It was an old establishment, well over a hundred years, set up by the very first nawab of the state. Successors to the throne had added to its collection of rare manuscripts, miniature paintings and books in several Oriental languages. The head librarian was a respected scholar, fierce in his devotion to the treasure house he guarded. His appearance, with his stately white beard, dark silk robes embroidered in rich colours and light piercing eyes, brought to Azeem's mind the wizards and angels that lived in the pages of the magnificent tomes of which he was the guardian.

Azeem was assigned as an assistant in the rare Arabic and Persian manuscripts section. The elderly librarian in charge of that space had a tender love for the books in his keeping and high expectations of all his apprentices. As caretakers and custodians of these rare treasures, they were to know the origins and antiquity of each book, the precise type of care needed for each depending on the type of parchment and binding, the exact movement of wrist and pressure of hand and fingertips to apply while turning the pages, and the specific placement of each title, flat or vertical, on a wooden, stone or metal surface.

There was a seventh-century edition of the Quran on parchment in Kufic script, another from the eighth century. There was a tenth-century version in the Naskh script and a fabulous thirteenth-century Quran by a master of calligraphy from Baghdad, ornamented in gold and lapis lazuli. Other rare manuscripts included early medical treatises and beautifully illustrated volumes from the time of the Mughal emperors Akbar and Shah Jahan.

Azeem learnt calligraphy and bookbinding as part of his training. The assistants were required to create copies of old manuscripts for the patrons' use, the originals too precious to be moved around. Teams of calligraphers and illustrators worked together with printers and binders to create copies that could be circulated, preserving the original from overuse and damage. Azeem liked working at the library. The universe of books surrounded him and filled him with a sense of magical possibilities, of spaces existing outside and beyond the tiny portion of the world allotted to each person to inhabit in life.

While at school, Azeem had put the past behind him.

His life was in no danger now. His family's tragedy was a forgotten tale, superseded by fresher intrigues at court, more recent acts of cruelty, injustice and violence. In his years in the boys' school, he had not entirely forgotten who he was, but his lost childhood was nothing more to him now than an old scrapbook of memories, once dearly beloved, now faded and rarely visited, its existence only a vague source of comfort.

Working in the library meant returning to the centre of the city. He rented a single room in a modest neighbourhood, close to Wasim chacha's house. The library was near the palace. His father's old office was in the area, a short walk away. Every morning as he passed the Durbar Hall, he remembered how he used to be fascinated with it as a boy. The noblemen, their horses and carriages, their grooms, the news of goings-on in the court, the musical and dance soirees—all this surrounded him now. Seeing it once again at close quarters made him restless.

It was disquieting to see with new eyes the world he had belonged to as a child.

He did not crave a nobleman's life any longer. It filled him with distaste, tainted as it was with his family's blood. Besides, it now carried the sweat of poor people. Having lived on the other side of the class divide, having belonged with those whose existence was defined only by what service they could render to the nawab and the nobles, he no longer wished to be part of it. His life as a library assistant was perfect in what it asked of him, a peaceful engagement with knowledge.

Azeem knew that he should consider himself fortunate. Yet, restlessness grew within him with each passing day.

The city centre—with its fine horse-drawn carriages, the occasional polo match he stood to watch, the royal stables with the smells and sounds of colts—filled him with an inchoate longing. He woke up to visions of mounting an Arabian mare and galloping along the banks of the Ramganga river. Stallions from his father's stables began to trot through his dreams, not alive, not quite dead either. The ghosts of horses past jumped over his bed all night long, urging him to ride them.

A thought began to form in his mind. That the horses were telling him something. Urging him to act. He did not belong in Rannpur any longer. His family had been murdered and wiped out. There were no ties holding him to the city. Besides, to survive in Rannpur, dispossessed, erased and hanging on the margins, was an insult to the souls of his proud ancestors.

If he was to make a life of any worth, the first step was to leave. To move to some place where he could walk upright; where he would be known as Azeem; where there was no yateem in sight or in memory.

At eighteen, he was an exceptionally handsome boy. Despite his nondescript work clothes, he stood out among his co-workers. His height, broad shoulders, aquiline nose, and the cleft on his chin all gave to him the bearing of a nobleman. The long, confident stride of his legs suggested one belonging to warrior stock. His looks had begun to attract attention. There were questions about his lineage from curious acquaintances.

Rannpur was a small princely state, surrounded by British-ruled India. Azeem began to explore ways to get a job in British territory, outside the borders of the state. Instead of avoiding the royal stables, he began to spend his free time in that vicinity. He got to know the grooms and the caretakers. He approached the horse grooms accompanying the royal guests from outside the state. He asked for jobs that might suit him. After a few weeks, he got the opportunity he was looking for. An English army officer, seeing his obvious rapport with horses, told him of a government horse breeding farm in Saharanpur and gave him a letter of introduction to the commanding officer at the centre.

Azeem packed his modest belongings, bid goodbye to a tearful Wasim chacha and took one last look at the city of his birth. He committed to memory the Jama Masjid with its three large domes and gold-tipped minarets, the majestic clock tower, the grand exit gates.

As he left, he knew he would never return again.

MADELINE

Middlesbrough to Jaunpur

1906

MARTHA EVANS PICKED up the day's newspaper every day before she headed home from the Middlesbrough Girls' School where she taught. She made a handsome figure in her dark tweed jacket, matching ankle-length skirt, stiff, high-collared white blouse and sensible sealskin boots. There was a wide-brimmed hat on her head, a newspaper rolled up in her left hand and a sturdy black umbrella tucked under her right arm. She was the first woman in this town of pig-iron foundries and steel mills to leave behind the fussy flounces of the Victorian gown and step into the 1900s with a trimmer, more sensible silhouette.

The late afternoon sun shone on the large bronze statue of the town's founder that stood in the centre of the market square. She stopped for a couple of minutes, her eyes glancing over the familiar text on the plaque under the figure.

JOHN VAUGHAN 1799–1868
MAYOR OF MIDDLESBROUGH 1855
DISCOVERED IRONSTONE IN THE CLEVELAND HILLS. FOUNDER OF THE IRON TRADE IN CLEVELAND. PARTNER OF BOLCKOW, VAUGHAN & CO. LTD
WHO BUILT
ONE OF THE FIRST IRON WORKS IN MIDDLESBROUGH IN 1840

Martha walked out of the central square at a brisk but unhurried pace and turned towards home. Madeline would be waiting for her. They went over the day's news together, and discussed it threadbare in the hour before supper, in their cozy parlour. It was something they had done ever since Madeline was nine years old. Madeline was nearly eighteen now, had completed school and applied for admission to college.

Martha's mind flew to the senior girls' class she taught at school. They were a mixed bunch, three parts frivolousness, one part earnestness. Sometimes, she felt she had higher hopes and greater ambition for them than the students or their parents themselves did. She wished for all of them to attend college, enrol in university and grow into twentieth-century women with careers, minds and opinions of their own. It hurt to see them dither over their college applications, uncertain of their plans. Most were willing to marry and settle with the first young man with a decent job.

Change, Martha consoled herself, looked slow in the here and now. It felt like a step by painful step affair when you were in the middle of making it happen, but take a long-run view of any situation, and you could see the full extent of it, the splendid drama plainly in view. It had only been a little over fifty years since John Vaughan had taken a stroll in the Cleveland Hills with his mining engineer and had found iron deposits in Middlesbrough.

Today, what was once a sleepy hamlet in North Yorkshire with less than forty houses, was a thriving industrial town, a melting pot of intermingled Welsh, Irish and Northern England cultures, different dialects, thriving jobs, burgeoning possibilities and an emerging shipping industry.

As Martha let herself into their small rowhouse at one quiet end of North Street, the sound of Madeline's singing wafted to her ears. The impassioned strains of 'Casta Diva' from Bellini's *Norma* floated in the early evening air and filled up the small sitting room. One wall was papered in a cheerful daisy pattern, making it a pleasant, comforting space. A slant of sunlight from the west window fell on a dining table set with two places. The housekeeper would have left the food in the oven and set the table for their supper before leaving for the day.

Tempra tu de' cori ardenti,
Tempra ancor lo zelo audace,
Spargi in terra quella pace

The words poured into the parlour in Madeline's clear voice, holding the high notes and the low ones too with ease. It was her daughter's Italian day today. Martha had been losing track of the study schedule of late, Madeline was mature now in handling it on her own.

She put the newspaper on the small round rosewood table in front of the worn-down damask sofa in the corner of the parlour and went to the privy out of the back door. When she came into the parlour again, after freshening up for supper, Madeline was already poring over the broadsheet, her hair cascading over one shoulder, an elbow on the table, a hand under the chin, the expression intent. Her eyes scrunched up; her lips puckered as she focused on a particular item of news.

'Mamma, the suffragettes have refused to stop campaigning and have chosen to go to prison again for six weeks instead. What do you think?'

Martha pursed her lips. She was among the large crowd of women who had gathered at the Liberal Party meeting last October demanding that male politicians make their stance on women's suffrage clear. She had gone to Manchester to participate in the protest. She could feel the thrill of the moment when the large white 'Votes for Women' banner had been bravely unfurled. Feelings of solidarity and sisterhood had filled the skies.

Then things had suddenly turned ugly in front of Martha's eyes, almost without a moment's warning. 'Will the Liberal government give votes to women?' someone yelled.

The young Mr Churchill ignored the question shouted out at him. Men had pulled the questioner down roughly. Annie Kenny, the young working-class representative, was being roughed up and thrown out of the meeting. Christabel Pankhurst entered the scuffle, and in support of her comrade spat at a police officer; she was hauled out too. When charged with rowdiness and obstruction, the two young women had refused to pay the fine and gone to prison instead. In court they had spoken eloquently at their trial, bringing many new supporters and the attention of the national press to the cause of women's suffrage.

'I don't know what to think any more, Madeline,' Martha sighed. Emmeline Pankhurst had decided that the violent tactics being advocated by her daughter Christabel, a young law student, and her cohort were the way to proceed. Being ladylike and showing good form hadn't worked. If they were serious about matters, the women's movement had to change strategy, escalate the issue.

Martha felt increasingly uncertain about everything, something discomfiting for a woman of her resolute nature. The movement was falling into the hands of young women operating out of London, some barely out of their teens, just a little older than Madeline. Martha could not bring herself to think it right to break windows, throw stones or wilfully attack public servants or property. But she had to concede that the peaceful campaigns had not yielded results. Women in New Zealand and Australia and many states in America could vote—even next door in the Isle of Man. In Britain, nothing had moved since Mr John Stuart Mill had raised the issue in 1865. It had been forty years! Perhaps, Christabel was right when she declared the vote had to be *taken*. It would not be given.

At the dinner table they ate silently. It was a practice Martha had introduced when Madeline was five years old and Norman was visiting home from India—he came every other summer. Unable to contain her excitement at seeing her father after a long gap and spilling with questions about his adventures in the East, Madeline would go from one meal to the next with stories and questions tumbling out of her mouth non-stop and scarcely a mouthful of food getting into her. The silence rule worked like magic and after dinner the small family always gathered at the tiny fireplace. As fair recompense little Maddy was allowed to stay up as late as she liked, chatting with her father. Madeline's appetite for stories was insatiable.

'More Papa, more please,' she begged even as her eyelids shut. Her dreams, Martha was convinced, were filled with brocade-clad nawabs and bejewelled ranis in purdah, teeming Indian spice bazaars and visions of tigers and cheetahs sprinting through mountains and forests. Her daytime prattle most certainly was.

Mother and daughter sat down on the sofa by the fireplace after their early supper was over. Martha liked to discuss Madeline's studies with her after the meal. 'Tomorrow is your day for Greek, isn't it? Which text do you plan to delve into?'

Madeline screwed up her nose and shrugged. She was a girl-woman now, honey brown tresses, hazel eyes, her father's delicate build and complexion, on the brink of beauty, her looks more piquant than lovely yet. To Martha, the curiosity shining out of her eyes was her most beautiful feature. There was nothing in the whole wide world more attractive than the light of intelligence streaming out of a pair of young eyes.

'Homer's *Iliad* again, I suppose,' Madeline sighed. 'Sadly, I have not found my way into its heart yet. I hear it as a faint story, it doesn't perform itself in my mind's eye, all splendid and bold. And I simply cannot bear that nobody will listen to Cassandra!'

Of the six languages she was well-versed in, Greek was the only one Madeline had some difficulty with. If only the Greeks had a proclivity towards opera, she would drown in its sounds and emotions with the same ease she felt with Italian, German and Spanish. Latin, of course, was her mother's subject so she had begun learning it very early. Martha had a varied mix of Latin-based word games they had been playing since Madeline was a little toddler and had scarcely started to speak in full sentences.

Martha smiled at her tenderly. Her unusually gifted polyglot daughter, precocious and bright from early childhood, was her greatest pride and accomplishment, the best outcome of her marriage with Norman. What a fine young woman she would grow up to be.

'I expect we will be hearing from Oxford soon. The news will be good. It can't be anything but.'

NORMAN EVANS WOKE up at the crack of dawn each day with the muezzin's call to prayer. He was not a Muslim, not even a particularly devout Christian. Four years ago, when the Indian Public Works Department posted him to its survey and canal division in the small town of Jaunpur, somewhere in the eastern neck of the vast North Indian plains, he found the deeply sonorous voice of the crier atop the minaret of the Atala Mosque more to his taste than the shrill trilling of an alarm clock. In Jaunpur, it had become a personal ritual to wake up to the dawn cry that floated down from the minaret and cascaded through the sleeping settlement to rouse the faithful to prayer.

The trill of the alarm clock was a sound he was averse to. It took him back to the school siren of his boyhood in Northern Yorkshire, a poor miner's son struggling hard to better his lot. The foreign sounds of the call to prayer, rousing and majestic, reminded him each morning that he was in some place far away and exotic. At long last he was a nobleman in his own domain.

Gobind, the bearer, his eyes still bleary with sleep, brought him a pot of Darjeeling tea, a sugar jar, a milk jug and two pieces of buttered toast, laid out on a tray with a white lace-edged cloth. Norman always took the same repast for his dawn tea. It felt pleasantly predictable and reassuring to him at the start of a varied working day supervising the different projects under him. The mild, muscatel aroma of his tea from the misty, rain-drenched green mountains of Northeast India never failed to remind him of the goodness of his life here. Later, when he returned from his ride, Abdul, the cook, would lay out a more substantial breakfast for him, with porridge, fruit, eggs, ham or bacon and more toast served with marmalade and preserves. Or upon rare occasion, should Norman request it, there would be an Indian breakfast of aloo paratha and dahi with jalebis or halwa-pudding on the side.

Outside the bungalow, the horse groom waited for Norman with the pony readied for his morning ride. Every morning, since his move to Jaunpur, he rode a five-mile route along the banks of the Gomti river, enjoying the flat, compacted, dun-coloured mudbank, the gentle sounds of the water, the soft river breeze, and the tall, feathery kash reeds that swayed gracefully by the river. As a young engineer setting out to serve in British India, he was advised at the Cooper's Institute in Surrey that exercise was essential to an Englishman's long-term sanity and survival in the tropics, as vital as careful discipline and moderation in the consumption of alcohol. Norman had heeded the advice in good faith for all the fourteen years he had lived in the country.

This morning, he stopped to gaze at the sixteenth-century stone bridge across the Gomti. It had been built on the orders of the great Mughal emperor, Akbar, and was something of a marvel of engineering. The city of Jaunpur itself was a couple of centuries older than the bridge and associated with the Delhi Sultanate. It was named after the most eccentric sultan ever known to India, Jauna Khan or Muhammad Bin Tughlaq, a mercurial genius with many ideas ahead of his time and what was, by all accounts of his reign, a slapdash, disaster-prone approach to their implementation.

Norman had struck up a friendship with the current nawab, a descendant of the thirteenth-century Sharqi rulers of Jaunpur, a well-educated, affable man with varied pursuits. He was always invited as part of the nawab's party for shikars or picnics. They also played chess on occasion. Norman was at home in this forgotten medieval-era town in India as he had never felt in any place before, in either England or India. Its sparsely cultivated countryside, its humble villagers, its quiet, unassuming river and especially its old monuments spoke to him. The beauty of the strong, stoic, sandstone architecture made by the Sharqi kings had laid a claim on his heart and mind. It spoke to him of many things—of humankind's innate impulse to build magnificent structures on the earth's surface, of the shared quest of rulers of all persuasions to leave their mark on posterity through architecture that combined beauty with functionality, of the inevitable, unrelenting march of time, and of how power was ephemeral, however absolute it seemed in the moment.

He rode around the Shahi Qila, the ancient stone fortress atop a small hillock, and headed back towards his bungalow. His thoughts flew to the time Lord Curzon, the viceroy, had visited Jaunpur for a day two years ago. Norman was a part of the local entourage deputed to take him around. Norman had taken the opportunity to bring him to the fortress and to make an impassioned plea. It was shameful to let historic monuments of such majesty fall into total ruin, in the absence of proper attention. When the Ancient Monuments Preservation Act 1904 was passed by the government, Norman had felt in its passage a small moment of personal achievement and satisfaction.

Upon returning, he dismounted from his horse in the driveway and handed the reins to the waiting groom. He squared his shoulders and strode indoors, exhilarated yet again by the generous proportions and quiet dignity of the limewashed bungalow with pillared verandas, arched colonnades, high-ceilinged, cool, airy rooms and ample gardens that was allotted to him. Most of his earlier postings in India were in remote encampments and had come with more modest lodgings. It was only in Jaunpur that he had gained the privilege of such an ample residence—a bungalow that stood in a salubrious tree-lined avenue, an easy ride from both the nawab's palace and from his club.

Norman enjoyed both the responsibilities and perks of his job equally. He travelled mostly on horseback, his pith helmet firmly on his head to safeguard against the harsh sun. It wasn't unusual for him to spend some nights in camp-mode before returning to the comforts of his home. He headed a team of well-trained and competent Indian engineers. The department hired a sturdy force of eight hundred labourers, whose wage roster and well-being he commanded. It was a hard life, touring with his subordinates, the villages and irrigation schemes falling in his jurisdiction. A hard life, but not an unrewarding one.

Once Martha and Madeline moved to this place, Norman would have no other happiness to ask of life. Even after two decades of being married to Martha, Norman had not stopped marvelling at the thought that a woman of her breeding, education and high taste had agreed to marry him. Of course, he had been an engineer with some prospects, but he was an engineer trained in a small county technical institute, while she had graduated with honours from the University of London, his working-class background no match for her family's status.

Martha had confessed to him several times that she found his humility endearing, his eagerness to learn and get ahead in life loveable. She held that his flexible and amiable nature was too rare a quality in a man to not appreciate. She could not have lived her life with a domineering husband who expected from her obedience and a constant kowtowing to societal strictures. It was Martha's encouragement and connections that had got him into the Royal Indian Engineers College in Surrey. He was glad to have been recruited into the India service.

It was odd how Martha had insisted on taking up a teacher's job and living in a small townhouse in

Middlesbrough, while he was here leading a lordly life in India, with cooks, bearers and attendants taking care of his every need. Over the years, he had pressed upon her to join him, but her dedication to Madeline's education came above every thought of comfort for herself. There was no denying that Madeline was an unusually gifted child and deserved the devoted mentoring her mother had provided her with by staying on in England. There was also the matter of his wife's increasing interest in the women's suffrage movement. He did not know what to make of it, but it did seem to be fashionable among a certain class of ladies in England.

Martha finally agreed to a year's visit to India. She was keen that Madeline should study at Oxford in twelve months. A year was a good start. Norman was hopeful that once they were here and saw for themselves the comforts and beauty on offer, their plans might change. It would have been good if they had come in November, at the start of the cold season, when ladies from home normally headed to India. A whole season of entertainment and engagements was planned out for them. But Martha needed to finish the school year and examinations, and thus they were delayed. The approaching warm weather could play spoilsport, of course, but Martha was a brisk, hardy woman and Madeline was young and eager. Norman was hopeful that they would adapt.

MARIAM DAS WAVED at her father out of the iron bars of the window as the train rolled away from the platform at Allahabad station. He was a dark-skinned man with a thick-set body, his right shoulder bent forward permanently from years of wielding a tall broom on the convent grounds. His eyes were curiously lit with an expression of pride mixed with fear. His figure became smaller and smaller, lost amidst a rush of families seeing travellers off, and bustling coolies and vendors hawking their wares on the crowded platform.

When Mariam had entered the train, the second-class compartment was packed with passengers seated on the slated wooden benches, their luggage stacked, precarious and unwieldy and in all shapes and sizes, on the narrow racks above them as well as under the seats. They looked at her with curiosity, taking in her dark brown skin with its reddish undertone and her plain ankle-length English gown. They allowed her place to squeeze into a window seat. She stowed her green canvas hold-all under her seat and settled in.

It was Mariam's very first time on a train, her very first trip out of Allahabad, the town she was born in. Her brother Vincent had been working at Jaunpur in the Post & Telegraph department for the last two years. He had sent for Mariam to come and interview for an ayah's position with a British family. She was headed there, grateful that a way out of her present job with a family in Allahabad had presented itself.

SPE LABOR LEVIS. Hope lightens work. That was the Latin motto of the charitable Convent for Catholic Girls where Mariam Das had studied. It was also her personal motto. As her train went thwack-clang-thwack-thwack-clang on the recently opened Lord Curzon Bridge over the mighty Ganges, Mariam felt hope bubble and dance through her bloodstream.

A shadow crossed her face as she thought of her current position, but she shut her eyes briefly and allowed herself to feel the excitement of new beginnings as the whistling steam train, with interlinked dark maroon-coloured couches and slatted iron windows, sped along urgently, moving eastwards on an elevated track. A furious, frothing blue-grey expanse of the river roared below. The sky outside the window was visible in slices through the massive slanting steel bars of the spanking new bridge. Further along the journey, little mud houses patterned with dung patties drying on their walls, wiry, bare-chested farmers with bullocks ploughing their fields and large stacks of hay passed by in a rush. Every now and then an elegant white egret could be seen surveying the countryside, daintily riding atop a black water buffalo, the beast oblivious of its own size and strength in comparison to the little bird lording over it.

The train stopped at a station and the cries of vendors filled the compartment. Her fellow travellers got off in a rush of coolies climbing in and large and small pieces of luggage being hastily pulled out. She settled in more comfortably in her corner, glad for the space. A new set of passengers hurried in, a large family. The man was bespectacled, his manner busy and officious as he settled in his wife, their three children, his parents and all their luggage into the compartment. He was perhaps a government employee. He looked as if he might request her to vacate her seat, leave the compartment to his entourage. Mariam looked out of the window, careful not to catch his eye.

When he was finally seated and the train was about to move again, he coughed loudly for her attention. His eyes were focused on the small oval steel locket hanging from a steel chain on her neck. Inside it was a picture of the Virgin Mary with Baby Jesus.

'Christi?' he asked.

She nodded briefly, even as his wife looked at her, her face full of curiosity. Her head and eyes were covered with the end of her sari which she lifted at a slant to peer cautiously at Mariam. The children stared openly.

'Nun?'

'Nanny,' she replied, after the briefest pause.

A vaguely puzzled look crossed their faces, not entirely sure of the word's meaning. She could have said ayah, had she wished to be clearer. However, she had disliked the man upon sight and didn't want to be slotted as a social inferior by him or his family. Gown-clad, convent-educated, fluent in English, on her way to a new job, she wished to hold her own.

The cries of the vendors offering *chai garma garam chai, paani Musalmaan paani, Hindu paani*—tea, hot-hot tea, drinking water for Muslims, drinking water for Hindus—drowned in the whistling and chugging forward of the train, out of the station. Mariam poured water into her white enamelled tin mug from her canteen and drank it. Mercifully, it was a short journey of four–five hours, and the water would last her. She had heard schoolmates tell terrifying tales of getting down to refill their flasks at a station and being unable to clamber back onto the train in time, obstructed by the crush of people at the train's door.

Faith in Mother Mary and her son Jesus was the mainstay of Mariam's life and though her hopes had been temporarily bashed around a few times by the vicissitudes of her life, for the most part the Divine Mother and Her Blessed Son had taken good care of her, well beyond the circumstances of her birth.

She had been born to a low-caste Hindu family in Allahabad, the younger of two siblings. Christianity had miraculously rescued them from a life of indignity heaped upon indignity due to an unexpected turn of events. Her father had been beaten up in an altercation with some upper-caste servants in the tradesman's house where he worked as a sweeper. He was badly injured and unable to work for over a month. The need to feed her two small children had taken Mariam's mother to the doors of the nuns who ran the convent for girls, begging for a job. As a low-caste woman, she was safer working in a convent than in the houses of rich tradesmen, who considered women like her game to be preyed upon at will. The sprawling red-brick convent with its long corridors, beautiful arched porches, courtyards, grotto and gardens—and its band of nuns in their stern black and white habits, completely dedicated to Mary Ward's vision of education for women—fortuitously took her in and extended a helping hand so she could emerge out of her miserable situation.

Mariam's mother had found not only a job for herself but a home in Jesus for her small family. Her husband was hired by the school as a sweeper for its vast grounds. The couple converted to Christianity at the nuns' suggestion. Their two children, Vinod and Meera, were baptized and rechristened Vincent and Mariam and enrolled into the charitable school for poor girls (the school was not averse to underage boys), which the nuns ran alongside the main school. The main school was for the daughters of the city's gentlefolk.

Mariam had prior experience working with white families. As soon as she had finished middle school the nuns had trained her and found her a job as nanny to a British family with three young children. Three more were born later. She had worked with the family for ten years before all the children had grown to the age of being sent back one by one to school in England. The Pinkerton-Smiths had treated her well, almost like a family member.

The next place she found work at had not been as happy an experience. However, she had steeled herself to stick on till a new prospect opened. And now here she was, an olive-green canvas hold-all with all her belongings rolled up under her seat, a glowing reference letter from Mrs Pinkerton-Smith and another letter of recommendation from the nuns at her old school in her reticule and an interview scheduled for the next evening with Mr Norman Evans, her prospective employer.

The aroma of mango pickle, sharply pungent and tantalizing, floated into her nostrils and filled up the compartment as the family travelling with her opened their tiffin boxes and began passing around food to each other—roasted parathas and a dry potato subzi which the woman must have woken early to prepare and pack.

Rocked by the motion of the train, Mariam felt calm and pleasantly lulled. A brief smile crossed her lips as she fingered the locket on her neck and tried to get some sleep.

NORMAN TOOK HIS evening tea on the front porch. He looked around idly, sinking into the comfort of a worn cane armchair. A pair of coffee-brown, yellow-billed mynah birds with matching yellow feet were scouring the flower beds in the front lawn for worms. Ram Deen, the gardener, clad in only a white vest and a flimsy cotton loin cloth, was bent over the beds hoeing and turning the soil. Norman's daftar, the papers and files he had brought home from office, lay piled on a small study table beside him, the rays of the late afternoon sun streaming past the pillars and creating a dappled pool around them. It was his practice to go through these at teatime.

After this was done, he would go indoors and get dressed for dinner. Gobind laid out a tailcoat, a boiled shirt, and a white waistcoat, with a stiff collar and a white tie, along with perfectly polished boots for him every evening. Norman scarcely ever ate dinner alone, preferring whatever company was on offer at the club, or frequently accepting an invitation from friends to dine at their home. It gave him a reason to change for dinner, dress formally as befitting a sahib. Setting the right tone before the natives was important.

He remembered he was to interview a young woman for the ayah's position. He glanced at his pocket watch—

the interview was scheduled ten minutes from now. He searched about his table for the handwritten paper on which the fellow at the post office had given him her name and details. Decent, well-spoken chap. This was his sister, apparently. Though, there was no saying for sure. In India, anyone from within a fifty-mile radius of their village was described by his labourers as a brother. Before his thoughts could meander any further, he heard the click of the wrought iron gate. She was early.

He watched her as she walked down the long driveway, her head moving to take into her gaze the hibiscus hedge and the garden beyond it. Her eyes rested on the rose beds and then moved to appreciate the speckled orange and yellow canna lilies standing tall in octagonal beds in the far corner. He noted with surprise that she was not wearing a sari but was clad in Western attire. She wore a plain, discreetly tailored gown in light blue cotton, lightly gathered at the waist, with a round collar and long sleeves—nothing showy or unbecoming about it. A tiny, inexpensive steel locket adorned her neck.

She came and stood in front of Norman, positioning herself before the study table, her hands folded in front of her in greeting.

'Mariam Das?' he asked, reading her name aloud from the note in his hand.

'Yes, sir,' she replied, meeting his gaze levelly. She proceeded to fish out some papers from the fabric reticule on her shoulder.

'My references. This, from Mrs Pinkerton-Smith. I worked with the family for ten years in Allahabad. And this reference is from Sister Superior at my school,' she said as she extended the papers to him.

She was twenty-eight years old. Had studied till class eight at St Anne's Convent in Allahabad. Her spoken English was good, with a sing-song Indian convent-school accent.

'And from your current employer?'

Her eyes clouded momentarily, and she looked down. She was wearing black buttoned boots with a broad front, well-worn, but of foreign make. Perhaps handed down to her by a previous employer, he surmised.

'I did not ask them for one. They are not very keen that I should leave.'

'But you are keen to leave their service?' he asked.

'For personal reasons, sir. My brother works with the P & T department in Jaunpur. I have spent my entire life in Allahabad. It is an exciting opportunity for me to work in a new city. My brother and his wife will be nearby and have assured my parents that they will look after me,' she replied, looking up with a gaze as clear as the blue sky above them.

He liked the quiet confidence with which she spoke. She was of medium build, had a round face with a snub nose, her hair pulled back in a low bun at the nape of her neck, her dark eyes observant and intelligent.

'My house is run well enough for my needs by my cook and bearer. Your job will be to attend to my wife and daughter. They are joining me here next month from England. You will have the usual duties of a lady's maid—serve them their morning tray in their rooms, make their beds and look after their bath, lay out their clothes, help serve their guests, run errands for them outside the house as required. I assume you are familiar with the work.'

Looking at her as he spoke, he realized he had never seen a native woman in Western attire before on all his various postings across India, though of course in cities like Bombay and Calcutta there were many Anglo-Indian women, of mixed blood, to be seen in English-style dresses. She made for a piquant change, this new applicant for an ayah's position.

'My daughter just turned eighteen last week. I would also require you to accompany her on walks and picnics and be a friendly chaperone to her,' he continued.

A group of tiny sparrows ventured onto the porch and hopped about delicately. A crow cawed loudly on the neem tree outside the gate. He wondered if he should offer her tea and decided against it. It might make her uncomfortable or be met with veiled hostility from his bearer or cook. He would leave it to Martha to set the tone for the family's interaction with her. As a Christian mission-trained, English-speaking person she would have to be treated appropriately. Above the other servants, but not so much as to annoy them or provoke them into treating her meanly.

'As I mentioned, I worked with the Pinkerton-Smiths for several years. The family has four daughters. I was fortunate that they considered me as much a friend as a servant. I have some understanding of how delicate the position of a lady's maid to a young lady can be,' said Mariam.

Once again, Norman was impressed by the dignity of the woman before him. As he asked her to sit down and discussed the terms of her employment with her, he felt glad to have found what seemed like a level-headed and very suitable person for the position. He hoped she would find favour with Martha.

THE POSTMAN HAD dropped two letters in the evening post. Madeline looked out from the window of their sitting room, drumming her fingertips on the pane to the tune of 'Are you sleeping? Are you sleeping? Brother John …' as she waited for Martha to return. The letters were lying unopened on the mantelpiece, one in a white envelope with pastel green stamps bearing King Edward's crowned head, the other in a large brown envelope with a red lacquer seal at the back. They awaited her mother's return. From the postmarks on them, she could guess the contents and the excitement was almost too much to bear.

As soon as she saw her mother turn the corner into their street, she picked up the two envelopes and let herself out onto the cobbled street.

'Mamma, look!' she called out. 'See what's come.'

Madeline wore a light lemon yellow and grey paisley printed cotton dress, holding its long skirt up a few inches in one hand to stop it from dragging on the street. The letters were held in the other hand. Her hazel eyes shone with excitement. Of course, Mamma would insist they go in and sit down in the parlour before they opened them. Even so. Now she knew the letters had come. The letter Mamma was waiting for was here at last.

'Goodness, child!' said Martha as they entered the house together. 'You've rushed me off my poor feet!'

Madeline looked at her expectantly. Surely, her mother would open the two envelopes before she did anything else!

As Madeline had predicted to herself when the letters arrived, Martha opened the letter from Oxford first. The second envelope bore the seal of the P & O Steam Navigation Company.

'It is exactly as I expected. Somerville College, Oxford, is pleased to offer you a place in its Bachelor's programme,' she said, a broad smile transfiguring her usually serious face. 'I am so proud of you Madeline!'

Madeline let out a sigh of relief.

'I'm so glad, Mamma. I would have hated to disappoint you and Papa.' She put an arm around her mother and leaned her head on Martha's shoulder, shutting her eyes briefly to savour the moment.

'Though there is still Girton College at Cambridge to hear from,' said Martha. 'All things considered I think I would be happier for you to head towards Oxford.'

Madeline nodded back sagely. The male students at Cambridge had fallen in her mother's esteem ever since they had burnt effigies of women scholars in the Market Square. They had destroyed property worth hundreds of pounds and manipulated votes to make sure women continued to be fobbed off with apologetic certificates instead of getting the equivalent degrees they deserved.

'It troubles me to think that the more privileged their position, the harder men fight to defend it,' Madeline remembered Martha saying to the senior girls' class. 'A sharpness of brain is no guarantee of a magnanimity of heart.'

'Mamma, do let's open the other packet!' She had a fair guess on what it contained.

This would be her father's promised eighteenth birthday gift to her!

Martha carefully opened the envelope with an intricately carved, delicately perfumed sandalwood paperknife brought back by Norman on one of his trips home. She took out two first class tickets from the Peninsular and Oriental Company from Southampton to Bombay and held them out towards Madeline.

Madeline clasped the tickets to her bosom and looked towards the ceiling, her green-gold eyes full of rapture, her hair falling in soft waves around her face and on her shoulders.

'Thank you, Papa. Thank you, life. Beautiful world, lay out your charms. Bring forward your sights and sounds. Madeline Evans is headed your way!'

Martha felt a strange disquiet as she watched her daughter pirouette, kissing the tickets repeatedly and laughing with unrestrained glee. It troubled her that Madeline was more excited by the prospect of travelling to India than by her hard-won admission into Oxford.

'Imagine, we are to travel to India in less than a month's time. To think I will celebrate my birthday sailing upon an ocean. Am I not the luckiest girl this side of the Suez Canal? And then when we are there, I shall count myself the luckiest girl *that* side of the Canal. Do you suppose we will meet a rajah and his entourage on-board? Papa travelled with one who had an entire harem travelling with him, and his dogs too. Do you suppose dogs get seasick? I certainly hope you and I won't!'

Martha frowned as she got up from the sofa to go to her room to change out of her work clothes and into her flannel nightdress. She wished she could share Madeline's enthusiasm for India.

'Seasickness is the least of our worries. I would hate to catch cholera or typhoid or some other terrible tropical fever. Or get bitten by a snake lurking under my bed,' she said. 'A cobra or a python.'

Several years ago, Norman had given her a copy of a book called *Tropical Trials: A Hand-Book for Women in the Tropics*. Just reading it had made her queasy. But, in all fairness, she had procrastinated and delayed this trip enough to try the patience of the mildest and most understanding of husbands. Madeline had finished school. She was eager to travel. Martha's own leave of absence for a year had been granted without any resentment by the school patron. The school knew itself to be lucky to have a woman of her class and breeding amongst its staff.

Martha had to rescue the tropical handbook from whichever forgotten corner of her book-lined parlour it was languishing in. It would put her in the right frame of mind for the impending trip. It might even provide a few practical tips as they prepared for the journey.

'You remember that heavy tome Papa brought me long ago, that last time we had plans for India, but we couldn't go? Maybe, we can read it together, a bit each evening, as preparation for the journey.

'There are snake charmers in India! Do you suppose we will encounter one? They play a particularly slow, mesmerizing sort of music to which the snake dances out of hiding. I read about it. And do you recall the story Papa told us about the bearer's children at one of his quarters who kept a pet mongoose in the compound?'

'Madeline, enough talk my dear!' said Martha. 'Let's sit down for supper now. And do bring out some sherry from the cupboard in the pantry, dearest. We must celebrate your admission to Oxford. You shall have just a wee bit, young lady, since you're not yet eighteen.'

MARTHA EVANS STOOD on the 'A' deck of the *SS Dwarka*, breathing the salt air deeply and grateful for the relative calm of the ocean. Norman had booked for them a rather well-appointed portside cabin. It was only concern about leaving Madeline unsupervised on the decks for yet another day that had made her come out of it.

Her first three days onboard had seen a terrible churning and heaving of her insides. Madeline, it seemed, had sea-legs. She was skipping all over the boat on them from the very first day, happy to converse with everyone, from crew to second class passengers to unattached gentlemen. As Madeline flitted in and out of their cabin full of stories to share with her mother, Martha decided she had better step out before Madeline acquired the reputation of being a very flighty young woman. She was a schoolgirl in her own head, but in the strict eyes of her fellow passengers she was likely to be misunderstood for a too-forward, ill-bred young lady.

Madeline bounced up from the deck chair where she had been poring over her atlas and came to greet her mother. 'Mamma, isn't it perfectly splendid to be out on sea? This air makes me ravenously hungry, and the food they serve onboard is so good too! Today you simply must come and have the lovely spread they lay out for the 4 o'clock tea.'

'You are not to mention food in front of me. I have only had coffee and two slices of dry toast since we left Southampton. Even that has taken no mean exertion of will power to hold down.' Martha shuddered. On Norman's suggestion, she had borrowed Chota Mem's book *The English Bride in India* from the library. As advised by the author she had brought along her old dresses for the early part of the voyage, to be discarded after they got smelly and soiled from seasickness. Probably the only useful advice in that book as far as Martha was concerned was on matters of wardrobe. The rest was about the management of staff, stores, household accounts and setting up house on a budget. She intended to stay clear of those, content to let Norman manage his household as he had been doing all these years without her.

Housekeeping was among the womanly virtues Martha had taken great care not to acquire. It was nothing but an invitation to women to pledge their creativity away at the altar of providing men and children with creature comforts, all in exchange for empty adulation at best, and more frequently titbits of patronizing affection mixed with frequent demands and complaints. She was most certainly better off doing other things with her mind and attention.

'Oh Mamma, how I wish the French had left things well alone instead of digging up the Suez Canal. Then we could have spent months on end on this beautiful liner instead of just three weeks,' said Madeline, breaking into her thoughts. 'And we would have gone around the Cape of Good Hope. Isn't it the most beautiful name ever? Just think—the Atlantic Ocean meeting the Indian Ocean in front of one's very own eyes!'

The captain had seated Madeline and Martha on separate tables for the entire duration of their trip. Martha did not know whether that pleased her or not, but she decided against requesting a change. Madeline would get an opportunity to make friends her own age. And Martha would have the pleasure of adult company, perhaps a much-needed opportunity to remember and revisit her social graces a bit before being dropped into the deep end at Jaunpur. She was mildly nervous about joining Norman's circle in India. His tales of his bridge and billiards playing club cronies and of hobnobbing with nawabs for hunts and picnics did not fill her with enthusiasm. The many years of living apart had made a happy recluse of her.

Back in Middlesbrough, she and Madeline lived a quiet life focussed on academic pursuits. That, and an occasional meeting or demonstration by the Women's Union that Martha attended. If she were the kind of woman who embroidered and hung frames with neat cross-stitch borders and pithy sayings in her parlour, hers would have read *Happy to Be a Bluestocking.*

At dinner, Martha found herself seated between a bird-like elderly lady from Germany who was an Indologist and a scholar in Sanskrit, and a gentleman who managed a coffee and spice plantation in the Nilgiris. Mrs Hilda Wilhelm-Burke travelled frequently to India. Mr Arnold too was an old India hand, suited and booted in great style, his elegant watch, tiepin, cufflinks and large topaz on the ring finger all suggestive of the healthy fortune to be made in plantations in India.

'Well, I must own up. This will be my first visit to the country even though my husband has been with the Public Works Department in India for almost fifteen years now,' said Martha, turning her head in either direction, bringing them both into the ambit of her confession.

'You will either love it or hate it. Most chaps I know grow to love it. India has its own rhythm and a certain earthy charm which draws you in after a while. But ladies, in my estimation, suffer much. Some find the heat intolerable, and then there are the discomforts of running a house in a foreign place. There is the matter of mosquitoes and houseflies. Also, a lot of the conveniences we are used to back home are simply not available. You will do well to learn a smattering of the local language. It will help you settle in quicker.'

This came from Mr Arnold. She tried to place his accent but didn't quite succeed. Certainly not public school. Not North England either. South or southeast covered with a coat of British sahib accent. It was a particular accent of clipped commands and authority that she had observed Norman acquire over his years in India.

'You must speak Indian fluently by now,' the lady sitting next to Mrs Hilda Wilhelm-Burke asked her, clearly finding the conversation of interest and keen to join in.

'I'm afraid I'm the most impractical of creatures, a scholar of ancient Indian spiritual texts. I'm working on a translation of the Atharvaveda from Sanskrit into German. Sanskrit is like Latin, you know. No one speaks it anymore. And though I expect you don't have any reason to know this, there is no such language as Indian. They speak dozens of other languages though. Too many if you ask me,' she replied. 'It's like the Tower of Babel.'

'Too many languages, too many faiths and gods too, a too-muchness of foods, festivals and rituals. But you don't have to let any of it worry you. The household staff is trained in our ways. You are unlikely to be meeting a whole lot of other natives. And if perchance you do, they will be ones from the gentlemanly class who speak English well,' Mr Arnold interjected, addressing both Martha and the other lady.

Martha found the dinner conversation more enjoyable than she had anticipated. The claret, a Château Talbot she had ordered on the steward's recommendation, had helped her relax. Mr Arnold had been courteous and attentive in an exaggeratedly gallant but not unpleasing manner, and Mrs Wilhelm-Burke had a fascinating history. Her family was long domiciled in England, although she was of German stock. She was a grandniece of Max Mueller. Martha couldn't wait to share that nugget of information with Madeline. 'My daughter is a polyglot and passionate about the study of languages.

She will delight in shaking hands with the grandniece of such a famed scholar. You must allow me to present her to you,' she said.

MADELINE STARED INTO the dreamy vastness of the ocean. The waves were sloshing energetically against the sides of the ship. The song of the sea was metronomic, slowly mesmerizing her. In the distance, the waves seemed neon threaded with silver. At the horizon the sea appeared stitched to the ultramarine sky with a silver light. It was as if their ship was a glistening white pearl, newly born and solitary, contained within the oyster lips of sea and sky.

All her life Madeline had been preparing to know the world, sedately, studiously through her lessons and her books—and here she was suddenly plunged into it, breathing it. The earth was no longer a construct in her head, or something showcased on a globe in her school library, or even something to discover inside the well-thumbed pages of the cherished school atlas she had carried with her. It was out here, and she was inside of it, its many experiences unpacked for her to touch, feel, and hear.

The ship was the whole world in miniature, a tiny replica of human society. She could catch the strains of many different languages in its air. They had scarcely been aboard, and she had conversed with different passengers on her deck in French, Spanish and German. Their cabin steward, a dark brown man whose lips parted frequently in a dazzling smile revealing teeth that shone bright, was from a colony called Goa and spoke Portuguese. She felt a stab of disappointment even as she tried out her few words of Portuguese with him. She had hoped he could help her with Hindustani.

She stole into the second class deck at the back of the ship after breakfast and sat in a corner, her face partially hidden behind her atlas, trying to tune into the conversations buzzing around her. She shut her eyes and let her body float in a pool of sound, the waves and intonations, the rise and fall of overlapping tongues washing over her. A sudden nudge of possible meaning touched her fleetingly like a small fish and then wriggled away, eluding her grasp as she reached out to catch it. She sighed in exasperation. Her luck in learning languages with ease seemed to have run out. Giving up the effort for the moment, she stared vacantly at the scene around her.

There was a contingent of nurses, another of soldiers, and a saffron-turbaned man in billowing robes, with long hair and a beard flowing to his chest. Next to him were two clean-shaven acolytes who were lovingly feeding him almonds dipped in honey with their hands, taking turns to do so. Apparently, that was all he ate. There was a big retinue of servants to some rajah, all in splendid crimson and yellow livery. There was so much she would have liked to ask them. But it was like being seated at a grand table with no cutlery laid out. Her mouth watered, her hands itched, her stomach growled, but she was to have no taste of it.

Back at their own deck she found her mother engaged in deep conversation with Mrs Wilhelm-Burke. It was nice to see Mamma making a new friend. She had been listless from the start of the voyage. The rhythm and salt smell of the sea made her feel heavy-headed and slumberous. She often fell asleep while she was reading on the deck but lay awake at night tossing in her bunk.

Mrs Wilhelm-Burke and Mamma were discussing how many young British women travelled to India each year, some of them with their wedding trousseaus packed into large chests and booked into the lower hold, hoping to find suitable husbands in the Raj. They were snidely referred to as the 'fishing fleet', setting out in November and arriving in India to a whole season of social engagements laid out for them to meet young men. Those who failed in their endeavour to catch a husband had to come back in March and were cruelly labelled as the 'returning empties'.

Madeline listened to them for a while before she spoke, unable to keep her discomfort to herself. 'But Mamma, isn't it brave to set sail like that, not knowing whom you will marry or where you will live, and what your life might turn out to be?'

'No braver or more adventurous, Madeline, if you think about it, than your father coming out alone to India on a new job. He went to where his work called him. Marriage just happens to be the job most young women are trained for. And if many marriageable gentlemen have gone to India, then the ladies must follow in pursuit to become their wives. Or be content to remain on the shelf!'

'Mamma, you do say the oddest things! You make it sound so unromantic and calculating!' Madeline protested.

'Dear Martha,' said Mrs Wilhelm-Burke. 'You do take a very prosaic view of things. It is all quite dashing and exciting, the dances, the picnics, the sporting events, the hunting parties. Though you will only be catching the tail end of the season, who knows—Madeline might find a charming beau and be swept off her feet.'

It never ceased to amaze Martha what elaborate courtship rituals society put in place to seduce young women into a life of unpaid housekeeping. She restrained herself from voicing the thought aloud. It was not good to be cynical in front of the young. Hilda was right about that.

'My dear Hilda, I truly hope that Madeline will eventually find a bright, young fellow to love and marry and spend her life with. But not yet. First, she must do justice to her *own* wonderful intellect, grow to be a full-fledged person in her *own* right. I wish that for every girl under my tutelage and most certainly for my dearest daughter. There is something slightly abhorrent about this whole business of young women being transported across the ocean to be mated.'

Mrs Wilhelm-Burke smiled at Madeline. 'There you have it, my dear. Though your mother speaks bluntly, there is some truth in what she says. Young women have been sailing to India in search of husbands for over half a century now, ever since the shipping routes became easier. Some are lucky to find love, but many must settle for whatever match they can find ... or take the long voyage home.'

Returning empties.

How achingly hollow, how wretched, how demeaning the phrase sounded. It made Martha shudder.

An unmarried woman in England was the subject of pity and ridicule, even if she had an inheritance or some independent income of her own. And those who were not provided for were not trained for any profession. They were thrust into being governesses or lady's companions to richer relatives, their lives relegated to a state of permanent abnegation. Martha had been dangerously close to being left on the shelf herself, till Norman fortuitously came along and asked her to marry him. She had accepted his proposal with great relief.

Of course, there had been some fondness of heart too on either side. She had struck lucky. Norman respected her.

'Madeline, my love. It's education, the vote and respect that women need most in this new century. Marriage cannot be the whole of a woman's life any more than it is a man's life.'

'Yes, Mamma,' Madeline smiled back. Her mother's views were known to her. Madeline admired her mother greatly for her forward thinking and independent stance on life.

'Have you made any progress with learning Hindustani?' Hilda Wilhelm-Burke asked Madeline. She had confided to Wilhelm-Burke her determination to learn three or four new phrases of Hindustani each day while aboard the ship and have the rudiments of the language in her head before she reached the country. A few words and phrases, many gestures, and listening, listening, listening, listening, listening—that was

Madeline's usual road map into the thicket of languages. You made the slightest of paths, the merest clearing and walked in ready to encounter whatever lay in wait, and sooner or later you reached a well-lit spot, a place from where you could look about and understand the shape of the entire forest.

'*Namaste, shukriya, maaf karna*—hello, thank you, excuse me—I haven't progressed beyond that, sadly,' she said with a rueful laugh.

One of the young gentlemen seated at her table had obliged her by teaching these three phrases. After that she reached a dead end. When she used them with the ship's staff they smiled indulgently and gently told her she could speak to them in English. Some even looked visibly distressed by her efforts. Apparently, it was insulting to assume they needed to be spoken to in their native language. It was a slur on their training.

THE AYAH'S ROOM in the Evans' bungalow in Jaunpur was a modest one at the back of the house. It was situated near the kitchen and stores. Its redeeming features were a good-sized arched window with a broad windowsill and a tall wooden door with brass knobs that opened out onto a private little veranda.

An old mango tree occupied much of the immediate backyard beyond the veranda. Its dark green branches and leaves provided a pleasant view from the window and the suggestion of a vast outdoor vista. Sheltered by the shade of the tree, the room was cooler than other parts of the bungalow. Dragonflies whirred in the backyard, spinning about in expanding circles. Little squirrels scrambled up and down the trunk of the mango tree. A crow dropped in every morning on the lookout for stale bread left out by Abdul the cook, next to it a beaker of water. A colony of little black ants busily occupied a crack in the veranda floor, marching to and fro holding aloft dead moths and beetles, dragging little grains of sugar or rice at other times. A fat, lazy golden tabby cat had marked out the backyard as his hunting ground at night. The single, somewhat wobbly, old cane chair in the veranda served as his bed when the sun shone. After a few days of warily watching from afar the new occupant of the hitherto vacant room, the cat reached a tacit understanding with her. She could sit on the chair when he was not using it.

Mariam Das stood staring at her own face in the small mirror she had placed on the window ledge. As she applied oil to her hair and combed it out before tying it into a low bun, she wondered if her appearance was pleasant enough. In her long years of service, she had learnt that it was an essential requirement for a position such as hers to look reassuringly pleasant. Not pretty or beautiful. Quite certainly not alluring.

But also, not too plain, and unsmiling. Plainness or a reserved demeanour was often confused for an unwillingness to serve. An ayah needed to find the correct balance between visibility and invisibility—within sight of the immediate family she was serving but not overly discernable to their circle of visitors and friends.

Mariam had been at the Evans' home a week. As the memsahib and the daughter were yet to arrive, there was little for her to do. Norman sahib spent much of his day outside the house. He had suggested that she take an inventory of the things in the house and tell him what other items of linen or furniture he might need to add to make his family comfortable. The bungalow had lain mostly vacant and was sparsely used in his years here. Which was a pity given how lovely it was.

Mariam wrote out a list in her neat convent school handwriting, cursive, looped and slanting gently to the right—just as the nuns had painstakingly taught each one of their students, rich or underprivileged. She went out to the front porch where Norman sahib would be seated at this time, going over his files and having his evening tea. The cook prepared for him a plate of deviled eggs or finely sliced cucumber sandwiches on most days. Abdul was eager to revisit his delicious teacake and fruit bun recipes once the ladies arrived.

'Here is the list.' She extended a small notebook towards Norman.

The whiff of her jasmine-scented hair oil assailed Norman's nostrils. He blinked beneath his spectacles, startled by it. This house had been a stranger to feminine fragrances for too long. He recalled the soft baby talcum powder smell of Madeline as an infant and felt a catch in his throat.

Mariam had put together a brief, sensible list. Just what he would have expected of her.

- Mosquito nets
- Additional candles and candlestands
- Hand fans

- Hand and face towels
- Sherry or port wine

'Very good,' he nodded. 'Is there anything else?'

'It would be good if you hired boys to pull the fans. The family will be spending more time at home than you do, and I expect there will be morning callers coming to pay their respects,' she said.

Smart girl. Didn't miss a trick.

For the moment, the big, airy, high-ceilinged rooms of the bungalow did not require anything. But in another few weeks the weather would turn. Young boys would need to be hired to sit outside, pulling with their toes the cord attached to the heavy draped fans on the ceilings.

'Very good. I'll tell Gobind to look into the matter. Thank you. If you think of anything else, let me know. I'm here for the rest of the week.'

Norman would be going to Bombay to escort his wife and daughter home. It was a long journey, involving a change of trains. He preferred to do it himself rather than depute a subordinate for the purpose. He wanted to gather Madeline's earliest impressions of India first-hand, as the country passed before her curious eyes, displaying its varied charms and its inherent chaos. He wanted to witness Martha's reaction too.

'There is the matter of the dhobi,' Mariam ventured. 'Memsahib shall not be happy to share a laundryman with other families. She will require one who visits more frequently than once a week.'

That was again something Norman had overlooked. The old dhobi who arrived every Sunday to collect

Norman's clothes, wash them on the riverbank, iron them at his home and return with them neatly stacked in a bundle on his donkey's back was going to find it difficult to cope. Two ladies in residence would mean a much larger load. There would be morning dresses for visiting and receiving callers, formal gowns for dinner, night gowns. Also, special attire for riding and playing tennis. Then, additional bedlinen, towels, table linen, napkins.

'I will ask Gobind to talk to him and see how we can work this out. Perhaps some relative of his can be hired separately for us,' he said.

Mariam nodded and stood there to see if he had anything further to say to her. Then deciding that their business was concluded, she bent down to pick up her notebook from the table next to him. He had put it there after glancing through her list.

Again, the slight whiff of jasmine. He reprimanded himself mentally for being so aware of it.

'I hope you are comfortable here,' he said.

Both Abdul and Gobind had conveyed a favourable opinion of her to him. She seemed to be a sensible young woman. Devout too, it seemed. She had brought along her Bible to read and had sought permission to attend church each Sunday with her brother's family. A separate afternoon service was held for native Christians at the local church.

'Yes sir, thank you, sir,' she replied.

He noted that she seemed to possess only two gowns. She was wearing the pale yellow one today. It agreed with her dusky complexion.

'If you need anything, please let Gobind know.'

'I needed one or two things. I have taken an old mattress and a spare quilt, after checking with Gobind,' she replied.

He had turned his attention to his sandwich platter, thoughtfully picking up a sandwich to eat. Abdul had perfected these to an art. The cucumber was finely cut and served between thin slices of soft, white bread with the crust removed. A thick coating of butter with just the right amount of coarsely ground black pepper were what made them perfect.

Receiving no response from Norman, Mariam discreetly walked away.

As he sat there with his evening tea, Norman Evans wondered what it would be like to have his family and a fully functional home in India. He looked forward to the hustle and bustle of day visitors and to entertaining friends in the evening for dinner. Even additional staff floating about the rooms felt like a pleasing novelty, after the many parched, quasi-single years here.

AFTER A STOP at Gibraltar, there was no sight of land for a few days, just an endless expanse of blue ocean and blue sky merging seamlessly on a distant horizon. It seemed to Madeline that blue was a language in and of itself, speaking in endless variations of tone and depth. She felt a pleasant kind of ennui staring into the sea. Even though she had thought she could go on gazing at it forever, she was relieved when Rose Eliot came on board the *SS Dwarka*.

The ship stopped at Marseille to take on board new passengers. They had travelled from England by train to Marseille to escape the turbulence of the Bay of Biscay on the initial leg of the voyage. There was the confusion of their bags scattered all over the decks until they were taken by the crew into the individual cabins. Among the new arrivals was a girl roughly Madeline's age with cases after cases of luggage. She stood there briskly supervising the stowing of her exceptionally vast baggage. It soon became apparent that she was not alone. She was travelling with an elderly gentleman, tall, upright, gaunt of face with a handlebar moustache that grew down to his chin before turning up in an impressive curlicue.

They were seated next to each other at breakfast the next morning. Her name, she said in a minty sweet voice that matched her toothy smile, was Rose. Rose Eliot. 'My Uncle George is setting up a school for the workers on his old estate. I volunteered to come with him, help settle him back there,' Rose explained to Madeline.

It was a curious tale. Rose's uncle had spent his life as a manager of a tea estate in India. After his retirement, he and his wife moved back to England. The wife had died shortly after, and Uncle George had developed a hankering to return to India, spend the remainder of his days in the mist-laden, rolling, green mountains he had spent his working years in. After a prolonged correspondence with his old company and his club he had managed to arrange a second innings for himself in the colony to his satisfaction. He would be starting a small school for the children of the tea-pickers in the gardens and had arranged to stay at a suite at the Planters' Club for the rest of his life. 'No place like India for an old India hand,' Rose laughed indulgently. 'Frankly, I miss it too.'

Rose and her sisters had spent their early years in India. It was with mixed feelings that the family had moved back to Sussex. The unexpected death of a cousin had left the minister's position in his village parish vacant for her father. He had taken it with relief tinged with only the slightest regret. The India years had been an exciting experience, but he and his wife were glad to ferry their large family comprising five daughters and two sons back to England, to the modest country estate now to be their home. The children were growing somewhat wild and difficult. They were running free and untamed through the large compound of the church, playing with the servants' children all day and paying only perfunctory attention to learning the lessons their mother strove hard to teach them.

'Do you remember any Hindustani, Rose?' Madeline asked.

'Oh, do I? How can I ever forget it? Hindustani was the first language I learnt to speak. My sisters too. Those first nursery rhymes that our ayah taught us still lift my spirits when I'm feeling doleful. There was this lullaby—*ninni baba ninni, makhan, roti, cheeni*—which we all loved hearing night after night. My sister now puts her babies to bed with it. And those cuss words the maali's son taught us—much to my mother's dismay. I remember them all!'

'Oh, please could you teach me Hindustani? I wish to make the most of my trip and want to surprise Papa.'

'Yes, of course. I'll teach you everything I know. Except the cuss words,' replied Rose with a wicked grin. 'I wouldn't want those traced to my door.'

Over the course of the next few days the two girls became inseparable, with Madeline vicariously living Rose's idyllic childhood in Ranchi and learning to twist her tongue around Hindustani. To her surprise, the ship's staff who had discouraged her own tentative efforts at speaking the language were very welcoming of Rose.

'They recognize a former missy-baba when they see one,' declared Rose triumphantly. Children who had grown up in the Raj mastered the art of making native attendants dance to their tunes even before they left their crib. They were undisputed stars in the eyes of their ayahs, cooks and bearers.

Madeline trailed behind Rose, happy and devoted, like a minor acolyte, content to learn by observing the master. Her mind looped and spiralled around the phrases and pauses, the turns of expression, as she listened attentively. Hindustani was complicated, its contours and exact form as confusing as a jalebi—and as sweet, flavourful and juicy on the tongue.

❋

MARTHA WAS GRATEFUL for the respite from the langour of being at sea when the *SS Dwarka* docked at Port Said in Egypt. Norman had booked Madeline and her on a two-day excursion. In addition to a viewing of the pyramids at Giza, there were to stay over at the famous Shepheard's Hotel in Cairo.

Life on board had fallen into a pattern of sorts. The sports enthusiasts had busied themselves with organizing tennis matches, the older gentlemen with playing noisy games of whist and the older ladies with watching the young people, who were fully engaged in evening parlour games and nightly dances hosted by the ship's captain. The passengers had gradually fallen into different cliques and groupings. And as had strangely become a pattern in her own life, Martha belonged not here, not there, not anywhere except inside her own head. Fortunately, there was Mrs Wilhelm-Burke. Dear, dear Hilda, more bookish than herself even.

Madeline and Rose were inseparable now. They were brimming with excitement at the prospect of sightseeing.

Rose had travelled this route many times before.

'Oh, Shepheard's is the very finest hotel in the world, I'm sure. My dear Mrs Evans,' she told Martha, 'you simply must see those stained-glass windows with their arches. Not to speak of their fine display of Persian carpets. And I do so love their gardens and terraces.'

Mrs Wilhelm-Burke had decided to remain on board and would not be accompanying them on the excursion, much to Martha's disappointment. When Martha went to bid her goodbye, she was catching up on her correspondence. She had in front of her a stack of postcards from the purser's room, beautifully illustrated with drawings and photographs of their ship.

'I stopped to ask if you might want something from the local shops.'

'Very thoughtful of you, dear, but I don't fancy anything. The older I get, the less I wish to possess. You might want to pick up a papyrus painting or two for your home in India,' she advised. 'Bargain a bit if you can bring yourself to. As you move East, prices get increasingly flexible you will find.'

'Oh, they inflate prices here? That is so terrible, so dishonest!'

'I don't know about that. Material objects have no value other than what's attributed to them by each person. In a cosmic sense, a different price for every person is more correct than the same price for everyone. Perhaps the East understands this better than the West, my dear.'

'I'd better be hurrying along. The girls are waiting.'

As she hurried towards the waiting Madeline and Rose, Martha puzzled over Hilda's viewpoint, not for the first time in their interaction. Hilda was a remarkable, scholarly woman but had spent too many summers under the Indian sun. Martha herself would rather deal with fixed prices than arbitrary ones. The slipperiness of eastern ethics was disconcerting to her.

As they disembarked from the vessel, Rose and Madeline made a fetching pair in their best gowns and wide-brimmed hats. They were carrying gaily printed parasols in case the sun got too hot as the day progressed.

Rose had been receiving much attention from a couple of gentlemen on board, desirous of courting her, but so far, she had shown a polite but guarded face to them. She divided her time between attending to her uncle—who was now part of a bridge foursome on the upper deck and required little attending to—and teaching Madeline Hindustani. Their time together had become one unending class, with Rose recalling more and more anecdotes from her childhood and Madeline ever eager to know and learn.

'You see, Mrs Evans, we are five sisters, and I am the youngest of us all. The older two are married, but Iris and Camellia are yet to make their matches,' she said to Martha. 'I am happy to wait and am glad for the chance to travel back to the dear, dear country of my girlhood and pursue something worthwhile. It is only going to be a charitable school for native children, a small two-room set-up with a tin roof, but I am very excited at the thought of helping Uncle George with it. We are carrying with us picture books, notebooks, charts and puzzles donated to us for the purpose.'

Martha smiled. Rose's ambivalent attitude to courtship reminded her of her own younger self. Not every young woman was enthralled and dizzy at the prospect of male attention and marriage, as society presumed they would be. Some were keen to live life by their own rules.

Only about fifty of the ship's passengers had opted for the excursion to see the pyramids. Some passengers had opted out as they were regulars on the route and had seen them before. There were others who, though first-timers, were not keen on either the heat or the expense.

Martha stood with Madeline and Rose in front of the pyramids of Giza. Three pyramids rose grandly against the sky. The sky itself was a brilliant and clear blue, almost an assault on the eyes, a martial, metallic glint to it. An eagle majestically soared and dipped above them in slow motion, as if sent out by a dead pharaoh to keep watch on the tourists flitting about his tomb. Colourfully festooned camels with their swaying gait and soulful eyes dotted the complex.

Madeline and Rose found the expressions on the faces of the camels a matter of much amusement.

'See that one. He is certainly a poet. He is looking about the courtyard with such a pensive gaze.'

'And that one has such a despondent look to him. Most certainly dissatisfied with his lot.'

'He'd rather be out on the dunes, solitary and undisturbed, than be called into duty here, decorated in these glad rags and required to carry foreigners like us around.'

'If we are to ride, let us pick that one. It has a friendly face. As if it finds the job of giving rides around the compound pleasurable.'

As she stood beside the girls, sweat trickled down Martha's back, making her gown a sticky nuisance. Her face was flushed red under her wide brimmed hat. Even as her daughter and her friend continued with their bantering, a dark shadow of dread descended upon Martha and wound its way into a corner of her listless heart. She could feel it heavy with certainty, impossible to dislodge. She was just not made for travel or adventure.

She was standing in front of one of the seven wonders of the ancient world. She was fully aware of the beauty of the scene before her. Yet, her heart ached for only one thing. To be back inside her cozy parlour at home, sitting on her favourite chair, reading a book.

This would not do, she chastised herself. She took off her hat, then shook her head from side to side before placing it back at a jauntier angle this time.

'Happy?' she asked, turning to Madeline. 'Is it how you had imagined it would be?' Madeline had been the reason Norman had booked them on this excursion.

'Oh Mamma! Isn't it truly enchanting? I wish I could sleep here in the open and watch the stars come out one by one. I wish I could walk here in the coolness of the night, hear the music of ancient times and listen to the stories ooze out of these golden tombs.'

The expression in her eyes was faraway and lost.

In Middlesbrough, Martha had always remarked on how much she and her daughter had in common. Madeline was, of course, an exceptionally gifted child. Martha had attributed a large part of her daughter's many accomplishments to the fact that her talents had been discovered early and carefully nurtured by Martha herself. This voyage revealed to her how unlike one another they were in essence.

Shorn of the familiar settings of home and school, Madeline seemed to be an altogether different creature, made of mercury to Martha's own lead. She felt the tiniest tremor of a cold ripple through her being as she stood under the blazing Egyptian sun.

Her daughter was her life. Had she already begun to leave her mother behind, drifting off slowly into another world?

ALL THE PASSENGERS stood on the deck as the liner docked at Bombay. Martha watched the city come into view—the silhouette of grey buildings against a blue sky rapidly turning a vivid pink and orange as the sun began to set. And then, as they approached land, the sounds of milling crowds on the shores broke into the picturesque sunset scene, and everywhere there were dark, wiry men, bright turbans on their heads, coolies loading and unloading the ships that had docked, vendors with baskets calling out their wares, others offering rides into the city in their horse-drawn carts. Everything moving, calling, shouting.

'Look, there is Papa!' Madeline squealed with excitement as she saw Norman on the gangway. Norman looked taller, more impressive to her eyes as he strode up in his tailcoat and top hat, his face clean-shaven and breaking into a smile as he saw them.

Martha and Madeline bid goodbye to their fellow passengers while Norman supervised the loading of their trunks onto the carriage he had hired for them.

'Rose, promise that you will write to me every week. I will too. I do hope we will meet again someday!'

The two girls embraced, holding each other close, tearful to be parting. Martha felt her own hand tremble ever so slightly as she shook it one last time with Hilda Wilhelm-Burke's. It was unlikely that they would meet again.

They were to rest in Bombay before they embarked on the over 900-mile-long train journey that lay ahead of them to Jaunpur. Norman had booked them at his regular hotel, the Watson Esplanade in the Fort area. He had been tempted by the prospect of checking into the newly opened Taj Mahal Hotel. All reports agreed that it was very grand indeed with German elevators,

American ceiling fans and Turkish baths. But in the end, loyalty had won the day. Watson was a 'Europeans-only' hotel, and the joke about it was that apart from English weather, everything else had been imported from back home including the cast and wrought iron frame of the five-storeyed building, its bricks, stones and tiles, as well as the fittings and furnishings. Even the waitresses in the restaurant and ballroom were English.

They settled into their room on the second floor and ordered for some light supper to be brought up on a tray.

'Why, Madeline has grown! She is quite the young lady now, no longer the child I met on my last visit home!'

She was certainly taller, more elegantly dressed.

'Wait till the tiredness wears off,' Martha laughed. 'You will find she's equal parts young woman and little girl. She made close friendships on board and some of her older friends have influenced her deportment. But she is still full of childishness. Gave the captain an awfully hard time, trying to practise her Hindustani with different members of his crew. I could sense that he would have preferred it if his crew were not encouraged to be familiar with passengers. But Madeline and her friend worked their charms on him, got him to agree somehow. She would prattle away, nineteen to the dozen, with everyone she could corner into a conversation.'

'Madeline! You learnt to speak Hindustani!' asked Norman, his eyes full of astonishment and delight.

'Papa, I was lucky that Rose was travelling on the same boat. She was my teacher and such a good one too. We had a lot of fun together. I shall miss her so, my dearest Rose.'

They spoke for a bit longer before Norman noticed Madeline curled up like a kitten on the sofa with her eyes shut. She had fallen asleep. They gently shook her and guided her towards the four-poster bed. Norman asked Martha to turn in early too. He would go down to the bar and come back up later and sleep on the extra bed the hotel staff had set up in the room. There would be plenty of time for them to be with each other now that she and Madeline were here.

'My dear, I cannot tell you what a happy man I am today. I cannot thank you enough,' he said, placing a tentative kiss on her lips before he headed out of the room. She smelt different, sea salt and sweat mingled with the Yardley talcum powder she always used. He found it oddly exciting.

Martha went into the attached bathroom and decided to fill up the bathtub. She lay there in grateful silence, happy to be on land, glad to be clean and cool at last, to be alone with herself. Half an hour later, feeling calm and restored, she slipped into bed next to the sleeping Madeline. Her daughter was smiling as if in a happy dream. The last three weeks had revealed to Martha many aspects of Madeline's nature. But what amazed Martha the most was the natural faculty she had for picking languages. It went far beyond Martha's own experience with teaching and learning.

Madeline did not learn a language as much as lead an expedition into it with all her senses following—she camped inside of it, inhabiting it from moment to moment, catching a bird of meaning here, lighting a fire of understanding there, diving into the flowing stream of it and coming up jubilant at the other end.

When Martha woke up in the morning, she found that tea had already been ordered to the room, and Norman and Madeline were in deep conversation. The morning sun was falling in a broad slant through the window, glinting on the silver teapot and hot-water jug on the table. A tall glass vase with red carnations adorned the centre of the table.

Madeline was describing in detail the Arabian Nights theme party on their last Sunday on board the *SS Dwarka*. Passengers had worn the most outrageous costumes and masks. Two on-board romances had culminated in formal engagements that night.

'Now that you even speak Hindustani, just think what a wonderful memsahib you will make. I will be so happy if you find yourself a beau among the many officers and gentlemen the colony has to offer,' said Norman with a laugh. He was only half joking.

'None of that sentimental talk of beaus yet, please,' said Martha. 'First, she goes to college. Somerville awaits Madeline next year, Norman.'

'Yes, dear,' said Norman. He knew this was a sensitive subject and one he should not pursue further. He changed tack. 'After breakfast, I should like to show you something of the city. There are some very impressive Gothic buildings in our immediate vicinity including Elphinstone College. And right across from it is the school of art.'

If Bombay's Rampart Row didn't impress Martha with the sophistication of its buildings and institutions, its clubs and hotels, nothing could. Bombay, given to Charles II as a part of Catherine Braganza's dowry by the King of Portugal in the late seventeenth century, was the jewel in the crown of the British Raj. Over the last century, its forward-looking Indian merchants and educationists had come forth to collaborate with the British rulers to create institutions that tried to replicate, with some success, the pedagogy and high standards of the colleges in England.

Norman decided he would take Martha and Madeline out for lunch at the Taj Mahal Hotel. Apparently, the architect had pulled off an eclectic fusion of European neo-classical and Indic architectural elements. He did not want to miss seeing it altogether. It would provide a nice talking point with the nawab as well as with his own set at the club back in Jaunpur.

MARIAM STOOD WITH Abdul and Gobind at the front porch of the bungalow in Jaunpur to welcome the family. The syce had gone to receive them from the station in the horse-drawn carriage. A local tonga cart hired from the station followed behind them with their trunks piled upon it. Norman alighted first and helped his wife down from the carriage. The daughter jumped off on her own, deftly gathering her gown up a couple of inches to avoid tripping. Her shoulder length hair fell in a mass of tangled curls, framing her pretty face, with eyes a colour Mariam had never seen before, not green, not gold, but something in between.

'Let me guess! You are the new lady's maid. And this must be Gobind. And this Abdul. I am so excited to meet you all at last!' she said in Hindustani. 'And my name is Madeline.' Abdul beamed, surprised and delighted to be greeted personally. Gobind, shy and taciturn by nature, bowed awkwardly and hurried towards the tonga to supervise the unloading of the luggage. At a peremptory clap of his hands, two boys appeared from the back of the house to help carry the trunks in.

Mariam curtseyed to Martha and Madeline.

'Welcome Mrs Evans, Miss Evans. I hope your journey was comfortable.'

'Yes, very good, thank you, Mariam,' Norman replied on Martha's behalf as he escorted her to a chair in the veranda. She looked pale and weary. 'Abdul, some nimbu-pani for the memsahibs please.'

'It was quite wonderful, thank you. What a spectacular country this is! I've never seen so much colour before. I think god must have begun making the world from east to west and quite run out of colours by the time he reached England,' Madeline replied to Mariam's question.

'Abdul makes the most refreshing lemonade,' Norman said to Martha. He fussed over her, proffering a cushion for her back.

'May I have some tea instead, please,' asked Martha.

'I'll go tell Abdul,' Mariam said.

'Wait! I'll come with you!' said Madeline, following Mariam.

Mariam paused, momentarily confused at the command. A brief, almost imperceptible nod from Norman gave her the go-ahead she needed. 'Come this way please, Miss. I'll take you through the parlour.'

The parlour was a high-ceilinged room with two worn but large damask sofas and four wooden armchairs, a table, some footstools and a piano in one corner. It looked empty, sparsely furnished for a room of its size. Above the piano was an oil painting of a busy bazaar. Madeline paused in front of it briefly, before following Mariam, who had already walked through a door leading into the dining room. It had a large dining table at the centre with an empty vase lying on a pink crochet lace doily. A portrait of King Edward VII hung on one wall and a larger one of Queen Victoria on another. Something about the dining room looked mournful, as if it had been many years since laughter and conversation had filled it.

A door leading out of the dining room led into a brick-laid winding path with a curved tin roof over it. It looked like something out of a storybook, something that might lead into a secret garden or an ogre's den. Wild grass and weeds were growing on either side of the path, lending to it a quaint, unkempt beauty. To Madeline's charmed gaze the path felt otherworldly and full of magical possibilities. If she stood still and listened keenly, she might hear elves or fairies whispering to each other.

Their walk ended at a stoic, square, limewashed brick building with a grey chimney, much to Madeline's disappointment. The kitchen was altogether too plain in contrast to the prettiness of the path leading to it.

'Abdul, Darjeeling tea for the memsahib. Make the larger pot in case the sahib wishes to accompany her.

With some biscuits. And nimbu-paani for the missy-baba.'

Abdul was smiling and bowing and bustling about in the kitchen, pulling out the biscuit tin, putting the water to boil on the stove, all at the same time.

In contrast to its white limewashed exterior, the kitchen was gloomy inside. It had no windows, only a small skylight. A humungous iron oven-cum-grill occupied one corner. The walls were lined with in-built shelves which held inordinately large pans, saucepans, kettles, stew pots and cauldrons of copper and brass covered with the weary patina of disuse. Some smaller pots and pans lay on the stone counter next to the stove. A large wooden cupboard in the corner opposite the grill held the crockery and cutlery.

'Would you like to see the pantry, Miss?' asked Miriam, leading her into a large space just behind the main kitchen.

'Pray don't be so formal. Call me Madeline, please. And I shall call you Mariam, dear Mariam. My friend Rose, who grew up in India, a proper missy-baba you know, told me that a lady's maid is often a girl's best friend and chief confidante in India. I do hope we will be fast friends while I am here.'

'Yes, Miss.'

The pantry was lined with provision jars, tins of milk powder and cooking oil imported from England and other large containers labelled rice, flour and sugar. Small tins of sardines and mackerel stood neatly aligned by one corner of a large shelf, like choir boys waiting to sing a few rousing lines in an otherwise dull production.

The kitchen building was almost as large as their home on North Street. And Abdul's smiling face was the only lively feature in it. Madeline thought of their tiny, well-lit kitchen at home with its neatly lined shelves and its dainty array of small pans. She wondered how Mamma would feel about this kitchen.

'Let's go explore the garden, Mariam. Thank you, Abdul,' said Madeline, as she walked out.

MARTHA WOKE UP disoriented each morning. They had been in Jaunpur for ten days now, but she still had to get used to what Madeline delightedly described as the 'night orchestra'. The crickets chirped and buzzed through the hours of darkness—a whining, squeaky, persistent refrain in the ears that went don't-sleep-don't-sleep-don't-sleep-please. And at 3 a.m., just as she was finally inured to their symphony, the male frogs would begin to vocalize plaintively their need for mates, each successive call more urgent, more pressing in its entreaty—comenow-noww-nowww-nowwww. Some nights belonged wholly to the hooting of owls, others to wild dogs baying at the moon and the worst ones to the howling of wild hyenas in the distance. Distant but not distant enough for her comfort. Martha tossed and turned all night, and just as she was falling off to sleep, she would hear Norman tiptoeing off to be served his dawn tea in the parlour. She had dispensed with the ritual of dawn tea for herself, asking Mariam to bring her a pot of Darjeeling at 8.30 a.m. on the front porch.

Madeline, flushed and full of news, would come back from her walk or her attempts to learn to ride from Norman's syce and join her. They would ask for breakfast to be served. Norman would join them on the rare day when he had not left for work already.

'Did you sleep well, Mamma?' asked Madeline as always. It was the second week of their stay in Jaunpur. She came in and sat down next to Martha, loosening the strap of the pith helmet she wore. Solar topees were an absolute must outdoors even in the early mornings. The sun gathered intensity without preamble.

'Better than yesterday,' Martha replied with a smile. Last night, two lizards had chased each other fervidly along the length of the bedroom walls and copulated on her ceiling. The fear of the lizards losing their grip and falling upon her had kept her sleepless and terrified. 'I really need to start sleeping properly and waking up earlier. This way your father and I scarcely get a minute alone.'

'Yes, aren't we busy beyond belief here?'

Martha had been taken completely by surprise at the level of socializing required of the families of British officials in the Raj even in a small Indian town. An elaborate system of personally visiting and dropping one's cards at the bungalows of senior officials' ladies and of judiciously going through the cards dropped by juniors and equals at one's own residence and inviting them for tea to get better acquainted with them was securely in place. Many young and single officers from the military cantonment outside the town, hearing of the arrival of a young lady, had hopes of wooing Madeline. Norman said they could ignore these for the moment. Martha would only be following protocol by prioritizing and getting to know the married ladies within the city first.

'What a relentless schedule of entertainment and intermingling they follow here. It is all taken so seriously that I live in perpetual fear of offending some senior lady or snubbing a junior one inadvertently and causing embarrassment to your father. Neither of the books we read tutored us adequately about the intricacies of seniority and rank or the stiff protocols to be followed morning to evening.'

'And the stiff evening gowns that ladies must wear every evening at dances and dinners,' Madeline chipped in. 'Mamma you had best accept Mrs Campbell's offer of sending her durzee over to make us a few gowns of satin and taffeta.'

'I thought the threat of catching malaria or cholera was what I needed to prepare for coming here. Not death by tea parties, dancing and dinner engagements and social exhaustion. Yes, dear, you are right. We may as well get a few new gowns each. No one must look at your father with pitying eyes for the lack of style in his ladies. Also, I'm intrigued by the notion of a nimble-fingered durzee sitting in my backyard like a magic elf producing dresses to order from pattern books. All for a few rupees.'

'Mamma do let us be determined to enjoy our India outing. Pray do not think it giddy and foolish of me, but I must confess I find it all very quaint and exciting. Mrs Campbell said we could leave word with their chowkidar, and he would send us the best boxwallah with bolts of fabric for us to choose from. He comes from Calcutta and has a whole array of muslins and satins and laces, and buttons too.'

'Certainly, my dear,' said Martha with a weary smile. 'Now, let us get our breakfast done, and I'll go get dressed for the morning's engagement. I am told it is perilous to be even a minute late when invited by the district police chief's wife for elevenses. She is second only to the district magistrate's wife, your father tells me. And very quick to take offence.'

'I wish I could go in your stead. Relieve you of this burden,' said Madeline, squeezing her mother's hand. Fortunately for her, young ladies were expected to spend most mornings at home doing art or needlework or reading.

As Martha stood staring at the petticoats, the stiff lace collar front, the layered gown and the large hat that Mariam had laid out for her in the dressing room attached to her bedroom, she shook her head briskly from side to side, trying to dislodge from her mind the annoyance she felt. All this formal dressing and elaborate ritual for some meaningless chitter-chatter in a stranger's drawing room.

With each passing day, Martha sensed Norman's disappointment in her but could not find in herself the means to alleviate it. This place was all too foreign to her, too sunlit, too grand. The life of a colonial memsahib in a remote Indian outpost was too different from her image of herself—entirely at variance with her ideas about womanhood and progress.

There was more staff in the house than she could mentally wrap her head around with any degree of comfort. They moved about barefooted and silent as ghosts through the house. Apart from the cook, the butler-cum-valet, the ayah, the gardener and the horse groom who stayed on the bungalow grounds there were many others who came in from outside—two (or was it three?) pankha boys who sat outside the bedrooms taking turns to pull the ropes of the fans affixed to the ceilings, a dhobi who came in every alternate day for the laundry, a bishti who appeared daily to fill water in the kitchen and bathrooms, and a mehtar who arrived to clean the latrine pits. It was impossible to step out of her room without running into one or more profusely salaaming or obsequious member of the staff. And this was just inside the house.

Outside the home, interacting with Norman's circle of friends at the club or at the lunches and teas they were invited to, she felt as if she had walked into the wrong century. Many of the people she met, senior civil servants and engineers like her husband, had moved to India twenty or more years ago. They, in their turn upon arrival, had adapted and fitted into the social rites and rituals of an even earlier generation of British settlers. Socializing followed the etiquette of the early Victorian age.

Norman had explained to Martha the necessity for the British in India to group together like this, become a cohesive social whole. Young men coming into work here would lose themselves to drinking excessively, gambling with locals, picking up bad habits like opium, becoming totally dissolute, useless to themselves and to their country, if left to their own solitary devices through the long evenings. Meeting others of their own race and station in life regularly, pursuing gentlemanly sports, being presentably dressed as per the standards back home was what saved them. As for the ladies, they did not even have the diversion of a job during the day. The frequent postings of their men across towns and cities, the troubles of living in a land where they knew neither the language nor the customs, the dependence on natives wholly for company—these things could lead to hysteria or a total nervous breakdown. What seemed to Martha as empty social activity served a much deeper purpose. It held a race—men, women and children—in the reassuring embrace of their own kind, their own food and customs, their own memories of home, their dreams of returning there one day.

Martha understood what he meant, but it didn't help her fit in any better. Not a whiff of Edwardian England with its ideas of modernity and women's emancipation had reached Jaunpur's British Indian society. Perhaps it was different in Calcutta or Bombay. But in a small settlement like Jaunpur, the conversations with its twenty-odd British families centered almost exclusively on diversions like sports, dances, parties or picnics or on household management, neither of which naturally interested Martha. She had spent the last few years unlearning the life of a lady of her class and teaching herself to become a woman of letters, a thinking woman who cared to understand politics and society, see beyond class concerns and empathize with the common lot of all women—in other words, a feminist who espoused the cause of higher education, employment and equal franchise.

Martha's learning, her opinions had no place here. She was required instead to kowtow to ideas of rank and social standing with a fierce rigidity, to conform in every item of dress, mannerism and social behaviour, to be an English lady of the upper classes in every step she took, every little utterance she made. Anything else would amount to letting down the side, disgracing her king and country; not being precisely British in food, dress and habit meant being seen as going native. It was a thought that made Martha shudder. This alien country was nothing to her, would never be.

Martha recognized that the possibility of young women from home losing their bearings in the seductive darkness of India was not a baseless, fearful imagining. When she saw Madeline with the ayah, chattering nineteen to the dozen, she felt alarm for her daughter. Admiration too. Madeline knew no discomfort with strangers, with the foreignness of everything around her. Sometimes she could hear her daughter's tuneful voice from her room singing strange haunting ditties. Madeline had heard Gobind singing to himself and had insisted that he sing the songs for her. They were songs of boatmen on the Ganges that Gobind knew from his childhood, and soon they were on Madeline's lips.

It was beautiful and terrifying to see her daughter in this new life. Madeline was special, but no one here would understand her daughter's eagerness to learn every new language that crossed her path, catch the music inside every song she heard.

The more she considered it, the more strongly Martha felt that it would probably be best to order new dresses for her daughter in the styles current here. She would get Madeline to accompany her on her social calls and fraternize with her kind. Tedious as it seemed, she had to be conscious of what was expected and do it. And then, Madeline would head home with her as soon as possible without wounding Norman's heart.

THE ARRIVAL OF the two memsahibs stole the quietness of Mariam Das's early days at the Evans' residence and filled them with a great deal more work. Their arrival also caused her some disquiet of mind, a tossing and churning of emotions in ways she had not envisaged. The mother and daughter were so different in their expectations and treatment of Mariam, that she found herself driven into wearing two different personalities and constantly switching between one and the other at short notice. Somewhere in the middle of these personalities stood the real Mariam Das, trying to be a balanced and loyal employee, trying to discharge her duty to the best of her abilities as tutored by the nuns at her convent.

Martha memsahib turned out to be distant and wholly uninterested in matters of the house. She wore a tired and tense look on her face most times, grimacing as visitors were announced, stoic and stern as she dressed up to go out. Even these unhappy expressions were reserved for the other sahibs and memsahibs. The staff in the house, Mariam included, were met with an expressionless gaze, as if Martha memsahib could not or would not see them for flesh and blood people. While Mariam went about serving her, bringing her meal trays, laying out her dresses, filling her bath, Martha looked through her with a cool indifference that Mariam found difficult to penetrate. In her presence, Mariam felt like a cardboard cut-out of herself, featureless, without voice. It was the same with other members of the staff. Mariam's friendly Good Morning and Good Evening greetings, Abdul's broad, whiskered smile, Gobind's solicitous deference, the dhobi's obsequious bending from the waist down, the pankha boys' cheery salaams all fluttered tentatively and fell to the floor, unnoticed by Martha as she walked past.

Martha had declined to discuss even the day's menu with the cook, leaving the job to Mariam. She wanted chicken soup and toasted bread every night. Apart from that, it was up to the staff. Fortunately for her, Mariam had spent long years with the Pinkerton-Smiths. She enjoyed the challenge of thinking up nutritious and varied menus. Abdul, the cook, too had a set of prized recipes from a family he had worked with earlier and could be relied on for useful suggestions. It was clear that Norman sahib was satisfied with their efforts. He had mentioned it to Gobind more than once.

Madeline presented a bigger challenge to Mariam's equanimity. She was difficult to deal with for precisely the opposite set of reasons as her mother. She was too warm, much too affectionate. She insisted on treating Mariam with an easy familiarity which made Mariam nervous and uneasy.

As they went out on their evening walk, Madeline sometimes reached out and insisted they hold hands, swinging their arms together while singing. She had a penchant for singing in her clear voice as they ambled along the river. Or she would pick up a flower and pin it on to Mariam's dress.

The first time Madeline clasped Mariam's brown hand in her own white one, the contrast in their skin colours jumped up at Mariam and filled her with dread. A wave of shock rippled through her body.

'You can't do that!' Mariam gasped.

'Why not?' asked Madeline, her brow furrowing, her eyes squinting up at Mariam in honest perplexity. 'You don't wish for us to be friends?'

'It isn't that. But you must see that you're white, and I'm not.'

'We are still friends, aren't we?'

'It's not done here.'

'But isn't the nawab married to a white woman?'

'It's different for nawabs,' said Mariam slowly. 'The rules are different for common folk. Besides, he's a man.'

'Nonsense, my dearest Mariam. Mamma says that it is our duty to fight differences such as these, the belief that noblemen are allowed some things that commoners aren't, or more pertinently, that men are allowed to do what women mustn't. If we can feel friendship for each other, why must we not express it openly? That is such a ridiculous rule. If anyone stops us, we will print out posters and stand outside the Jaunpur Club in protest. I'm certain Mamma will join us too.'

Mariam was bemused at the thought of Martha memsahib doing something like that. To Mariam, she looked proud and listless both, as if every effort to please her left her unmoved. Mariam secretly felt sorry for Norman sahib saddled with such a cold, unfeeling wife. He hid his disappointment well, but he must undoubtedly feel it.

'When we get home, I'll make us both crowns of flowers picked from the garden. I am sure Ram Deen will not resent our taking a few red hibiscuses from that glorious bush near the back gate. We will wear our crowns and stroll arm in arm in the garden, as royal as royal can be. We shall declare we are female nawabs and can do as we please,' said Madeline. 'What is a female nawab called anyway?'

'Begum,' replied Mariam. That was the closest word she could think of. Nawabs were nawabs and begums were their wives. Noble wives were called begums but often so were commoner wives. There wasn't a special word to denote a woman of power. It probably hadn't been needed badly enough. Women's power mostly derived from who they were married to and how their husbands treated them.

As they walked along the riverbank hand in hand, she couldn't help thinking that Madeline's impetuous behaviour could get her, Mariam Das, into serious trouble. As an ayah, the blame for any such forward behaviour would land at her door, never mind that she herself had done nothing to encourage Madeline. Her previous positions working with British families had already taught her this lesson. Enough to last her through her remaining life.

She should mention it to Martha memsahib, but Madeline's mother had grown only a little less unapproachable as the weeks passed, conceding a slight nod in response to Mariam's greeting in the morning.

It was a subject that Mariam could not bring up before her with any degree of confidence. To raise it with Norman sahib would be awkward. Familiarity between white and brown people was a subject she was loath to broach with a man. There were layers of subtext in such a conversation, between master and maid.

Mariam shrugged. Here, along a quiet riverbank, friendship with a young white girl who was only visiting temporarily could not be such a dangerous thing perhaps. Madeline was different from anyone she had known before. She reached out for the person inside of Mariam, paying no heed to her position or her race. Ram Deen, Abdul, Gobind, they were all living, breathing humans to her with hearts and histories, songs and stories. She had even adopted the fat tabby in Mariam's veranda and named him Luka. On most days Luka curled up and slept at the foot of her bed, the two cosy together under a mosquito net wafting in the breeze of a gently moving rope pankha.

As weeks turned into months, Mariam found herself growing terribly fond of the girl. She wanted her for a friend.

NORMAN EVANS PRESENTED his visiting card to the tall, strapping, middle-aged durwan—the rather prepossessing doorman at the Nawab of Jaunpur's city mansion. It was a joke that he had shared with no one, but no less funny for that, that on his first visit to the nawab's residence many years ago, he had mistaken the moustached, turbaned doorman with his distinguished-looking silver hair, trimmed beard and exceedingly fine raiment to be the nawab himself. When he was ushered into the nawab's presence, he was a bit let down to find that the actual nawab was casually dressed in a plain white, button-down shirt and trousers and spoke English in a British public school accent.

The doorkeeper returned shortly and asked him to wait in the study. As Norman walked past the main hall, his footsteps echoed through its vast silence; the ornately framed family portraits on the walls watched him unmoved. He turned left into the nawab's study and exhaled deeply. Across evenings, the study had been the site of lively discussions and debates and the battleground for some intensely fought games of chess. Norman's eyes went to a half-played game on the chess table towards the corner of the room. The nawab did not lack partners to play with, though Norman himself had become a scant visitor since the arrival of his family in Jaunpur. He flushed to think that only his own worries had now brought him on this long overdue visit. But the nawab was a friend. He would listen. He would understand. And if he could help, he would.

A bearer came in with a glass of khus sherbet on a silver salver with raised brass handles. Though it was overly sweet and a curiously lurid shade of emerald-green, Norman had grown to appreciate how cooling the drink could be on a hot sunny day such as this one.

'Please make yourself comfortable. Nawab sahib will join you presently.' The stately bearer bowed deeply and walked out on soundless feet.

Norman was staring at the ivory and black pieces on the marble chessboard in deep concentration. His sherbet held in his hand, his back to the door, he was trying to guess who had been facing the nawab at the opposite end of the chessboard and in how many moves his friend would take the game.

'New chap called Milton. Forest department. Not quite as good as you,' said the nawab as he entered. 'Care for a game?'

'Gladly. I have been missing our evenings of play.'

The nawab rang the bell for the bearer. The on-going game was carefully lifted and placed on a small end table. It would be resumed whenever Milton returned. A new walnut wood chess board was brought and its exquisitely carved pieces laid out. Norman and the nawab nodded to each other, and the game started. As was their way, it proceeded in complete silence. In a moment of carelessness, Norman lost his rook. In this part of the world, the piece was called an elephant. It was checkmate for him two moves later.

'Not paying attention today, are we?' said the nawab with a laugh, pleased with his easy win. 'How's the family? It's a pleasure to run into young Madeline ever so often in the library. Junaid sahib tells me she's the most earnest and dedicated student he's had in many years.'

'It is very kind of you to allow her use of your library. And very kind of Junaid sahib to take her under his wing.'

Madeline was learning the finer nuances of Hindustani from the nawab's librarian. Though she remained heartily grateful for Rose's lessons on board the *SS Dwarka*, her subsequent conversations with the nawab's librarian made her realize that the Hindustani she spoke was a 'memsahib' version of the language—functional, but not as beautiful and fluid as the tongue she heard spoken around her by native speakers. She enlisted herself as his student and lost no opportunity to make her way into the library for his guidance and instruction.

'Don't mention it. Junaid sahib is happy with the task. How is your wife? Does she like being here? It's getting quite warm now.'

It was an opening. The precise one he needed. Norman decided to take it.

'It is not going quite as well with Martha as I had hoped. She is restless and uneasy, not used to the formality of our ways here. She finds social engagements tedious and tiring. She misses home. I'm afraid that the hot weather here is beginning to be her undoing. I can see her chafing under the skin already, unable to get a good night's sleep. I suggested that she and Madeline might like to move to the hills for the rest of the summer, but they are unwilling to do so. They say they came here to be with me, not to be packed off to another place hundreds of miles away.'

'You're in a tough spot, old chap. Is there no way you can convince them? Shimla or Nainital are the places for ladies to be in at this time of the year.'

'I did have an idea that might work. That is my selfish reason for calling upon you today. I need a favour.'

'Tell me.'

'If I could accompany them, they would agree in a trice. I had a notion of how that might be arranged. You are aware of the work I did in Nainital after the second landslide in 1898. There have been problems with the design and execution of some elements. The Public Works Department had left the culverts to be done by the municipal body. The proposal for onsite assistance by the PWD has been floating around for a long time. If you could put in a word with the commissioner, he could possibly ask for me to go on lien to the municipal board for a few months and get the work done. God knows, the sooner they have the culverts and drains reinforced the better.'

'That's a capital idea. Gracie holds me in high regard from our time in Harrow. I was his senior by a couple of years. Looked out for him against the bullies. Besides, he's likely to see the good sense in this. Nothing to be gained from yet another landslide. How about your work here?'

'It's really the best time to be away. Half the labour force will be absconding soon, going to their villages to get the fields ready for planting before the monsoons.'

'Fine then. I'll write to Gracie. Meanwhile, make sure you get a clearance for undertaking this assignment from whoever needs to give you permission to proceed to Nainital,' said the nawab.

Norman felt a weight lift off his shoulders. It was going to be all right.

'Care for another game?' the nawab asked.

'Of course,' Norman replied.

AZEEM

Saharanpur

1904–06

LUSH GREEN FIELDS of oats and gram surrounded Azeem's new living quarters. All over the stud farm there were large, fenced paddocks for the horses and mules to graze. Gigantic haystacks dotted the landscape like straw houses from a fairytale. A muster of peacocks roamed the fields freely, roosting in the trees and perched atop the haystacks, their distinctive cries and screams filling the evening air. Further afield, there were stags, blue bulls and black bucks.

The Stud Depot, Saharanpur, was set up in 1843 to use advanced breeding techniques to improve the stock of horses for the British army and keep them supplied with mules. The year Azeem joined, it had been reorganized, expanded and renamed as Remount Training School and Depot, Saharanpur. Azeem had to undergo a test of physical fitness and appear for a written Indian Army Tradesman Examination to make the grade for the position of syce or horse groom. Some 200 miles from his hometown of Rannpur, located outside the city of Saharanpur, the horse breeding farm was a world unto itself. It had over 2,000 horses and the entire farm stretched over a matching acreage.

The syces were housed in individual accommodations scattered across the vast campus. After living six to a dormitory in his school and then being crushed into a tiny windowless first-floor room he had rented in the bazaar area of Rannpur, the square, sparsely furnished, stand-alone chamber that he was allotted with its sloped slate roof filled Azeem with quiet joy. Sitting or sleeping on the lone cot that came with the room, he felt like the nawab of a vast realm, all the sprawling acres outside the door his to gaze upon.

Saharanpur, the small town outside which the stud farm was located, was named after a Sufi saint from the medieval era, Shah Haroon. Something of the Chisti mystic's spirit still seemed to blow gently over the city. Its streets and houses, its bazaars, its city centre all felt different from Rannpur. There were no grand palaces, mosques and pleasure gardens, no awe-inspiring city gates, no fortresses. Saharanpur rolled out into a countryside of farmlands, mango orchards and sal forests, unannounced, unchecked, without gates and cannons, its citizenry free to move and merge, a seamless part of a large nation going about the business of life. There was no grandeur and no abject penury. After the court protocols and formality of Rannpur, Saharanpur felt like a symbol of freedom and dignity to Azeem, a town with wide open arms and gently scattered hamlets to accommodate common folk.

Known for its woodcarving, Saharanpur's bazaars were full of intricately chiselled timber furniture and screens—adorned with filigree work and floral motifs, and with stone inlay patterns. The doors of the houses in this city were special. They were carved by master craftsmen with an array of swans, lotuses, gods and goddesses. In the streets of the bazaar, Azeem saw brightly painted lacquer toys. On one trip to the city, he bought himself a pair of bright green parrots with shiny red beaks to place in a small alcove in his room. Sometimes, the maulvi from his school came to him in his dreams and shouted *Lahaul-vila-quwwat*. The old maulvi in his dreams would be happy to see the lacquered parrots in this new room, if dreams and reality gazed upon each other as he slept.

Apart from the horses and mules bred in the stud farm for routine activities of outfitting cavalry regiments and moving materials and munition across the country for the British army, the farm also kept in reserve five hundred Australian horses—a miracle of equine breeding. Their first ancestors, English thoroughbreds and Spanish horses, had survived long and arduous sea voyages to reach New South Wales in 1788. Further importation—of Arab stallions from India, mares from Chile and Peru, Welsh mountain ponies and other prized breeds from across the world—went into the bloodline, creating a breed unsurpassed in symmetry and endurance. They were a combination of strength, athleticism and intelligence, making for excellent cavalry horses, capable of travelling long distances on scant rations, and powerful, adept, versatile in the battle or sporting arena. Azeem watched them endlessly, marvelling at their sheer beauty, wondering how it must feel to master a horse like that.

These horses were kept ready to be sent out on special assignments, to welcome viceroys, generals and other top officials, and to perform at important sporting events in Calcutta and Bombay. To be a trainer to these horses was a sought-after job among the syces. Azeem had set his heart upon joining this elite group within the farm someday.

He went well beyond the call of duty to keep the pack ponies in his charge exercised, groomed and fed. And he spent his free time watching from the sidelines the training of the grooms assigned to the Australian Walers, taking in the manoeuvers and tricks taught by the officers. Sometimes, he attempted gymnastic poses on one of the horses in his charge, taking care not to injure either himself or the animal.

Major Wilby, the commandant, had over his many years as station in-charge developed the practice of riding through different parts of the vast acreage at odd hours, unaccompanied and unannounced. It helped him know the rhythm of the station more intimately, the mood in the ranks, the atmosphere in the stables, the peace or unrest under the different men commanding the lines and barracks.

It was almost on instinct that he stopped short when he heard a man's voice muttering endearments in Hindustani in a soft, dulcet, almost musical whisper. Had one of the syces sneaked in a paramour from the local bazaar? Major Wilby reined in his horse and watched unseen in the dwindling light of a dusty evening as a young man, a recent recruit he did not know, gently cajoled his pony to pirouette on tiptoe while he vaulted up on one arm, his body in a parallel line to the length of the horse, the other arm outstretched in front, his legs stretched out behind. For a perfect minute or so, the boy and the horse moved down a narrow forest trail into a sky turning a dull purple. Then the screech of a roosting peacock from a tree above startled the pony, and the syce lost balance, landing with an ungainly thud upon the horse's back. He scrambled hastily to the sitting position, taking care to calm the startled horse, murmuring love and apology in words the major could not quite catch.

'Boy! Stop!'

The command rang out in the sky like a gunshot.

Azeem turned around to find himself caught in the piercing gaze of the station commandant. The prayers his mother had taught him aeons ago, a forgotten lifetime back, suddenly pulsed through his being. He sought protection for his job, his life here. To lose it would be a calamity.

He clambered off the horse and stood at attention, saluting the officer.

'Where did you learn to do that?'

'Here, sir.'

'Who taught you?'

'I've been watching the trainers.'

'You taught yourself?'

Azeem nodded.

'What is the name of your supervisor?'

'Jai Chand, sir.'

'I shall speak with him.'

Three days passed after the incident. It seemed like they were thirty as Azeem waited to be told he had been fired. The sound of horse hooves going past his door, the clip of feet walking on the tarred road, the ordinary, everyday summons to share the duty roster, the very voice of his immediate supervisor became triggers for a gnawing anxiety. Azeem lived in anticipation of a hand on his shoulder. He'd have to raise his eyes to meet his supervisor's and stoically take the news, ignoring the sympathetic glances of his fellow syces as he packed up to leave. He dared not ask Jai Chand if any action was being taken against him. He did not want to bring the incident to his supervisor's notice unless he was compelled to.

Some part of him fervently wished and prayed that the station commander in a moment of charity had decided to overlook his transgression.

On the fourth morning, Azeem's supervisor came to him and asked him what he had done to attract the station commander's favour. He had been shifted to the unit in-charge looking after the Australian horses. The sports and ceremonial units were being expanded in anticipation of the visit of the Prince and Princess of Wales to India later that year. During their five-month tour they were to travel extensively through the country and to Burma. Preparations for their welcome were underway. The Remount Depot, Saharanpur, would be required to supply well-trained teams of horsemen in various places.

The boy called Azeem was on his way to becoming a very accomplished syce. His childhood dreams, crushed in the turning wheels of time on a sudden fateful morning long ago, had leapt to life again on an equally unforeseen evening more than a decade later. It seemed as if his lucky star had found him after a gap of many bleak and obscure years.

HE WAS FAR away from the life he was born into. This was a different world, with foreign rulers, foreign rules. Its pomp and protocol were of a scale that made the Nawab of Rannpur seem like just another walk-in part in the world's grand tableau of riches and royalty. Participating as part of the equestrian gymnastics team from the Remount Depot welcoming Prince George and Princess Mary, Azeem travelled to many cities in the northern plains. It was an exhilarating time for him.

Standing in a small lane in the Aishbag bazaar of Lucknow, he sighted a bookshop. It was only as he entered the small shop that he realized that he missed the days he had spent as an apprentice in the royal library. He missed the smell of books, the touch of different parchments and papers, his calligraphy pens and inks. There were no ancient manuscripts in Arabic and Persian and palm-leaf collections inscribed in Sanskrit and Pali in that small shop. However, there were many volumes of Urdu poems. Lucknow was a city steeped in poetry and music, its culture and etiquette a yardstick that no other city, not even the old Delhi of the erstwhile Mughal emperors, could match up to.

As he walked out of the shop after paying for two volumes of poetry, its young proprietor—with whom he had just had an animated conversation about his days as an apprentice at the royal library in Rannpur—called after him.

'Wait, Azeem bhai. Take this book too.'

He was holding out a small, slim volume titled *Umrao Jaan Ada*. It was written by a Mirza Muhammad Hadi 'Ruswa' and bore the stamp Gulab Munshi & Sons Press, Lucknow, 1899.

Azeem flushed. He only had a few coins in his pocket, saved up for a meal. He was loath to part with them for a book with the drawing of a woman's legs, her feet adorned with a courtesan's anklets. The aroma of boneless mutton kebabs being roasted on skewers and fresh bread baking in the clay oven was wafting in from the neighbouring lane.

'I … I don't read …' He searched about for a word but could not find one to describe the book being urged upon him.

'Take it, my friend. I tell you … a book like this has never been written before. Ruswa sahib is an Islamic scholar, a professor at Christian College here, no ordinary scribe. This is a work of sheer genius.

'Lutf hai kaun si kahani mein
Aap beeti kahoon ya jag beeti?

'Ah! Those words!

'What story is more pleasurable?
Shall I tell my own or the world's?'

The line sprung out from the throat of the bookseller and drew an invisible circle around Azeem, holding him within its gravitational field, causing a constriction in his chest. Truly, what tale was more compelling that of a life unfolding or that of the world's wheel turning? Azeem took the book from the bookseller and leafed through it. It seemed to be a courtesan's story as narrated to the author, its pages sprinkled with couplets of poetry. He put his hand in his pocket to bring out the money.

'No! No! Azeem bhai! This is a gift from me. You came as a customer. You leave as a friend. Wherever you go, the beauty, the grace, the romance of my beautiful city will go along with you once you've read Umrao Jaan's story. You will remember this small shop, this humble shopkeeper in your prayers always.'

Azeem was unable to read the book for many weeks as their contingent moved from Lucknow to Agra to Delhi, welcoming the royal couple. It was only once he was back in his room at the Remount Depot, the excitement of the royal tour firmly behind him, that he remembered his Lakhnavi friend's gift and settled down one afternoon to read it. It still looked curious to his eyes, this slim volume, so unlike the books in the Rannpur library—heroic epics and dastaans, stage dramas and long ballads, with their intricate illustrations.

It was a moonlit night in summer. Munshi Sahib had had the terrace sprinkled with water to make it cool. Carpets had been spread on the floor and covered with white sheets. Surahis fresh from the potters, fragrant with a smell of earth and fresh water, were lined up on the parapet. The pan had been delicately scented. The stems of hookahs had garlands of flowers twined around them and their smoke pervaded the atmosphere like heady incense. The only light besides that of the moon was of a candle flickering in a glass shade, the shama which was placed in front of the poet whose turn it was to recite.

Azeem was transported immediately to a terrace in a building in Chowk Bazaar in Lucknow. He was sitting with the author and his friends, inside a night of poetry. A retired courtesan lived in the upper-storey flat next door, her life solitary, the heavy drapes on her window always drawn. She heard the author recite a couplet she liked and invited him to her home.

'Who will listen to the tale of my woeful heart?
I've wandered much, I have much to impart.'

She had been a poet herself, an accomplished singer, a famous and wealthy courtesan once. That moon-drenched, poetry-flamed night, Mirza Ruswa persuaded Umrao Jaan to let him narrate her story.

And what a story it was! Amiran was a young girl in Faizabad, much loved and indulged by her family; her father was a supervisor in the Nawab of Oudh's employ. A dacoit, Dilawar Khan, was angry with her father whose testimony against him had resulted in a jail sentence. On his release from jail, he kidnapped young Amiran, took her in a bullock cart to Lucknow and sold her to a brothel. An act of revenge.

Her story was his story. Innocent children plucked out of a happy family and home and thrown into a cruel world to fend for themselves. Amiran. Azeem. They were destiny's children.

Said the bird to the fowler:
'It is my first night in the cage
Let me beat my wings against the bars.'

Destiny had made a courtesan out of Umrao Jaan. And yet, through the many storms in her personal history, the many twists of fate, the ironies of love and relationships, the political upheavals in the state of Oudh, she had held on to the core of her being. She was Umrao Jaan 'Ada'—a woman of learning, of high culture, of classical music, of ghazals and poetry. In the end what remained was neither the innocence of the well-born Amiran nor the world-weary wisdom of Umrao Jaan of the high-class brothel, courted and desired by rich patrons. What remained was a creature of pride and dignity, alone in a rooftop room, buoyed by memories of her lived experiences and words of poetry.

Life had happened to Umrao Jaan, but Umrao Jaan too had happened to life.

Azeem vowed to himself that he would keep his inner self sacred, separate from his circumstances. Fate had made him first an orphan, then a library assistant, now a syce. Destiny and chance were big influences—this was undeniable—but so too were strength of character, determination and choice.

Where would he be at the end of his days, Azeem wondered. In the time since he had left Rannpur he had already seen so many different cities, met people from varied walks of life. The world was much larger than he could have possibly imagined as a boy sharing a tiny windowless room with five other lads in the orphanage behind the mosque.

IT WAS A dull day at the end of May 1906 that Major Wilby received a request from the Public Works Department. A team of four—two engineers and two syces—was to be sent on assignment for a period of four months starting July, to help carry out a survey of the entire watershed surrounding Nainital during the monsoons. They would be required to study the run-off of rainwater and identify weak spots that needed to be buttressed in the event of a natural disaster. The hill station had suffered huge losses of life and property in recent earthquakes.

The Australian stock horses from the Remount Depot were the obvious choice for such a demanding assignment. Their intelligence and adaptability would be put to good use. Major Wilby reckoned that like the horses, the syces he sent for the job would have to be both intelligent and athletic—for they would have to quickly learn the job of measuring and mapping contours and gradients, recognize rock and soil types and identify weak spots that indicated the possibility of recurrent breaches. The engineers would no doubt lead the survey but given the heavy downpours in the monsoon and slippery nature of the terrain, the syces would need to be able to fill in for them should the situation demand it.

After giving some thought to the matter, he decided to depute Azeem and Raju for the job. They made an odd duo—one tall, handsome and with an irrepressible adventurous streak to him; the other diminutive, taciturn, extremely cautious in all his dealings. Curiously, they were good friends, often to be found together. Considering the length of the assignment and the fact that they would possibly have to share quarters for four months, Major Wilby summoned them to his office to brief them about the job and its requirements. He would let the pair decide if they wished to apply for the opening as a team.

As the two syces walked out of Major Wilby's office, Azeem read in Raju's demeanour a resounding 'no' to the question they had been asked by the officer. He saw it in the grey clouds gathering on Raju's swarthy face, in the stiffening of his back as if his body were preparing for an unwelcome attack, in the deliberateness with which he dug his heels into the ground. Raju's expression was guarded, his stance one of a person who did not wish to be swayed.

They turned the corner from the road that led to the office, stopped and faced each other.

'Why don't you want to do this?' Azeem asked.

'It sounds like trouble. We're not trained to do this kind of survey work. There may be mistakes, or worse still, some accident, a broken leg or a damaged spine. It's going to be raining hard and continuously in the mountains,' Raju replied with a frown.

'The major chose us because he thinks we're capable. Why doubt his judgement and our own abilities?' urged Azeem, perhaps too vehemently. Even as he spoke, Azeem realized he needed to be careful. He so wanted to do this assignment, but pushing Raju was a strategy that never worked. His friend liked to do things slowly, cautiously.

'We will be alone with two British engineers for months on end, under their direct command, at their beck and call. If they turn out to be terrible masters, we'll be stuck like lackeys. This isn't like travelling to Delhi or Calcutta in a contingent for a sporting or ceremonial event. I don't want a black mark against my record for failing at being a field assistant to some unknown white sahib.'

One bad report could derail their entire career. Raju wasn't wrong about that.

'Raju, friend, don't do this,' Azeem pleaded. 'Don't imagine the worst for no reason. Here's a chance to do something different, learn new skills, travel to a new place. I have dreamt of those hills all my life. And you want us to say no to an invitation to spend months there. When do people like us get an opening like this?'

'Exactly. It's not for people like us.'

In the end it was a couplet from *Umrao Jaan Ada* that won the argument for Azeem—

'Not in the same state of mind can a man
pass all his days ...'

The friendship of Raju and Azeem had begun with Azeem's accidental discovery of a small stash of books lying on top of the metal trunk in Raju's room. The books had tantalizing titles—*The Loves of Satan, The Bleeding Lover, The Murderous Dame*. But what had held Azeem's attention was the name of the author—Mirza Hadi Ruswa. Further conversation revealed that Raju was a Lucknow lad, his home a two-minute walk from the very book shop in Aishbagh from where Azeem had got his copy of *Umrao Jaan Ada*.

Different as Azeem and Raju were, one conversation led to the next and then to the next. Their comfort with each other grew over time till they were fast friends.

ALFRED

New York

1959

THE YEAR OF becoming a widower was moving like a glacier on some unwatched high mountain pass, frozen and still, its surface a featureless sheet of ice. With Rose by his side, the passage of years had been swift, full of urgency and lifeblood. They had started their publishing house in 1915, adding a new imprint every few years. They had moved through successive apartments in Manhattan, had two sons and a daughter, and built this home in Brooklyn together. There had been no sense of time's passing. One moment had rushed into the next to create a mosaic of a rich and varied life. There had been plenty of challenges but none that their partnership, professional and personal, had found insurmountable.

Norman Jr called on Alfred almost every other day, ostensibly to seek advice on the publishing business, but in fact to see if he was holding up alright and say bracing things about Alfred's managing just fine. Norman Jr seemed to have a morbid fear that Alfred might drink himself to a slow death. He was overwhelmed by the sense of responsibility that came with being the firstborn. The younger son, Alfred Jr, and the youngest, his daughter Sarah, checked in on Alfred in their own ways. The former deluged him with gifts of fine wines and collectors' editions of old books. The latter insisted on taking him to some new musical or theatre performance every Saturday.

Rose and he had raised them right after all, he supposed. Rose had never stepped back from the publishing business except for the duration of her confinements, and he had never stepped back from the business of parenting, never cut himself any slack for being a man. On the ship to America, they had promised each other a new world, with new values, new ways of living and loving. And they had mostly made good on those promises.

It had snowed last night as he slept. The first snow of December was piled up outside. Alfred shook off the numbness and shovelled the snow off the path leading to his broad wooden doorway.

Christmas was almost here. The children did not think that their mother would approve of skipping the occasion this once, or even of celebrating it in a low-key way. The structure of every functional family stood on a scaffolding of rituals. Celebrating Christmas and birthdays together over formal family dinners was an important element of Rose's legacy and one that her children were determined not to neglect after her passing. They were keen that everything should be as it had been in years past—the roast turkey, the six-course meal, the giant decorated tree with its fuss of buntings, fairy lights, angels, stars, socks filled with gifts for the younger grandchildren and the customary exchange of gifts between the grown-ups.

The phone in the hallway rang, interrupting Alfred's bleak thoughts.

'Daddy, what a miserable morning this is! I'm sure you are moping. Serena and I propose to drop by for coffee at eleven. And Serena is keen to spend the rest of the day with you, if you will allow her, helping you with the Christmas presents.'

It was his daughter Sarah, nagging him in her gentle, steadfast way to gear up for Christmas. And offering him as a bribe the company of her older daughter. Serena had been closest to Rose, a clear favourite among the many grandchildren, the inheritor of her grandmother's friendly nature among other things. She was an adopter of stray cats, a rescuer of abandoned puppies and an avid reader. Her latest obsession was learning to play the guitar. She had an exceptional singing voice.

It was just as well that Serena was coming to assist. Alfred knew the precise chest in the basement in which Rose would have stocked up gifts for them all. She was particular about finding the right present for each person. She started collecting them many months ahead of time, sometimes picking up treasured pieces out of her own jewellery or book collection to bestow on a member of the family. They would need to go through her pile, fill in the gaps where gifts might be missing. Rose would be a hard act to follow; still, there was no putting off the job any longer.

Alfred was still in his dressing gown when the doorbell rang at a quarter to eleven. They were early. Sarah would frown at his dissolute appearance. His sartorial elegance had gone into hiding of late. He must watch out, lest he become a cliché—a man gone to waste for the want of a good woman.

Serena stood alone at the doorstep, flushed and excited. 'Mamma had to take Catherine for her violin lessons. The class got rescheduled. You are to excuse her, she says. Which means that I have you all to myself today!'

Serena breezed in, shrugged off her coat and hung it on the stand.

'I must say you look very modish,' said Alfred. 'Is that the latest fashion?'

She was wearing a straight shift dress in a bold geometric print and white calf-length leather boots. Her hair was held back with a matching broad white hairband and fell straight to her shoulders, setting off to advantage the white shell hoops she wore in her ears.

'Yes, isn't it a perfectly smashing get-up? I bought these boots with the cheque you gifted me for my birthday. Horribly expensive, but absolutely necessary you'll concede! And there is still some money to spare, so I'm taking you out to Katz. We are going to have the world's best pastrami sandwiches, and you are going to be grilled by me. I have so many questions to ask.'

'Slow down. Let me get you some coffee first.'

'I'll make coffee for us both. And while I do, please get yesterday's beard off your handsome face and dress up nattily so that we can step out in style.'

Over lunch, Serena was full of questions about Rose and Alfred's early days in New York.

'You see, Granma only wished for me to listen to Madeline's story. She did not have the strength to talk about other things. She was sinking, her mind kept slipping, and she was only coherent when she spoke of Madeline. I listened and took notes and promised that I would write the story one day. I hope I will be able to do it justice.'

'I'm sure you will. She would not have picked you unless she had faith in you.'

'But I also need to know about you and her. Alfred and Rose. What did you both do once you reached New York?'

It had been difficult, very difficult.

'It's never easy starting over in a new country. But we weren't alone. It was a time for emigrants. The city was full of them. There were millions of people moving in from Italy and Ireland. Other places too. We just joined the tide. It helped that your grandmother spoke Italian fluently. We rented rooms in the Lower East Side. She worked two jobs while I set about exploring business opportunities.'

'How did you decide to become publishers?'

'After Norman was born, Rose had to stay home. She started doing translation work for a small press and got work home. She did that for a few years. She had tenacity and great ideas, your grandmother. Her mind worked at a feverish pace around the business of books. Her employer began to rely on her suggestions.'

'She said it was you who put together the idea of starting your own publishing house.'

'I just struck lucky. I was the right man at the right place. I got a tip-off that a cargo of good printing paper was being sold for a pittance at the docks. There was some disagreement between the exporter and the buyer. The deal had fallen through. I took a gamble and acquired it, entirely on credit, with an agreement to pay in six months. Rose's employer was transitioning to an offset press. They were the latest breakthrough in publishing just then, destined to change the face of the industry. He gave us his old machinery for next to nothing. We got started in earnest.'

'Just the two of you?'

'Yes, Rose put together the initial stories. I did the illustrations and the production and binding myself. We sold out of trunks at fairs and on streets to start with. It was a miracle, but it worked.'

Serena was looking at him with admiration, her eyes full of awe. He felt the depression of the last few months dispel. Rose and he had built something good and lasting together, a business, a family, a life of beauty and meaning. He must not let Rose down now.

'Pick up the cheque, young lady, and let us get some work done for Christmas. We must make your grandmother proud,' he said.

Back at his house, he led Serena to Rose's gift chest. It was a large, wooden trunk with an antique lacquer polish in bronze and gold. Inside the chest, there was a pile of gifts with a notepad and pen placed on top. Some gifts were already wrapped, others lay inside shopping bags. There were rolls of bright red wrapping paper patterned with green mistletoe wreaths and spools of white satin ribbon and tiny gift cards in envelopes, all lined up and waiting to be used.

Serena and Alfred sat together for a few hours matching the unwrapped gifts against their intended recipients, aided by the jottings in the notepad. He watched as Serena efficiently wrapped the things and affixed a small card with the to-be recipient's name and stacked them on a nearby table. It struck him yet again how much care his wife had given to each member of the family. And how much she had left behind for him to love in this world.

After Serena left, he continued to sit there. Being with Serena had made time move once again, fan him with a soft breeze.

Serena spoke with her hands as much as with words, flinging them expressively in every direction, tossing back her head and laughing frequently. Wrapping the gifts in her company, he had felt closer to Rose than he had in the months since her passing. Some residual fragrance of the orange blossom perfume she had worn every day lingered in the room, citrusy floral, fresh and sweet.

As the evening deepened, he felt melancholic, full of an inchoate grief. He felt grateful for the tears that welled up in his eyes and rolled down his cheeks. He felt he had turned a corner.

There were presents still to be bought for the three youngest grandchildren. Serena and he had another lunch date and shopping spree planned out. He was looking forward to it. The shops and streets were festooned with Christmas decorations. Strangely, they did not make him wretched. Grief and the festive season could coexist in the same time and space. The human heart was larger than he had imagined it to be.

'I wonder what Gran left me for Christmas. She told me it was her most treasured possession ever, and though it was mine I should leave it with you for as long as you wished to keep it,' said Serena when they met again. She had spent a lot of time with Rose after the latter had taken ill. Mercifully, it had not been a long-drawn illness. The end had come soon and was not painful.

Alfred had seen a large envelope marked with Serena's name somewhere. He was not sure where. In the study perhaps. 'I am sure she would have wanted you to wait till Christmas morning,' he said, waving an admonishing finger at her in mock sternness.

Serena left after embracing him in a warm hug and kissing him on both cheeks for good measure. She extracted from him a promise to take her out for lunch again. The post-war pall had lifted. New York was booming once again. Dozens of new eateries and cafes had sprung to life. Serena insisted on introducing him to them.

Back in his own home, Alfred sat by the fireside, dozing intermittently. He was feeling better than he had in a long time. His granddaughter had a goodness of heart, a grandness of manner that was so reminiscent of Rose that it had planted a seed of hope inside of him. Even though Rose was gone, she would always remain with him in the many things their love had created and given to the world.

Evening shadows were falling on the library floor in a crisscrossing pattern from the window grille, when he remembered Rose's gift for Serena. He was curious to know what Rose had left her. He lumbered across to her little study, switched on a tall floor lamp and sat down on a stool in a soft pool of amber light, next to the wooden chest of drawers where Rose sometimes kept things.

He found what he was looking for at the bottom of the last drawer. Inside a large yellow manila envelope bearing Serena's name in Rose's neat handwriting, he found two old books, their pages curled with age, and crumbling.

One was an old school atlas. The top right-hand corner bore the name of its owner written by hand—Madeline Evans. The other was a slim book in Urdu, the script running right to left. It had no name written on it.

It had belonged to Azeem.

Two young people ahead of their time. He was grateful to Rose for holding their memory sacred.

Rose had told Serena the details of Madeline and Azeem's story. Someday, perhaps, that story would be written and told to the world. He brought the two books near his forehead and held them to it reverentially. Then he gently put them back in the envelope, his eyes faraway as he did so.

MADELINE

Nainital

1906

NORMAN EVANS WAS waiting to receive his family at the Kathgodam railway station. This time around, the separation had been a brief one. They had all travelled together from Jaunpur to Bareilly. Then leaving Martha and Madeline to recuperate for a few days at a friend's home there, he had proceeded to the Public Works Department rest house at Ranibagh to set up his office for the survey work and to arrange for his family to stay in Nainital.

Nainital served as a summer capital for the United Provinces. Spread around seven hills surrounding a freshwater lake, its topography and weather were like that of the Lake District in England. Many British families moved into the town between April to October each year to get away from the bristling heat of the North Indian plains. The hill station had on offer horse riding, rowing, sailing, roller skating, and walking trails for their pleasure. Local clubs and hotels organized sporting fixtures and social gatherings for the summer crowd. The boarding houses and eateries served excellent fare. The music in the assembly rooms was always lively with many talented Anglo-Indian performers, and on some days theatre enthusiasts staged burlesque comedies for the evening's entertainment.

Mr and Mrs Croft, his friends from previous visits to the town, had agreed to provide them with excellent lodging for the next four months. The hot season in Jaunpur would be well behind them by the time they returned home in November. Norman wished to spend Christmas in his own residence with his ladies at his side.

He was planning to host a splendid lunch to reciprocate the many invitations he had received on Christmas over his many years in India. But for now, he was grateful that his stratagem of getting a work assignment to bring them all to the cool climate of the hills had worked out.

He had written in advance to the tonga superintendent at Kathgodam to book a full horse carriage for the travellers. They would go by road for the better part of the climb to Nainital. The two ladies and the ayah, along with their luggage, would travel by tonga, while Norman would ride alongside, accompany them to Nainital and settle them in. He would retain his room at the Ranibagh rest house but hoped to spend as much time in Nainital as his work allowed him.

The train came to a slow, almost sighing halt in the tiny station with an unusually clean platform, free of hawkers. A few coolies in red shirts and flimsy white dhotis stood in a disciplined queue near the first class compartment, not hustling or rushing about. The ersatz European toy station feel of Kathgodam, with the train standing like a friendly caterpillar against the leafy green backdrop of the mountains rising behind it, was a happy promise of the things to come. Madeline waved to Norman from her window as soon as she saw him. She was a blur of honey-coloured hair and both arms moving behind the slatted bars. On alighting, she threw her arms around her father in an affectionate hug.

'Papa, I have missed you so!'

Martha too looked more relaxed. As she kissed him fleetingly on the cheek, Norman sensed from her smile that the prospect of heading into the mountains was pleasing to her.

He led them into the first class waiting room.

'I'll have the luggage put in the cart and see that the ayah is taken to the tonga. Then I'll come back for you.'

Martha was glad to stretch herself out on the easy, generously proportioned reclining chair with a cane back and wooden arms that could be extended out to serve as leg rests. She was dozing lightly by the time Norman returned to fetch them.

The Public Works Department rest house was located along the cart road to Nainital, a few miles from the train terminus. He stopped there to pick up his raincoat. It looked as if it might rain anytime.

They halted briefly at the bridge as Norman pointed out to them the spring-fed Gola river gushing underneath them. 'Excellent trout by the dam. Riley and I have already been fishing twice,' he said. The prospect of good fishing in the vicinity had put the Ranibagh rest house many notches up in his estimate as the base camp for his team. Madeline said delightedly to Martha:

'I chatter over stony ways
In little sharps and trebles
I bubble into eddying bays
I babble on the pebbles.

'Doesn't it remind you of this poem, Mamma?'

'"The Brook" by Lord Alfred Tennyson. It was in our Radiant Reader in Class 7,' said Mariam from the back of the tonga.

Martha turned around to give her a curt nod of acknowledgement. The young woman was obviously proud of her education. There was a quiet poise in the ayah's demeanour that Martha found disconcerting. Yet, she was always respectful and was good at taking orders. There was nothing to complain about. Martha just felt more self-conscious in her presence than she did with the other natives working at the bungalow. What mattered really, she reminded herself, was that Mariam was a good companion for Madeline, who genuinely seemed to enjoy being with her.

'I can already smell the pines,' said Madeline.

There was the hint of coolness in the air, the merest of breezes.

'I think this was a good idea. I'm so glad to be escaping the worst of the summer, dear Norman,' Martha said. She could feel herself unclench, the crease in her brow easing with the withdrawal of heat from upon her skin.

She was wearing a newly tailored gown, a soft pastel flowered print in chintz. One of the few people who had earned her approval in Jaunpur was the durzee who set himself up with his Singer sewing machine at the back of the bungalow and made dresses to order, his skills equal to copying the most elaborate patterns shown to him in magazines.

It was the middle of the rainy season in the hills. The lower slopes were full of wildflowers; tiny white and yellow daisies and bursts of spiky red and purple salvia adorned the slopes. Pine trees rustled in the wind. Clouds with puppy faces chased each other in the skies.

They stopped for a quick lunch at the Vergomont Hotel. It was the first stop for changing the ponies.

'What a pretty place this is. Could Mariam and I walk around and explore a bit?' asked Madeline. Beyond the fence of the hotel, a wild patch of baby pink and white rain lilies beckoned invitingly.

'Madeline, first come in and eat a bit. I ordered minestrone soup and mince pies to be kept ready for us. I'm so tired of the dak bungalow chicken curry the cook serves us every day.'

After the meal was over, Madeline, accompanied by Mariam, strolled around the hotel grounds. It began to rain a short while later. Madeline came rushing indoors, into the parlour where Norman and Martha sat with a tray of tea. She took off her bonnet and shook off the few drops of water that had gathered, before putting it on again. The sudden but swift downpour delayed their departure by half an hour.

When they did leave and move higher, the hillside turned dark green with moss, fern and giant oaks, the underside of their leaves a furry white. The oaks stood in hoary old congregations, giving to the surrounding forests a suggestion of deep wisdom, of some quiet knowledge older than time. Every now and again, mountain springs burst into sight and then vanished again into the thick undergrowth, their water gurgling and swirling icy cold.

The second horse change stop was at the Roman Catholic Mission. The mission ran an orphanage and school for native children.

'Is this the kind of school you studied in?' Madeline asked.

Mariam stood silent for a moment, searching for the correct answer. 'A little different. Our school was part of a bigger school for girls run by the nuns. We were just next to the main school which got students from very rich families. It had a large compound with many different buildings, its own chapel, beautiful gardens.'

'Were you always Christian or did you become Christian on account of studying in a Catholic school?'

Martha frowned at her daughter.

Madeline's curious questioning was something that Martha had encouraged in her from early childhood. Against the familiar backdrop of an English town, it had seemed like an intelligent, very desirable trait. In the uneven terrain of a foreign country, complex with different faiths and classes of people, Martha found herself embarrassed more than once by Madeline's inquisitive probing.

'Oh, Mamma. I didn't mean to be rude. Forgive me, Mariam, if I offended you. I just find it unusual that Mariam is Christian.'

'My parents converted from Hinduism to Christianity,' said Mariam quietly.

'But there are people in India who have been Christians since the time of St Thomas the Apostle. There is a church in the Hindu holy city of Banaras which is said to date back to the time of St Thomas's visit there. Banaras is not far from Jaunpur. Maybe we can plan a trip once we go back,' said Norman. He was trying to draw the discussion away from Mariam, sensing her awkwardness.

'Isn't Banaras where the cremation ghats are? I saw a feature in *The Times* once. I'd rather we stay as far from there as possible,' said Martha.

'Martha dear,' began Norman. Then thinking the better of it, he kept quiet and proffered his arm to walk her back to the tonga. It was too early to explain to her the stark, solemn, undying grace of the ancient space, the oldest living city in the world, where devout Hindus went to die, believing it offered them freedom from the cycle of births and deaths.

Soon everyone fell into silence, lulled by the rhythmic movement of the horse carriage. Martha was dozing lightly. Madeline was watching the scenery intently, as light green terraced fields alternated with dark green forests, and the circuitous cart road wound up, up and around the mountains.

Mariam was deep in her thoughts. Her faith in Christ was the deepest part of her being, her devotion to Him utter and complete. Yet she felt wretched and unsure of herself when anyone probed its antecedents. She realized that Madeline's questioning was innocent, but it had touched a raw nerve.

Madeline knew nothing of the caste system in India that had driven people like Mariam's parents into Christianity's welcoming arms. It promised to wipe clean a past of demeaning jobs and social ostracism. And yet discrimination followed them. 'Rice Christians'—that was the pejorative used for them. They were derided as being followers for the sake of receiving alms from the church.

The final coach stop was the brewery, where Norman's acquaintance, Mr Burke, had arranged a little picnic tea for them. The cart road did not go any further from there. They would be leaving the tonga and travelling by dandi. Coolies would carry each of them separately along the bridle path, in the local version of a sedan chair. If Norman had been alone, he would have walked the last two miles, enjoying the challenge of the climb. Before leaving the guest house, he had asked his syce to come and collect the horse from the brewery.

The evening tea at the brewery included buttered scones with plum jam, apple tarts and the finest Darjeeling tea, which was served under a large flowering jacaranda tree with dark blue, almost violet flowers. It was as if they were seated inside a painting by Van Gogh.

Martha struck up a conversation with Mr Burke's wife who walked up to Nainital once a week to return books from her library and take out new ones. Martha had the feeling that Nainital would suit her much better than being in Jaunpur. It felt good to know that the town they were headed toward boasted of not one but two excellent libraries, each with a wide selection of periodicals and books in English.

The small library at the Jaunpur Club had only back issues of gardening and knitting magazines, a few classics and the worst kind of penny dreadfuls by way of reading material. The nawab's personal library, which had Madeline in its thrall, had a bias towards Oriental works. Martha was happy to admire it from a distance.

Mariam was chatting with two other ayahs. They were accompanying another British family travelling up to Nainital. They sat in a separate group a little distance away. The other ayahs were dressed in bright, gaily printed saris. The family they worked with owned a summer home in Nainital to which they retreated each year. The older children studied in boarding schools in town.

Madeline was returning from a visit to the facilities located at the back of the main building when she saw a young man, about twenty years old, standing in a side garden and talking to her father. He was tall, a good two or more inches above six feet, broad-shouldered, clad in khakis, with brown boots, dark hair, dark eyes and a cleft on the chin; his skin was very fair by native standards. A strange awareness flooded her body. She felt her heart skip a beat, her breath catch in her throat, a slow flush spread through her body. Who was he?

His conversation with her father concluded, he walked at an unhurried but smart pace towards where her father's horse was tethered and led it out of the compound. She fought down an urge to shout—Ruko! Stop!—thus compelling him to slowly turn around and look towards her. Instead, she watched his receding figure till he was completely out of sight.

'That's my new syce. I asked him to come here and take the horse back to my rest house,' her father said.

His new syce? What business did a syce have looking like that!

'Oh good. I am looking forward to my riding lessons here. Mamma got the tailor in Jaunpur to make me a new riding habit in the latest style,' Madeline said, her tone deceptively light.

The prospect of riding lessons seemed suddenly fraught with risk and adventure.

The last two miles by dandi were arduous. The climb was extremely steep.

'The poor coolies. I feel guilty to be using them so,' Madeline said. It struck her as unjust to expect the coolies to carry their party uphill.

'It is a job they are well-trained to perform and happy for the earnings from,' Norman replied.

It was difficult to discuss the matter further, seated on separate dandies as they were. Madeline decided to keep her peace. She knew she was trying her father's patience. She had already annoyed him much by asking why Mariam was not allowed to travel in their train coach or sit with them in the railway waiting rooms.

There was a long queue at the toll before they could enter Nainital. There was nothing to do but endure it.

'Tired?' Norman asked Martha and Madeline. 'There will be a warm bath at your lodge. Some hot soup and bread too, should you want any. We'll make an early night of it.'

Past the toll, a beautiful marble head of a cow gushed water into a large trough below. The ponies of those who had ridden up the bridle path stopped to drink their fill and the coolies washed their hands and faces from under the spring. Ferns grew out of the cracks and crevices of the trough, the steep wall verdant with moss and foliage.

They entered Nainital through a busy market, which opened out to reveal a view of an emerald lake surrounded by high peaks. The evening shadows covered one half of the lake; the other half was curiously light still. Rowboats moved in a smooth, slow motion here and there. In the distance were a couple of yachts with brightly striped sails. The rain had stopped. There was the perfume of wet soil and sodden leaves in the air, moist and earthy.

'I think I'm going to love being here,' said Madeline, inhaling deeply and then exhaling a soft, sensuous, slow breath out, her body arching skyward.

In her mind's eye, she could see herself riding out on a winding mountain trail to the highest peak and taking in the view of mountains and meadows spread out all around. Standing beside her was a native man in khaki pants and brown boots, the setting sun casting a warm glow on his face, his dark eyes staring intently into her own tawny golden-green ones.

ADJACENT TO THEIR cottage in Oak Park, Mr and Mrs Croft kept rooms for lodgers to rent in the summer season. A sense of relief flooded Martha at the prospect of living in a boarding house over the next few months. The bungalow at Jaunpur had drained her of all emotional energy. She could neither accede to the claims the large house made for her attention nor ignore them with a good conscience. As soon as she woke up each morning, she felt burdened by the unvoiced expectation of receiving orders by the many members of Norman's household staff. The watchful, nervous expression on Norman's face as he waited for her to take charge of the bungalow only added to her sense of inadequacy.

In the early days, she had made a few feeble attempts to fulfil what was expected of her. But by midday, her resolve to be more actively engaged would lie in a crumpled heap in some corner of her head, while the rest of her just struggled to get through the dull, sultry day, with its plethora of well-meaning morning visitors and its tedious evening engagements. The house continuously made her feel dour and brittle, a cold woman of clumsy gait.

Mrs Croft was a wonderful host, friendly and full of useful tips for her guests. Printed menus of the more popular establishments on Mall Road, hand-drawn maps of routes to various nearby picnic spots, the rate list for hiring horses, tongas, boats and coolies—practically everything of interest to a visitor could be fished out from the large box-file lying on the carved walnut wood table in the main parlour. Guests could eat in the dining hall, request food trays up in the rooms or could take their lunch and dinner at the excellent restaurants and cafes dotting the high street that ran along the length of the lake.

It was not just the Englishness of the climate that made Martha feel more at home in Nainital. The town was assembled out of a sensibility that was entirely British. Its homes, hotels, shopping establishments, many churches, schools and sporting facilities had sprung afresh around the pristine lake that one Mr Barron had chanced upon in 1841. There was a promenade all along the lake, lined with willow trees and benches to sit on and gaze from. The main road with its traffic of hand-rickshaws and horse carriages ran parallel to it at a slight elevation.

Across the lake was thandi-sarak—a cool, dark, shadowy road. It was devoid of buildings and traffic. Its leaf-shaded length was favoured by horse-riding enthusiasts. It allowed them to take their horses for a canter or brisk trot without the impediment of shoppers or rickshaws. At the northern end of the lake was a huge flat expanse called The Flats that boasted of a theatre, a bandstand and sports grounds.

Around eleven each morning, Martha and Madeline took a stroll along Mall Road, walking past establishments selling coats and fine Pashmina shawls, carved wooden furniture and objets d'art, clocks and watches, among other things. Walkers nodded pleasantly to each other, stopped to exchange a few words about the weather and moved on. The town felt both intimate and impersonal to Martha.

'Mamma, should we take a boat ride again today?' Madeline suggested a week into settling in.

Rowboats were available at a minute's notice for one anna an hour. Martha enjoyed rowing. She had a strong set of arms. The rhythmic movement of the oars over the gently rippling water relaxed her, helped her build up an appetite for lunch.

Madeline waved to a wiry old man with a flowing white beard. She recognized him from their last outing on the lake on his boat. He had a glistening but uneven set of teeth through which he smiled broadly and frequently, his grey eyes narrowing into a squint each time he did. After launching the boat into the water, past the line of canoes standing on the shore, he was content to let his oars idle while Martha and Madeline took charge of the small wooden canoe.

Madeline marvelled at the town spread out around them as they boated companionably. It had the feeling of an enchanted toy town with its colourfully roofed houses and picturesque clubhouses. Yachts and rowboats bobbed on the opaline lake, the willows weeping into the water. Walking along the lake were gentlemen in top hats and suits and ladies wearing grand dresses. It all seemed as if it had been conjured magically out of the surrounding hills.

'Mamma, isn't it strange how different this is from Jaunpur, from all the other places that we travelled through? It's like a different country.'

The country she had seen when the *SS Dwarka* docked in Bombay, and while travelling by train to Jaunpur, was different. Jaunpur, with its medieval fort, mosques and crowded bazaars, had been teeming with people and history, many centuries worth of living spilling out. In contrast, history was conspicuous by its absence in Nainital, as if the locals had no claims on the place.

'It was discovered and developed wholly by an Englishman. There was some taboo about living around it among the locals.'

'I wonder if our boatman will know more. I'm curious to understand why they would not live in such a scenic location,' said Madeline, turning towards the old man.

'Chacha,' she said, training her gaze on him, smiling to convey her friendly intent. She had learnt that you addressed everyone here as an intimate—an uncle, brother or grandfather—if you wanted to start a conversation. Addressing the boatman as shriman or mian, the English equivalent of mister, would be considered awkward in Hindustani, a non-starter as far as opening a dialogue with someone went.

The old man looked back at her, the merest ripple of interest passing over the furrows on his face, his gaze waking to alertness. Once she had his attention, she directed her question at him, slowly separating each word from the next so he could navigate her Hindustani, which, despite her best efforts, was still heavily accented.

'Why did your people not build homes around this lake? Why were the first settlers around the lake English people?'

He looked at her warily.

'Tell me, please, Chacha,' she repeated gently. 'I just want to know.'

He pointed with his finger to a temple at the edge of the lake. The temple was that of goddess Naina, after whom the lake was named, he told her. It was Naina Devi's sleeping place. People were allowed to gather at the lake only once each year to pay homage to her. They believed the waters were sacred and had to be kept pure. Until a local coolie was tricked by an Englishman into revealing its location, the locals had guarded the place zealously, kept it a secret. They did not wish for their goddess to be disturbed.

'You know it's only a story. Local folklore,' said Martha when Madeline told her what the boatman had said. Madeline could be very impressionable, unable to tell fact from fanciful tales.

Madeline nodded in assent but continued to frown to herself. The boatman's story troubled her. She wondered how the goddess felt about the intrusion on her centuries of peace.

She remembered the story more than once as she walked on the promenade. Of course, when she wasn't thinking of the goddess, rudely disturbed out of her sacred slumber, she could not help loving the dainty little hill town—being glad that it existed and that she was there enjoying its many pleasures.

NORMAN FOUND HIMSELF busier than he had anticipated. The rapid development of Nainital, in the years since Mr Barron had discovered and claimed it for the British settlers, had been somewhat too eager and ambitious. No one had considered the fragility of the mountain ecosystem. An earthquake followed by a landslide had razed an entire hillside. It had brought complete buildings crashing and tumbling down into the lake and killed many Europeans and Indians in its wake.

After the landslide in 1880, the Public Works Department that Norman worked for had intervened to line six ravines with masonry work and contain the damage from the occasional deluge. However, another landslide occurred in 1898 and caused widespread destruction again. Two drains recently built by the municipal board in another part of the settlement had been destroyed.

Norman was heading a survey team to help the municipal body design culverts, roads and canals to avert future disasters. It was a challenging job. It required him to travel along narrow mountainous paths with his junior engineer Riley, examining the points where slips had occurred, studying the debris, collecting contour data as well as soil samples. A team of four horses and two syces from the Remount Depot at Saharanpur had been issued to him and his junior engineer.

As he rode up and down treacherously steep and narrow trails, made more dangerous due to the rains, he was glad that the department had the foresight to send such well-trained, able horsemen. Azeem, the chap allotted to him, was a keen, very accomplished rider, alive to the possibility of the slightest danger. He steered the team clear of the trickier spots, offering to collect the samples and measurements needed on his own from the riskier locations. As they worked together, Norman found himself developing admiration for the boy. He was exceptional at his work.

Apart from escorting his family to their Oak Park lodging, and staying for three days to settle them in, Norman had only been able to make fleeting visits to Nainital. He could sense their disappointment at seeing so little of him.

Now that the first segment of the survey was done and they had some measure of the problem, he decided it would be useful for him to plan a longer stay in Nainital, to impress upon the town's authorities what dangers they were repeatedly courting with unplanned construction.

Once divested of the large trees that held the mountain slopes with their roots, the soil itself was like oatmeal—dry, porous and capable of soaking in rainfall to the point that it grew unimaginably heavy. The whole town could come tumbling down again. Its fancy hotels could become tombs for their occupants, as had happened in 1866, 1880 and 1898.

Norman arrived at Oak Park one afternoon, after bifurcating his survey team into two units—one half consisting of the junior engineer Riley and his syce, to be located at Ranibagh; the other, comprising him and his syce, in Nainital. He was only half-disappointed to find no one at the lodge. Another part of him was pleased to think that his family was settling in well and enjoying their time there.

Martha was the first to return. She was accompanied by Mrs Burke. They had run into each other at the library, and Martha had invited her home for tea. As he sat having tea with his wife and her friend, a deep sense of contentment filled Norman. It was good to see Martha had made a connection here. She was comfortable, clearly like her earlier self, full of intelligent conversation.

'Where is Madeline?'

'She must have gone walking with Mariam. They do that on the afternoons Madeline has no skating class.'

'Ah. So, she decided to continue with the lessons!'

On his last visit Madeline had been on the brink of giving up. She had been discouraged by her many falls and bruises. She feared she had no talent for skating and could never learn.

'Apparently, she's gliding across the wooden rink quite nimbly now. She says it makes her feel like a ballerina pirouetting to classical music on a dance floor.'

'Well, I'm glad she's enjoying herself. Let me go and see Mrs Croft about lodging for my syce. Perhaps we could all go out for an early dinner tonight.'

'That will be a wonderful change for us,' said Martha. She and Madeline dined in the Crofts' main dining hall. It was cozy in an everyday way. She loved the thought of dining out in town. The lake was beautiful at night, twinkling with the reflection of the town's lights, as if completing the star-studded night sky, joining it to create a perfect shimmering sphere.

'I'll be getting along now, my dear Martha. I have a long walk ahead of me,' said Mrs Burke. Martha saw her to the door, thanking her profusely for her company. She settled down in an armchair and looked through the set of books she had borrowed from the library. They really did boast of a very satisfactory collection.

'It looks like your father is here!' said Mariam when she and Madeline reached Oak Park after their walk.

There were two horses stationed outside their lodge.

Inside, her mother was reading, ensconced in her favorite chair. Papa was nowhere to be seen.

'Has Papa come? I saw ...'

'He's gone to see Mrs Croft about living quarters for his syce. He intends to stay here now,' Martha told her.

The syce! The image of him leading Papa's horse out of the brewery flashed across Madeline's mind. She shook it out of her head.

'That is simply wonderful! I've been missing Papa so!' she said. 'Let me go and find him!'

As she walked towards the lodge, she saw her father making his way back to their rooms. Behind him was the syce, walking with an assured gait, clad in khakis and boots as before. Their eyes met for a moment, and then he lowered his gaze. Had he flushed or was it just a trick of the early evening light?

As she greeted her father, she saw the syce lead the two horses away.

'Papa, may I go riding tomorrow morning?' she asked. Her voice wobbled ever so slightly.

Her father did not seem to have noticed the wobble. He summoned the groom back and ordered him to come in at 7 a.m. in the morning to take the young miss riding. They would not be starting work till later in the day.

Madeline would ask Mariam to lay out the riding dress on the sofa in her room that evening itself.

MUCH TO HER delight, Madeline's riding habit had the desired effect. It enabled her to ride astride Papa's horse and gave her courage to canter at a ripping good speed along thandi-sarak. She imagined she saw more than one envious glance directed at her from the two other women riding side-saddle on the road that morning.

It was good to have a mother like Martha, who encouraged her to look at comfort and practicality first when it came to dressing. Mamma had no patience with trailing long skirts, tight corsets and dresses that constricted a woman's body or restricted her movements unnecessarily.

She stole a few sidelong glances at Azeem—whose name she had learnt from her father—walking by her side. Her heart had lurched momentarily this morning as he had walked towards her and given her charge of the horse's reins. She noticed that he had artistic-looking hands with long tapering fingers, nails neatly clipped and clean.

'What is his name?' she asked, looking towards the horse, taking special care to make her Hindustani sound dulcet. She saw the syce's eyes flicker for a second, surprised at her use of Hindustani.

'Steel,' he replied. He continued to stare ahead at the road. They were returning to the lodge.

She felt strangely chagrined at the horse's name. Steel was so prosaic. It must be the colour, she concluded. He was a beautiful grey with a swishing black tail.

'Just stay here for a moment while I go in and fetch him a lump of sugar. He's been most well-behaved. He should get a reward,' she said, as she got off the horse and let Azeem take charge of him.

The horse nibbled at the sugar and looked up at her with limpid eyes, imploring her for more. After giving him a second lump, she gently stroked his neck with her fingers and he nuzzled her, leaning towards her trustingly. They were going to get along, she could tell.

'How beautiful you are, Steel. I hope we can be friends from today,' she said, turning her head from the horse to the groom before going in. She had pronounced khoobsurat exactly as the librarian at Jaunpur had taught her. If Azeem noticed her superior diction, his face betrayed no signs of it.

Her parents were already having their breakfast.

'Did you have a good ride?' asked Norman. 'You look all flushed.'

'It was wonderful. I could gallop freely all the way from the lower stands to the upper end of the lake without any need to rein the horse in,' she said, hanging up her bonnet on the hook near the umbrella stand in the veranda and sitting down at the breakfast table laid out outdoors. It was covered with a tablecloth—a bright yellow and green flowered print on a dull ivory backdrop.

She finished her cornflakes and reached out for the toast. She began to butter it.

Perhaps she could tuck in an omelette too. Riding made her ravenous.

'Some jam?' asked Norman, pushing three little jars, set on a small wooden tray, towards her. Plum. Peach. Apricot. All made by Mrs Croft's cook. There were many fruit trees on the estate.

'What are your plans for the day, Madeline? I have promised Mrs Burke that I will spend a few hours at the library today helping the new librarian understand the Dewey system better. Papa is going to be busy meeting members of the municipal board, and then he and I are lunching together at the clubhouse. Would you like to join us for lunch?' asked Martha.

'I think I'll stay in and write back to Rose. She waits for my letters as eagerly as I await hers. There is so much to tell her since my last letter. I'll call a lunch tray up to my room.'

'Are you sure, my dear?' asked Martha. It was unusual for Madeline to wish to spend a bright, sunny morning alone in her room. 'Convey my regards to Rose. I'm really glad to hear that her uncle's school is finally off to a start with its first pupils enrolled.'

'I will, Mamma. You enjoy your outing. I may go walking with Mariam to post the letter once I'm finished.'

'Sounds like everyone is set for the day then,' smiled Martha. 'I'm looking forward to doing some useful work for a change.'

'I thought you liked being here, dear,' said Norman, with his lopsided, endearing smile, a searching look in his brown eyes.

'I do. I shall like it even more for being engaged at a task which needs doing,' replied Martha with a laugh. 'You know indolence doesn't become me. I am much happier playing worker-bee than butterfly.'

Norman smiled back at his wife. Happiness transfigured her face, made her seem gentler. When had Martha become such a serious, solemn woman? Perhaps she had always been so in essence. Youth casts its own veneer of joy on a face; time peels it off year by year.

Alone in her room, Madeline settled down to write to Rose. After a few falsely bright sentences describing the new friends she had made in her skating class, she gave up with a sigh. She needed to confront the elephant in the room before she could write a single truthful, coherent sentence again. She needed to confront the confused feelings her father's syce stirred in her. A strange longing to speak to him, an urgent desire to know him better coursed through her.

If only Rose were here. It was impossible to write to her about Azeem without causing alarm. She pushed the letter pad away and exhaled deeply. Madeline would need to talk to Madeline, after all. As a single child, she had much practice being her own chief confidante, having extended conversations with the girl in her mirror. She had grown out of speaking to her over the years. But today, she needed her back, that friend of her childhood fantasy, the alter ego who was able to see things differently, give consolation and counsel as needed.

'It's alright, Madeline. You're just a friendly person. It's quite simple, really. You like knowing people. You talk to Mariam, to Gobind, to Abdul, to Ram Deen, to the boatmen, to everyone. So why not Azeem?' she said aloud to herself.

Azeem. She said the name aloud a few times, just to make sure it would flow mellifluously off her tongue when she addressed him the next morning. There was no use pretending to herself that he was no different from Gobind or Abdul or the pankha boys or the dhobi with his donkey.

'Remember, you are talking to yourself. There is no point to this conversation unless you are truthful,' she chided herself.

Something was happening to her, something unfamiliar and unsettling. It wasn't just that she was acutely aware of Azeem, sensing his presence in the vicinity even before she saw him, picking up the sound of his footsteps distinct from all others as he crossed the compound, her nostrils quivering as the scent of him, woody and pine fresh, reached her. She had become extremely aware of herself, constantly seeing her person through his eyes, conscious of every aspect of her appearance and speech, imagining how she must look and sound to him.

This was sheer madness, this edge of excitement she was walking on, her sense of self all tremulous and uncertain. It was best if she stayed away from the syce. She could always resume riding lessons once she returned to Jaunpur. She must nip this unseemly attraction in the bud.

'Madeline Evans, if you saw a beautiful mountain view, would you not admire it? If you smelt an alluring perfume, would you not want to know its source? If you found a poem that spoke to your soul, would you not memorize it by heart, and repeat it to yourself again and again? When you tasted a mango for the first time, didn't you let its sweet juices fill up your mouth? You didn't ask yourself to spit it out! Why then are you hiding in your room and deciding that you will never go near Azeem again?'

For much of her life, she had been a girl who hurled herself at new experiences with enthusiasm, never scared to engage.

'This is different, altogether too risky,' she replied to the girl in her head.

The very climate of her being was changing, slipping out of her control. Only fools went out heedlessly into impending storms. When you could see the weather ahead was inclement, you stayed home till it passed.

She put on her bonnet resolutely. She would go find Mariam, and they could go to The Flats in search of some diversion.

Mariam, when she found her, was buying wool. One of the other ayahs would be teaching her how to knit. A vendor on a donkey, from a high mountain village, had come on the road outside the lodge hawking colourful bales of wool and an assortment of knitting needles of different counts. He was a delightful, toothless old shepherd with a craggy, deeply lined face and a tinkling bird-like voice. He came down each summer to sell the yarn spun and dyed by his family.

'My brother's wife is expecting her first baby. A woollen blanket will be a welcome gift. Winter in Jaunpur is cold, unlike its long, sweltering summer,' Mariam told Madeline. 'There isn't much for me to do here. This will fill up my time nicely.'

Madeline felt a twinge of guilt. It was true. There were many days on which neither Madeline nor Martha needed her. Mariam must feel lost for things to do. Well, today would be different. They'd spend time together, just like they did in Jaunpur.

THERE WAS A polo match in progress on The Flats, three players to a team. 'Do let's watch it,' Madeline said to Mariam.

There was something about the horses on the ground that moved her deeply—their trotting and galloping unfolding like elements of a ballet performance, their hooves pointing downwards, their legs rising in the air. The swift flying and slow landing of their bodies with so much grace was enchanting. It felt as though they were moving to some music audible only to them.

As Madeline sat in the amphitheater watching the match in progress, her gaze softened, blurred out of focus. She felt that strange restlessness assailing her again. Instead of the riders in front, she was seeing Azeem. He was flying across the field to cheering from the watching crowd. She shook herself awake and focused her eyes on Mariam, sitting beside her.

Mariam was wearing the paisley lemon and grey gown that Madeline had insisted she take from her. The tailor had altered it to Mariam's size, taking it up an inch in length and letting it out at the bodice. It looked good on her. On Madeline's suggestion, she had piled her hair up into a high knot. It made her look taller. Almost fashionable.

The polo match was over. The players shook hands with each other. The grooms led the horses off the field. Madeline and Mariam strolled to the end of The Flats and bought roasted corn on the cob, hot off the coals, from the man who stood roasting and fanning them with a hand fan on a wooden cart on wheels. It was deliciously charred and seasoned with Himalayan salt and freshly cut lemon. They sat down by the lake to enjoy the corn.

A family of ducks glided at the near end of the shore, while tiny mynah birds hopped in and out of the branches of the trees above, making a vaguely musical sort of racket. It began to rain, a soft, lacy drizzle to start with. As the rain increased, they pulled out their umbrellas.

They continued to munch on the corncobs and gaze at the lake.

A whispery mist was beginning to descend on the water, making the red and yellow row boats seem like apparitions in a floating dream, now there, now vanished in the moisture-laden haze.

'Mariam,' said Madeline impetuously. 'Have you ever been in love?'

Mariam stared at Madeline in surprise. In all the time she had known Madeline, the girl had not lost her power to startle. She was infinitely curious. She flitted lightly from one topic of interest to the next like a butterfly did from blossom to blossom, probing expertly for the nectar within, not content to move on till she had had her fill. She drank deeply of existence, yet there was a delicate beauty to her, a sweetness of nature, an eager interest in the business of life. Everyone's life, not just her own.

Mariam found she could not resent Madeline's inquisitiveness. Mariam wasn't alone here. In Jaunpur, Madeline had everyone eating out of her hands—from the cook, the butler, the tailor, the fan pullers, the sweeper, to the nawab and his librarian.

'Once,' said Mariam guardedly. Only the first instance hurt, the second time was so forgettable, it didn't qualify. So 'once' was true enough. 'It was long ago and does not matter now.'

Madeline caught the littlest inflection of pain in Mariam's voice, the merest clouding of the expression in her eyes, and stopped herself from asking Mariam any more questions. She reached out for her hand and squeezed it instead.

She thought of the friends she had made onboard the steamer. She wished she had paid more attention to their conversations about men and love. There had been discussion aplenty on the tumults of the heart, the quickening of breath, the flushing of cheeks. But Madeline had not been even remotely curious. She had been wholly focused on learning Hindustani from Rose and practising it on the ship's crew.

'Love, really, must be the wretchedest thing. I have no personal experience of it, Mariam. Though I have read plenty of books that dwell on it. And opera, which I passionately adore, doesn't veer too far from love either. Love seems to pervade all the arts. But it's all so woefully tragic. Though I must confess heartbreak makes for the finest arias. You and I are best off keeping a distance from love. All death and destruction, warring sides and the drinking of poison—that's how it ends,' said Madeline.

The distance from love is loneliness, thought Mariam to herself bleakly. When love pushes you away, loneliness embraces you. There's a dejection of spirit which sits in one corner of your being, no matter how brisk and cheerful the rest of you might be. It wasn't much of a choice.

She wondered at the suddenness of Madeline's question. Where had it come from? Had she taken a fancy to one of the dashing young polo players? They were mostly British men, army captains and lieutenants, stationed in nearby cantonment towns in the plains. They came up for an occasional game. Her father would not mind. She sensed in Norman a wistful desire to keep his daughter close. Martha's repeated reminder of Madeline's future as a scholar at Oxford always elicited from him a half-hearted response. Mariam had noticed a slight shadow of disappointment clouding his eyes.

'PAPA, IF YOU are not working today, I would like to ride to the top of Cheena Peak with Azeem. I believe the view is magnificent,' said Madeline. 'Apparently, you can see as far as Tibet on a clear day.'

Cautious, circumspect Madeline had put up a resolute battle against the rebel who lived inside her head for three whole days and finally conceded absolute and total surrender to her point of view. She simply hadn't travelled ten thousand miles across the ocean to hide inside her room. She was not to be a scaredy-cat and a silly goose. If exotic new experiences beckoned, she was to walk towards them, open the gates and see what lay across on the other side. Azeem was clearly no Count Dracula, she was no milky little Victorian Miss about to be ravished. There was the smell of damp oak leaves and woodsmoke in the air and something outside of words calling to her spirit. There were mountains to climb, forest trails to explore, friendships to be forged. There was life asking to be lived.

Norman looked up from his plate. He seemed to be contemplating her request gravely. There was a slight uncertainty written on his face. He spoke after an elongated pause. 'The paths up can be tricky in the monsoon season. But Azeem should be able to lead you up and back safely. Listen to him, don't be impulsive or in a hurry.'

'Thank you, Papa. I promise I'll be very careful. I'll ask Mrs Croft if I can have a picnic basket. It's a lovely sunny day. Why waste it?' said Madeline.

Azeem rode a dark brown stallion named Copper.

As they began the climb up, from the Upper Bazaar side, Madeline reined in her horse and waited for Azeem to catch up with her and take the lead.

The long dirt path rose steadily through oak, cedar and rhododendron forests. She had to dismount and walk with Steel at a couple of places. Once, Azeem had to tether Copper to a tree and come back to lead her horse up. He told her to remain seated as he guided the animal up a tricky stretch.

There was a stretch of plateau on top, and from there the snow-capped peaks of the Himalayas were clearly visible, a view of breathtaking beauty. Azeem pointed out the peaks to her by name. Visible from the other side was a bird's eye view of Nainital, the teardrop shaped lake at its heart, and around the lake, buildings with their red and green sloping roofs, their steeples, spires and clock towers glinting in the sunshine.

'I have a packed lunch for us. Let's sit there, near that tree,' she said, pointing to a majestic cedar rising tall from the plateau's edge. In this informal setting, perhaps she would be able to strike up a real conversation with him, other than the stiff 'Yes Miss, No Miss' that he rarely went beyond as he escorted her on her morning ride.

There were wildflowers all around—dainty yellow buttercups on the meadow and tall slashes of wild hyacinth rising against the blue sky in scattered clumps. From under a large boulder, tiny pink rock roses peeped out. Madeline pulled out the tablecloth and laid the sandwiches, apples and flask of water upon it.

'Thank you, but you please eat. I will eat in the bazaar later,' Azeem said. He spoke formally to her, his voice low and deep. There was something regal to his diction. It made her self-conscious about her own Hindustani. She sometimes flung her words about in quick abandon, without a thought to their rhythm or flow, just small stones hurled out to connect with her target, the listener. When it came to speaking Hindustani, he was a lofty archer, she a barefoot girl with a catapult. But speak they would today, she had made up her mind.

He was still standing at the same place, a slight frown furrowing his forehead, his dark eyes distant. His face was a shut door. She needed to find the magic words to open it. Once inside, what did she hope to discover? Perhaps stories of an ancient land washed in valour and grief, or old poems in a sun-kissed, moon-soaked language, the words falling like dark raindrops on her light skin. Maybe rituals for slaking the thirst of wandering souls, for feeding hungers older than time itself.

'I insist. You must understand I am not a typical memsahib. You are not to treat me like one. I wish to be your friend. I have asked you to come here with me so that we can be friends. I seek your friendship.'

There, she had said it. Dost. Dosti. Simple words. It was their magic she sought to invoke. All she wanted from Azeem was this—to know him. Why was it taking so long for him to comprehend?

Azeem just stood there, statuesque, staring ahead, unmoved by her request.

If she tried, would she able to read the thoughts racing through his mind? *Who was this girl? In the stories he had read, there were seductresses and witches—white-skinned, green-eyed temptresses leading soldiers and sailors to their doom. But this girl, there was nothing ethereal about her. Her hands waving in the air as she spoke, her nose twitching at every fresh scent on their path, her eyes eagerly watching every passing expression on his face—she was all too real. You could not mistake the candour in her eyes. Doṣti? What made her imagine that friendship was possible between a person of her race and class with one of his, even if he was to forget that in his culture men and women could never be friends, only relatives or strangers?*

Finally, Azeem shrugged and sat down at a small distance from her, his back resting against the boulder, one leg stretched out and the other folded at the knee, his brown boots somewhat muddy from the ride, not shining any longer as they had done in the morning.

A short laugh of exultation escaped Madeline's lips. She brought her palms together and bowed in a mock 'thank you' gesture.

'May I ask you a question?' he said after a while. He was sitting more comfortably now, his edginess had dissipated. A flock of little white-throated laughing thrushes called after each other, chattering, muttering, cackling, filling the air with their friendly chorus.

'Yes, of course,' she replied. She looked into his eyes. Her gaze was attentive and frank.

'How do you speak our language so fluently?'

A triumphant tinkle of laughter left her lips once again. She knew she was behaving like a silly creature, but she felt much delight at his question. It meant she had piqued his curiosity—despite all the indifference he had shown her earlier.

'The few British officers and their families that I know from a distance at the Saharanpur depot speak a bare smattering of Hindustani words, the odd sentence, if that much. You are newly arrived, yet you can converse with ease.'

His Hindustani, as she had already deduced, was different, more formal than hers. His voice, when he spoke at length, was as she had imagined it might be. Gravel. Husk. Woodsmoke. Starlight. Something muted but resonant with the silent music of the spheres.

'I learned to speak Hindustani on the ship, from a girl called Rose. She and her sisters lived here when she was a child,' Madeline replied.

'But everybody comes here on a ship, don't they? They don't all speak Hindustani.'

'I have always been interested in learning different languages. My mother is a teacher. She teaches in a school in Middlesbrough, the town where we live. She discovered that I was naturally gifted and put me under special instruction when I was only five. I already knew six languages before I came here. This is just one more I'm learning.'

'Six languages!' Azeem exclaimed, a boyish enthusiasm transfiguring his face. 'You are like Mirza Hadi Ruswa then!'

'Who is Mirza Hadi?' Madeline asked. Her face was now cupped in the palms of her hands. She was beginning to enjoy this conversation immensely. They were going to get along quite well after all.

'He is my hero, my favourite writer. In addition to Urdu, he can speak Persian, Arabic, Hebrew, English and Greek. He teaches philosophy, mathematics and Persian at Christian College in Lucknow. He has a keen interest in chemistry, alchemy and astronomy,' Azeem replied.

'You like reading books on alchemy and astronomy?' Madeline asked, wrinkling her nose. A scholarly syce, who would have suspected?

'No. I'm a fan of Mirza Hadi Ruswa's novels,' said Azeem. 'All his academic work doesn't fetch him any money. His teacher's salary is very modest. He has expensive taste and runs up bills that need paying. Lucknow, the city he lives in, is a very cultured place. I was there for some time last year. It's full of the finest pleasures—food, poetry, music, dance. It is rumoured that Mirza sahib dictates a new novel every time a creditor is at his door and refuses to leave unless he is paid.'

Azeem was speaking in Hindustani, his voice rising and falling, weaving images in the air.

Madeline only half-understood what he was saying but was reluctant to interrupt him.

Printing Mirza Hadi's books was like printing rupee notes, Azeem said to her. Readers loved them and couldn't have enough of them. No one before had written that kind of literature. His stories were racy and real, full of life-like characters drawn from his own experiences.

Azeem's face was animated as he told Madeline of Mirza Hadi. He had finally lost the 'native man on duty escorting the white boss's daughter' expression that he always wore. Seeing her smile to herself, he stopped abruptly, suddenly conscious of how much he was speaking.

'I'm sorry. I ...' He flushed with embarrassment.

'Which languages do you speak?' Madeline asked, eager to keep him talking.

'Only Urdu,' he replied. 'That was what we studied at our school in Rannpur. I only came to know of Mirza Hadi Ruswa and his books recently. It is difficult to believe, but he lost his parents when he was young and went to school for only a short time. Most of what he knows, he has taught himself at home! I thought there could never be another person like him, a master of many tongues. And now I'm meeting you. And you know six languages too!'

She frowned. It was six-and-a-half now if you counted—what was it?—Urdu? Hindi? Hindustani? It had taken her a long time to understand why a language that sounded the same to her wore different names. The librarian at the nawab's library in Jaunpur had explained it somewhat. Yet, not enough for her to be certain.

'I sometimes wish I could learn English,' Azeem said. 'But I don't know where to begin.'

He looked serious, a little wistful. Without English, he would remain forever stuck in a syce's stirrups. Always deferentially standing outside the gates of the world that opened into privilege and opportunities. Always removed from the circles of conversation that seemed to move and magically realign the world in favour of those who spoke the language.

'I bought myself an English primer but did not know what to do after memorizing the alphabet,' Azeem continued.

Madeline looked at him thoughtfully. Perhaps she could help him.

'It can be very difficult to learn a language from the beginning. A new script is so hard to decipher that you can get totally mixed-up and overwhelmed. The best way to learn is by conversing with someone. You will be better off understanding and speaking the language first. Once you are somewhat familiar with the flow of English, of how the language curls and curves upon the tongue, rises and falls on the eardrums, how it sits inside spoken sentences, you can attempt reading and writing it,' she said.

A thought was beginning to form in her head. A thought that made her heart race to a silly, zigzag, miss-a-step, double-thud-thud, jump-a-step, skip-a-beat tune. Someone was going to get himself a new English teacher.

Azeem would learn Madeline's language, and she would get better at his, and between them there would never be any silences other than the ones they desired.

THE FIRST STEP was to get Mariam to understand her role. Mariam was to be the designated English teacher to Azeem, spending an hour each afternoon talking to him in the language. Madeline would keep a friendly eye on their progress, helping and encouraging them. She didn't foresee much of a problem on that account. Mariam was the sweetest, most obliging of creatures. Besides, she must be bored senseless, sitting on the steps outside her room and knitting blankets and baby clothes for a niece or nephew yet to be born. Madeline couldn't think of a duller pastime.

'But Madeline, I don't read and write Urdu. I was taught English and Hindi at school,' said Mariam when Madeline broached the subject to her. 'I might not be able to help Azeem at all.'

Madeline tried to recall what the librarian in Jaunpur had explained to her about Hindustani. Centuries of influences were layered into the language spoken by the common people of North India, drawing from earlier tongues like Sanskrit, and later day entrants like Arabic and Persian. Hindi was Hindustani with a greater proportion of Sanskrit words. Urdu was Hindustani with more Persian in it. It had been one language but was now crystallizing into two. Hindi was getting associated with Hindus and Urdu with Muslims. It had seemed odd to Madeline that language should be partitioned into different boxes based on religion.

The British government had some role to play in this. Papa had conceded as much when she asked him about it. After the Mutiny of 1857, the British rulers influenced the education of the locals, now under the crown. Printing presses came up quickly, and with them textbooks for teaching. Books with more Persian words—such as the Quran—were printed in the Persian script, and those with a greater number of Sanskrit words—such as Hindu religious texts—were printed in the Devanagari script. Urdu texts were distributed to some people, Hindi to others.

Madeline couldn't help but think what a curious situation it was. Though Mariam and Azeem were united by a common spoken tongue, they were divided by script.

'You are not to worry about that, dear Mariam. I will not be asking you to use Hindustani-to-English dictionaries or teach him to read and write. You are simply to teach him as Rose taught me to speak Hindustani. I need you to talk to him in English, point out and name things, tell him what you did through the day, ask him simple questions in English about his life and work, encourage and help him to answer back and correct his mistakes. You are not to be his teacher as much as a friend who speaks to him in English. Someone he can trust, who will give him a hand as he stumbles through a new language.'

Mariam looked at her dubiously. 'Why …'

'Mariam, I know you want to know why you should teach Azeem English. But instead think why not! If someone is thirsty for a glass of water, you would give them water if you had any to spare, wouldn't you? If Azeem is thirsty for some knowledge and you have plenty of it, why would you withhold it? Does your Christianity not teach you to help your neighbour?'

Mariam flushed at the mention of her Christianity. It was true. Gifting her and her brother Vincent with an education in English had been the greatest of the many kindnesses the nuns had done to her family. It had opened employment prospects for them, made their situation in life more comfortable and secure. To resent teaching Azeem would be churlish on her part, a refusal to share with her fellowman what had been so generously bestowed on her.

'I do not think your parents will approve of my spending so much time with your father's groom,' she said after thinking upon Madeline's plan. While there were no restrictions on the staff from talking to each other, the kind of prolonged engagement Madeline was suggesting with Azeem every afternoon was bound to be frowned upon.

'Leave that to me, Mariam. I will only ask you to do this if Papa and Mamma don't object. In fact, let me go and talk to Papa now, before Mamma returns from the library committee meeting.'

Norman was seated in the small parlour, bent over some topographical maps, a pen in his hand, a notebook at his side.

'Papa, may I have just two minutes of your time?' asked Madeline.

'Yes, my dear. Come and sit. Tell me what's on your mind. I was just about to get up and go find Azeem. I need him to ride out to Khurpa Tal and verify some measurements we took the other day. Something is not looking right in the gradients Riley and Raju have recorded.'

'Azeem is exactly who I wished to talk to you about!' said Madeline. 'Papa, Azeem wants to learn English. It will help him in his job, working with English bosses like you. I think I have just the plan to make it possible. Mariam is the right person to teach him. She is at loose ends here in Nainital. She doesn't have much to do. I'd like to sit down with them both and see if Mariam can help Azeem learn to converse a bit in English. It will be good for her to do something other than knit. Frankly, I can't think of a more tedious pastime.'

Norman looked at his daughter in bemusement. What exactly was she up to now? It was difficult to predict or understand the way Madeline's mercurial mind worked.

'Madeline, I hope you don't have any silly romantic notions in your head.' Madeline's eyes flew to her father's face in alarm.

'Azeem is a Muslim. Mariam a Christian,' Norman continued. 'They come from entirely different backgrounds. To you, all Indians might seem the same, but India is really many countries contained in one. Besides, I suspect she's older than him. Any kind of romantic liaison between the two would cause a terrible brouhaha here. If that is what you have in mind, please perish the thought immediately. Nothing good can come of it.'

Norman saw Madeline's nose wrinkled up in distaste at the idea; her lips tightened. What a sensitive, intense creature his daughter was, throwing herself into everyone's life heedlessly, eager to help.

'It hadn't crossed my mind even, Papa. Like you said, Mariam is so much older than Azeem. And she is such a serious-minded creature that I didn't think you would look at it like that, that anyone could. But you are right. People may misunderstand the situation. I will seek Mamma's advice. She will know how we can best go about this.'

'My dearest, I must get this work done now, before it gets dark. Please don't start anything without consulting your mother.' He got up in search of the syce. He hoped that Martha would come up with some tactful way of diffusing Madeline's enthusiasm for the upliftment of the native staff.

When Martha returned, Madeline listened patiently as her mother shared the details of the library committee meeting. Martha had volunteered and been taken on as an ad hoc additional member of the committee. There had been much discussion this afternoon, over tea and biscuits at the club, on a revised list of periodicals and magazines to be subscribed to. With readers of all ages and both sexes, it was no easy task to arrive at a list which would be seen as being representative and fair.

'Mamma, it is so lovely that you can do something useful with your time here. When I watch you and read Rose's letters about the hard work she is putting in to help with her uncle's school, I almost feel envious. I love being here, but I can't help thinking that morning tea parties, afternoon picnics and dance and theatre evenings are all very well—but is this all I should go to Oxford with to show for my year in India?'

Martha's face broke into a broad smile. It seemed that she hadn't lost her little girl entirely to this frippery. Madeline was keen to get off to a good start at university and create a favourable first impression there.

'Don't forget, my dear, you'll be returning with one more language to your credit than in your application letter. That too an Eastern tongue completely different from the languages you were formally tutored in. It's no mean achievement. I still marvel at the speed with which you started speaking in Hindustani.'

'Mamma, I have an idea that I wish to seek your advice on. Papa's syce told me he is keen to learn English. It struck me that I could pair him with Mariam for an hour every afternoon when Papa is home for lunch and doesn't require his services. Mariam could familiarize him with English by speaking to him in it, just like Rose helped me learn Hindustani. I could take notes on the syce's progress, see if the method of pairing up two people as conversational partners has pedagogical possibilities. It would be so interesting to do, something meaningful to show for my time here.'

'Why, Madeline. That's a very unusual and interesting train of thought ... though I'm not sure how much a syce will be able to learn or how good a teacher you can expect the ayah to be. You and Rose were a different set of people, from a vastly superior educational background.'

'But Mamma, this is precisely what I need. To see if the method works with different people, in varied situations. If a foreign language can be learnt in the same way that a baby learns to speak, by listening and associating. It will make for such a fascinating research paper. I could write it up on our voyage back.'

'Try it then, dear, if the idea beguiles you so.'

Madeline sighed deeply. 'Both Mariam and Papa are against it. They think it would cause unnecessary gossip among the staff if the two are seen to be spending time together. Isn't it sad how the small-mindedness of people can make the simplest of learning exercises so difficult?'

'Let me see if I can ask Mrs Croft about how we can tackle that problem. We shouldn't have to sacrifice our academic ambitions for the sake of needless staff chatter. I will make it clear that it's a project that you are working on for your university. I shall ask Mrs Croft if we can put out a small table in front of the bench under the pear tree in the back garden. It will be best if you also join the two of them occasionally and oversee the arrangement, at least for a few days at the start.'

'Mamma, you are the best,' said Madeline.

'It is perfectly alright to be a bit sly for the sake of a good cause,' the girl who lived in Madeline's head told her that night as she put out the oil lamp and made herself snug under her light wool blanket in her small room in the lodge. 'Well done. All in all, you tackled Mamma and Papa adroitly on the matter of teaching Azeem English. And if you can give him a new language, it is most surely a noble cause.'

Madeline had the pleasantest of dreams that night, a happy nonsensical dream of horses conversing in English and a glorious opera being staged in soft, sensuous Urdu, the tenor wearing polished brown boots, the mezzo-soprano with sparkling hazel eyes and dark honey-coloured curls. The chorus was sung by laughing thrushes, their white collars perfectly suited to the part. The audience—cotton wool had been placed on everyone's eyes—was clapping in slow motion.

THE CLASSROOM UNDER the pear tree was inaugurated with some fanfare by Madeline. Mrs Croft, Mrs Burke, Martha and Norman were invited as guests of honour. Madeline began with a small speech.

'I am so excited to welcome you all to our classroom under the pear tree. I have always considered myself a very lucky girl. I was lucky to be born with an ability to pick up different languages with ease. I am lucky to have a Mamma who recognized my talent early and encouraged me in every possible way. I am lucky that Papa works in this beautiful country and that I've got an opportunity to visit it. I am lucky that on the ship to India I made a wonderful friend in Rose Eliot, and she agreed to teach me Hindustani. I am lucky to have made the most wonderful friends in India like Mariam who is a gentle companion and Azeem who is the best riding teacher possible. I am excited to announce that Mariam and Azeem have agreed to participate in an experiment that I have thought of based on my experience of learning Hindustani from my friend Rose. It is so kind that Mrs Croft has given us permission to use this place as our classroom and Mrs Burke has promised to be an independent judge of the success or shortcomings of our experiment. May I ask for a round of applause for all of us here and request you to join us for tea and biscuits?'

After tea, the guests retreated to sit in Mrs Croft's main parlour, leaving Madeline alone with Azeem and Mariam. Azeem looked wary and uncomfortable. She wondered how much of her soapbox theatrics and grandstanding he had understood. Had she overdone her girlish gushing a tad? Mariam also wore a slight frown on her face.

Madeline sat down on a chair that had been placed in front of the bench. She waited for Azeem and Mariam to settle in. Mariam was clearing the teacups while Azeem kept standing, staring moodily into the distance.

'Won't you please sit down?' she asked Azeem gently in Hindustani, even as Mariam picked up the tray of used cups and headed towards the kitchen.

Azeem sat down on the bench tentatively, as if it were a barbed wire fence.

'Mariam, come back quickly, please. We should begin now,' said Madeline.

Once the two were seated in front of her, Madeline began to speak to them, this time in Hindustani. 'I know from your faces that you are both not happy to be here. You are probably asking what is to be gained from all this. I urge you to stop thinking like that. Perhaps nothing at all will be gained, except the time we spend together, getting to know one another better. But I do believe our experiment has potential. Anyway, how will we know for certain unless we try? I am willing to do my best. All I ask of you is to give it a chance. Will you?'

Mariam nodded her head in an uncertain manner. It was not clear if she was saying yes or no.

'No,' said Azeem stonily.

The agreement between Azeem and Madeline was of a quiet, out of sight friendship; that was the dosti she had asked of him. What she had just proposed to the gathering was outrageous. He was not willing to be the dancing bear wearing a gaudy skirt in her vaudeville show, held by her on a chain, performing for spectators.

Madeline looked at Azeem in consternation. She had not thought to ask him! She had clearly offended him. Presumed too much.

'But you can't just say no after I have planned it all out!' she said in a hollow voice. He shrugged. As if to say he could. He had.

'You said you wanted to learn English, didn't you?' she accused, boring her eyes into his, challenging him to deny it.

I do. I did. But not like this. Not like an exhibit in a zoo.

'I don't wish to now,' he said stiffly.

'Mariam, say something. Explain to him, please. It will only feel uncomfortable for a day or two. Once we settle into it, everything will be alright. We will all get to spend more time together. And Azeem, I promise you will speak English before Mariam and I return to Jaunpur.'

'Madeline, I'm afraid …' Mariam began.

'You are afraid! He is afraid! What is this sudden epidemic of fear?' Madeline stopped her impatiently before she could continue. 'No one ever died of trying to learn another language. Believe me, I speak many. What are you scared of anyway? Talking to each other? Maybe making a few silly mistakes? That is all I'm asking of you! Is it so hard?'

Mariam and Azeem exchanged a look. Mariam gave him a bemused smile. Madeline was all spit and fire, like a very angry kitten that had been ruffled and teased. Azeem found himself smiling back. Perhaps, he needed to lighten up.

Madeline noticed the easing of the tension with an inward sigh of relief.

'It's really very simple if you will both stop being nervous. Azeem, just remember you've done it before,' she said. 'When you were a baby, no one taught you how to speak. You listened, you saw, you made associations between sounds and meanings, you started speaking on your own. You can do it again. For the time you are in this class, just assume that there is no other language except English and speak whatever gibberish that comes to you, use your hands and objects, if need be, to communicate. Learning will happen on its own. And Mariam, you are to feel no pressure to teach him anything. Just speak to him in English.'

'What am I to speak about?'

'Whatever comes to your mind. Your family, your day, your time in Jaunpur, anything at all. If nothing comes to mind, recite a poem you learnt at school or sing hymns. Just be there every day. Answer the questions Azeem asks you.'

'Could I just read to him? From the Bible or any other book of your choosing? It will be easier for me. I'm not sure I will have so much to say.'

Madeline considered her question for a moment.

'No. The book will be about unknown people, a distant place. We need a connection between what is being seen and heard for the language to start making sense to Azeem. Since this is our first session, let me take the lead, show you what I mean. What would you like me to talk about? Azeem, you suggest a topic.'

'Your journey by sea,' he said, after a moment's thought.

'Very good. Let's begin then. Remember from this point on, we will speak to each other only in English. Let's all pretend we don't know any Hindustani. Agreed?'

NORMAN WAS PLEASED with Azeem. The boy was disciplined and capable. He was an excellent rider and guide as he accompanied Norman on survey work. Norman had been worried that his English lessons might give him ideas about being favoured and encourage him to have airs.

But Azeem remained as he had been from the start, obliging but distant. He seemed to have mastered the knack of being aloof without seeming rude, attentive to the work required of him but not constantly in the way. He was an unusual fellow, proud without coming across as arrogant. He carried himself as if he listened to everyone but in the end answered only some voice inside of himself.

Norman had had more than one discussion with Martha about the odd threesome their daughter, her ayah and the syce made under the pear tree in the back garden of Oak Park. But Martha remained staunch in her support of Madeline. Should any of the other lodgers at Oak Park remark on the scene, Martha was quick to tell them of Madeline's gift with languages and her desire to use her year in India doing something worthy. She also let slip that Madeline would be attending college at Oxford in the coming year.

'Norman, I know she looks grown to you, and you wish for her to behave like a young lady in society, but behind the smart new dresses and pretty bonnets is the same curious little Maddy who wouldn't stop asking you questions about India when you came home each summer. Let her enjoy the last of her girlhood. She's always been special, more advanced in matters of learning, less focused on social niceties. There will be time enough for her to act more grown-up and ladylike,' said Martha. 'Frankly, I am happier for her attention to her experiment than to the dashing officers in town. She is too young. Let her get to college first, make something out of her remarkable brain.'

Martha was right, of course. Madeline had a bright future ahead of her in England. If Norman succeeded in persuading Martha to stay back in India, it was enough for now. Madeline could visit them each summer. There would be time enough for her to find a match. She would have both officers of British India and the gentlemen attending Oxford to choose from.

'Is Azeem making progress with learning English?' Norman asked Mariam one morning, as she sat at the bottom of the three broad steps leading into their lodge. She was knitting while waiting for Martha to come out and give her instructions for the day.

Mariam laughed.

He noticed that she had a pleasant laugh, sparkling white, even teeth in a generously parted mouth with pink-brown lips.

'Madeline is very different from the teachers I had in school. She says we are not to worry about Azeem making any progress.'

'I hope that you are finding the lessons more enjoyable than knitting,' Norman said with a friendly nod as he walked into the house. He wondered what the poor, stoic horse groom was suffering at the hands of his zealous daughter, and whether Azeem would soon be requesting him to be let off from the lessons.

Mariam smiled to herself. She found knitting most enjoyable. Its gentle, repetitive motion was calming. She liked the reassuring feel of the colourful yarn. The soft balls of wool were soothing to the touch, pleasing to the eyes, and there was a thrill to completing a blanket and imagining its warmth enveloping her brother's newborn. Knitting was a simple pleasure—simple to learn, simple to do, simple to know the purpose of.

It was Madeline's enthusiasm to make an English speaker of her father's syce that Mariam found unfathomable. The afternoon sessions had been very difficult to start with—a wooden, expressionless Azeem and Mariam herself awkward and unable to converse with ease. Yet Madeline showed up full of some bright story from her childhood or happening from her day, drawing them out of their shells.

Even though Azeem had very few words to show for their sessions under the pear tree, Mariam could feel something changing under the surface. He now seemed to be an integral part of their conversations, present with his eyes and his ears, his face reflecting a keenness of understanding which felt more acute for its wordlessness. He had started to bring to the class a sketchbook and calligraphy pen. On most days, he sat there quietly writing out all their names in the Persian script, embellishing them with fine patterns of birds, fishes and snakes, and geometric arrangements of ellipses, circles, triangles and squares. He'd make delicate borders around the page. Mariam wondered where he had learnt to draw like that.

Azeem was something of an enigma to Mariam, his bearing proud, his words few and far between. It was not clear who exactly he was and what he was thinking. He was a good syce, there was no doubt about that. But there was more to him, Mariam suspected. If only he would let go of his reserve.

MADELINE AND MARIAM trekked up the two miles to Snow View with a growing sense of anticipation. Upon reaching the top, they stood holding hands, Madeline's milky white fingers firmly clasping Mariam's chocolate brown ones, watching the twin peaks of Nanda Devi and Nanda Kot glowing rose pink in the evening light.

'Mariam, won't you sing something please while we wait? Who knows how long they will be?' Even as the distant peaks flushed pink and orange, a chill was beginning to settle on the air around them.

Mariam's repertoire was modest and contained only the hymns and psalms she had learnt at school . She sang with a sincerity that Madeline felt moved by each time.

Her voice wasn't beautiful so much as it was filled with faith, inflected with a deep honesty of feeling. A yearning for goodness streamed out of her. When goodness was being handed out to souls headed earthwards, little Mariam Das's most likely queued up for a second helping.

'Join me, then. You know this one,' said Mariam, as she began singing 'Joy to the World'.

Madeline joined her, picking up the chorus a moment after her to resounding effect. Her heart was thudding with excitement. Her parents would be shocked if they found out that she had left the polo match early and dragged Mariam with her to this rendezvous on Snow View.

'It really feels as if heaven and nature are singing here. I do think this is my favourite hymn ever,' said Madeline.

Mariam's favourite song, the one that defined her life, was Psalm 23. The Lord was her shepherd, truly. How else would she be standing here on this mountaintop, watching the sun's rays glinting off the snow-capped peaks of the Himalayas, holding hands with a most unlikely and unusual friend, and singing on top of her voice, while inhabiting a perfect moment of happiness and camaraderie?

The sound of horses cantering up the path made them both turn around. They were here!

Azeem burst into their vision on his horse, strapping and handsome, followed by another young man, darker and more diminutive. Small clouds of dust rose from the dirt track as they dashed in at considerable speed. They were both wearing bright red ceremonial caps, probably from one of their past tours together. They brought their horses to a stop and doffed their caps to Madeline and Mariam. Then, they threw the caps into the air with a flourish, letting them float to the ground like tiny red-breasted robins trying out their wings for the first time.

'Okay, Raju. Ready, steady, go,' said Azeem.

Mariam inhaled sharply as the two boys stood up on their horses and began a vaulting performance, perfectly balanced, and poised, their arms stretched open, while the two horses started to walk away from each other. They executed a sharp turnaround at opposite ends of the ground and trotted smartly towards each other, picking up speed. Together Azeem and his friend performed a sequence of gymnastic feats atop their horses, leg splits, knee bends, bodies balanced sideways on one arm, the other arm pointed skywards, men and horses perfectly synchronized with each other. The two boys came together to form arches and bridges of great beauty, standing tall and fluid like sculptures of magnificent strength. All this against the backdrop of snowclad mountains.

Azeem brought the show to an end with a headstand atop the horse, his legs parted in a victory sign, his boots his crowning glory, shining brown against an azure sky. Horse, man, saddle all melded together into a single moment of triumph. Raju had stopped at the previous position. He sat on his horse and slowly began to clap to signal the end of their show.

Madeline picked up his cue and began to clap fervently followed by a bemused Mariam.

Mariam now understood what Azeem had meant during his outburst in yesterday's class under the pear tree.

Azeem had acquired a fair vocabulary in English, but he only spoke in single words, that too strictly to Mariam. His reticence to speak in Madeline's presence was marked. He was still to utter a full sentence in English, and it was clear to them both that Madeline was beginning to feel increasing doubt and disappointment in him.

'Perhaps we should give up,' she had said the previous day, a note of irritation in her voice. His uncooperative silence was getting under her skin. 'It was foolish of me to expect anything extraordinary.'

Azeem had got up suddenly and broken the rules of the class to speak to them in Hindustani. He had stood there with a flushed face and said he was tired of listening and just for once he would like to speak, and that Madeline should listen.

Madeline was always telling him to listen, to let the patterns inside the language he was hearing talk to him.

'Speak then,' Madeline had said, taken aback by the blaze in his eyes.

'Not here. It's Sunday tomorrow. Come to Snow View after lunch. I will get my fellow syce Raju. Together, Raju and I will show you something special, our unique language. You can admire its movement and patterns for a change.'

'That was marvellous!' said Madeline to Azeem, as he dismounted from his horse and stood leaning against it casually, casting a probing look at her face, one hand stroking the horse under its neck.

Madeline's eyes stood large in her face, dazzled, thunderstruck. This Azeem, and his mesmerizing beauty! It was casting spells on her again. How often had she tried to persuade herself that he was just an ordinary boy with a handsome face whom she was obsessing over unnecessarily. That there was nothing special about him. How determined he seemed to refute that internal dialogue.

Listen to me speak, he had said.

She had just heard him out, and her whole being was in tumult.

I'm not an ordinary boy, he had just screamed at her in his own way. *I am my own special. That's who I am. You may know many languages, but even if you knew all the languages in the world, it would all only be words. Being has its own essence, its own presence. Words are just birds soaring and swooping, capable of marvellous flight, but they are not everything. Being is the whole sky.*

❋

DID LOVE COME at first as a slight stirring in the air ... or did it fall like the apple in front of Mr Newton, with a thud? Perhaps it started off as a little disturbance, and if you attempted to shoo it away as you would a bothersome fly, then it hit down hard—no mistaking its existence.

Madeline was all alone with her questions, in the absolute quiet of her little room in Oak Park. The girl in her head had fallen into a stunned silence by the turn of events. Things had gone much further than she had anticipated. She had urged Madeline to step out of her fears and tease out a few experiences, romance the East lightly, walk briefly on that edge of excitement, flirt a little with being young and abroad. Flirtation. Friendship. What was it called? Dosti. Who had expected her to fall over the edge, irrefutably in love. Love. Liebe. Amor. Amore. Amour. Eros. She would not be able to explain it to her parents in any language she knew. She had landed in a place outside all dictionaries, a world composed of inchoate longing and an uncontrollable urge to drown inside another being.

Three days had passed since Azeem's equestrian performance with his friend Raju. She had not met him since. The evening at the hilltop ended shortly after the show staged by the syces. Both she and Mariam had been fulsome in their praises. Raju, once he dismounted from his horse, was an awkward lad. He was uncomfortable in their presence, his gaze reluctant to meet theirs. Azeem, too, seemed restless, wishing to end the evening, conscious perhaps of his friend's discomfort.

'We'll stay here for a while. This is Raju's first time at Snow View,' said Azeem. The junior engineer Riley and his syce had continued to stay at the Public Works Department rest house in Ranibagh, unlike Azeem who lived in Nainital now. Azeem had gone down to Ranibagh in the morning to fetch Raju.

Mariam and Madeline said goodbye to the two.

'Enjoy the sunset,' said Mariam to Raju kindly, as they were walking away. She could understand his fear of being seen with Madeline. Indian lads like him were safer not fraternizing with white girls. They could get beaten up, dismissed from service or jailed even.

They had only walked a few yards when Azeem called out after them. 'Wait!'

Madeline had dropped her handkerchief on the ground. It lay fluttering there, a white cambric square with delicate pink lace, initialled with an embroidered M in one corner. Azeem rode up towards it. He swooped from the horse turning upside down. He picked up the handkerchief between his teeth and straightened in a flash. He held it out for Madeline to take. His eyes danced in merriment at her shock at the daredevil manoeuver.

Madeline's hand shook as she took the kerchief from him. Their eyes met—the meeting not unlike a primeval sport, a combat of spirit and mettle. She felt as if she had been uprooted from the world of words and thrown over a cliff, to flounder or fly in a space where sensations ruled, where language had no currency.

And now here she was, holed up inside her little room, trying to restore some order to her mind before she stepped out again to deal with the Azeem situation. What exactly was the Azeem situation? She had repeatedly gone over the bare facts. Azeem was handsome. The way he looked sent her heartbeat racing. Fact. He was perhaps much more than handsome. Fact. The more time she spent with him the more drawn she felt to his persona. Fact. She felt alive in his presence, and she hadn't felt that way with anyone. Fact. She was committed to teach him English. Fact. To call off the lessons now would be to renege on her promise to him. Fact again.

The English lessons themselves were not going too well. The problem—as she was beginning to see—was that she was a better learner than a teacher. She was adept at plunging into the sea of languages, flailing, floating, somehow coming up and hanging in there, any which way, till she reached the shore. But her attempts to push Azeem into the deep end only left him resentful of her. To her chagrin, he made better progress when he was alone with Mariam, but Madeline felt unable to let the class go on without her. Despite her best resolve to stay away, she was pulled to take her place under the pear tree.

On their way back from Snow View, Mariam had remarked how she had not realized earlier that there was a show-off locked up inside of Azeem. He was normally so restrained. That last dangerous act of picking up the hanky from the ground with his teeth was the one that had earned him Mariam's disapproval. He could have smashed his head to the ground.

Madeline bristled with guilt. Azeem was not a show-off, anything but. She had pushed him by making him feel stupid during her lessons. She had to find a better way of teaching him. As a good teacher, her first job was to make the student comfortable; the rest would follow. It's what she had seen Mamma do.

Madeline was not ready to declare her project a failure.

'I don't know where I'm going to find the courage to go on with the classes as if the evening at Snow View did not happen, but find it I will,' she told the girl in her head. 'You told me not to be a scaredy-cat and a silly goose, didn't you? Well, thank you and same to you.'

She decided to go look for Mariam and ask her if she would like to walk up to the Church of St John in the Wilderness. It was one of the oldest buildings in Nainital, built in the Gothic style. It would be empty at this hour. Nainital had so many beautiful churches, and it was Madeline's desire that Mariam should visit them all, one by one, before they returned to Jaunpur.

Mariam attended service every Sunday at the St Francis Catholic Church on Mall Road. She had not seen St John's yet. She would love the Belgian stained glass windows with their depiction of scenes from Christ's life. Madeline wanted to spend some time at the back of the church compound near the graveyard. She wished to read the brass plaque at the memorial with the names of those who had lost their lives in the landslide of 1880. Forty-three Europeans and one hundred and eight Indians. It was a sad spot, but also, infinitely peaceful amidst the tall cedars and pines.

If Papa could have his plans for the city carried out, as he hoped they would be, there need not be any future landslides.

IN A BOAT every man could be, at least for a brief time, an island, complete unto himself. In this case, every woman, Martha thought to herself.

Buoyed and gently rolled from side to side on the tranquil, softly rippling green lake, solemn with evening shadows, she felt awash with serenity. They had left the boatman on the shore, and Madeline and Martha now rowed in tandem, the brightly coloured wooden canoe with its long oars splicing the water. It was something they enjoyed doing together, in rhythm with each other, in their own two-person mother-daughter universe. Each was content to be quiet with her own thoughts. It was difficult, in any case, to talk above the lapping sounds of the water and the noise of the wind.

Martha was enjoying herself better than she had expected. Her circle of friends was steadily expanding. The sisters at All Saints' School—a girls' day and residential school—had invited her for an informal chat with the teachers and students. She had liked the walk up the Ayarpatta hill, past the stately Governor's House, to the school's new campus. It was flush with flowers and ferns after the monsoon rains.

She felt her enthusiasm for life bounce back as she conversed about the education of young women with the nuns, over tea and biscuits. The sisters were dedicated educationists. They were determined to offer the best of the English educational system to their students in India. They used the same readers and textbooks that Martha did in her school in Middlesbrough.

Martha found the sisters somewhat conservative. They were training their students to merely be well-educated wives and mothers, refined upper-class women. A few of the girls from less well-off families would, of necessity, get trained as teachers or nurses. But those were only a handful in a school like this.

When Martha put to them that they owed their students something vital—they had to teach them to aim higher, to aspire to become lawyers, doctors and architects—the sisters simply smiled at her, not interested in taking the discussion further. Yet, they had agreed with Martha's suggestion that they have an inter-house debate on the topic: 'The new century calls for women to take up new roles'. Martha looked forward to being a judge and a guest of honour for the debate. She hoped to leave the students with a few thoughts and dreams; to plant the seeds of creative discontent in their minds.

Madeline, on her part, was thinking of her last meeting with Azeem. She had asked him if he would teach her to perform the tricks he could on a horse, and he had declined saying that she wouldn't be able to learn. He didn't want her broken bones or crushed spine on his conscience.

'Do you find me lacking in cleverness? I am a fast learner,' she told him. She was piqued by his dismissal.

'Yes, but a broken bone is a broken bone, and it hurts no matter which language you say it in,' retorted Azeem.

He went on to tell her of Mirza Hadi's broken collarbone. The good Mirza considered himself a genius at learning things. When the bicycle first appeared in Lucknow, he decided that if others took many hours to master it, it should be a matter of a few seconds for him. He started to ride one without any assistance, suffered a nasty fall and fractured his collarbone. Which, of course, he went back home to set himself, maverick that he was.

Azeem had a gleam in his eyes when they spoke of Mirza Hadi. Watching his enthusiasm, Madeline was struck with an idea about how to proceed with his lessons. She had just issued out John T. Platts's *A Dictionary of Urdu, Classical Hindi and English* from the library. With Mirza Hadi Ruswa on one side, and Mr Platt on the other, perhaps she could try making a fresh start. It was a somewhat indirect route to take, but she was sure it would work. When her lessons were done, no one would remember, not even Azeem, that he wasn't born into the language.

She let out a sigh. This was going to be fun for them all. Madeline had asked Azeem to get *Umrao Jaan Ada* with him when he came for the next lesson. She was the eponymous heroine of the Mirza's most famous book. Azeem would read, Madeline would listen, and then together they would scale the barriers of language. With help from Mr Platt, of course.

'Mamma!' Madeline tried speaking over the lapping sound of the lake. 'Do you think you would like to stay here for longer?'

Martha pulled herself out of the drift of her thoughts and answered. 'The boatman will want his boat back. It's close to an hour since we took it.'

The sun was about to set. The sky was turning coral and rose pink. Flocks of starlings crossed the sky above in patterned formations, bidding a spirited adieu to the vanishing day.

'No, I mean here in India,' Madeline said dreamily.

'I've been thinking about it, dear. I know your father would certainly like it if I did. I could take up a teaching job. All Saints' School would take me on as a teacher, I suppose. There are others as well that would welcome someone with my teaching experience.'

Martha wondered what made her say that. Yes, she liked Nainital well enough. But not enough to leave her life in England. Had she been needlessly dishonest or were a few white lies permissible in the cause of sharing a loved one's enthusiasm for something?

'That would be so lovely, Mamma. I could visit you and Papa each summer and meet Mariam and Azeem. This could stop being a dream holiday and instead become my real life,' Madeline said. Her eyes shone brilliantly; her face was transfigured in the evening's glow, her hair windswept in the lake's breeze.

Perhaps, a holiday is a dream holiday only because it is not a part of one's real life, Martha thought to herself. She did not want to dislodge the stars in Madeline's eyes or dull the sheen of her daughter's new experiences with her own practicality. The child would return happier to England with her treasure chest of exotic Eastern memories.

And yet, Martha couldn't help feeling a stab of betrayal somewhere in her heart. Madeline showed no signs of missing home or of looking forward in excitement to the whole new life of learning that awaited her.

Madeline's heart was dancing to music Martha could not hear.

MARIAM WAS SITTING in pitch darkness in her small, windowless ayah's room at the back of Oak Park. She had woken up at 1 a.m. after a few short hours of restless sleep. Memories of pain, betrayal and heartbreak that she had put behind her were surfacing to her consciousness at odd times of the day and night these past few days, gutting her with their intensity.

She was reeling from the force with which she was thrown into a maelstrom of past hurts remembered. She had just woken up from a fierce nightmare in which Madeline and Azeem were feeding each other pears sitting on a bench by the lake, when the ducks had suddenly gone into a terrible squaking—high-pitched and ominous. Everything turned dark, a storm descended, and with it a flurry of flying oak leaves and trembling trees.

In her dream, Azeem had jumped on to his horse and ridden off at breakneck speed, up, up, up the mountain, onto Cheena Peak and right off its edge. She watched dumbstruck as man and horse plummeted down towards a certain death.

'Mariam! Warn Azeem!' her insides screamed as she woke up in a cold sweat.

The cause of her panic was a small scene she had witnessed three days ago. Another ayah had come down with fever and Mariam had been stuck in the staff barracks, taking care of her, unable to attend the afternoon class. Relieved from her nursing duties after an hour and a half, she had walked to Madeline's room to explain her absence. Not finding her in, Mariam had gone outside to look for her. As she approached the orchard behind the cottage, she saw Madeline and Azeem seated side by side on the bench, bent over a book. He was sketching for her and explaining something, she was looking at him, her face strangely glowing, her eyes brightly lit.

It had dawned on Mariam with a sudden, absolute clarity. Those two were in love with each other. What was obscure to her till now was suddenly startlingly obvious. How could Mariam not have gleaned it earlier? How had it escaped Madeline's parents' notice? How had nobody realized what was staring them in the face?

The eyes do not see what the mind is not aware of, it was as simple as that. To their mind, the spaces that Madeline and Azeem occupied in the world were so removed from each other—different races, different nationalities, different religions, different social classes—that the possibility of love had not occurred to the onlookers.

Yet, Mariam knew it inside of her bones, in the inchoate fear and restlessness she had been feeling, in the ragged-edged and sharp memories of Clive that had been bothering her of late. There was a fragility, a fraught quality to the air, a delicate fractured awareness in all exchanges between them, that could only signify newborn love, tender and vulnerable.

Madeline had devised a new routine for her English lessons. They began with Azeem reading aloud for them a few pages of *Umrao Jaan Ada*. As he said the words in his well-modulated voice, the Urdu tripping off his tongue with ease; as his utterances rose and fell, pausing dramatically and bursting forth again, Madeline and Mariam were filled with the magic of Amiran's story.

The twists and turns in her fortune kept them riveted. The peaks and troughs of her emotional life, its sadness and anguish, its moments of triumph, its poetry and its music came alive.

After the reading, the three would sit with a dictionary, and Madeline would attempt to tell the story in English. Azeem and Mariam would join her in her efforts. Azeem was getting good at stringing together whole sentences.

The courtesan of Lucknow had drawn the three inside her magic circle of light, into a story full of pathos, poetry and philosophical musings.

Some days, Mariam, Azeem and Madeline sat with Madeline's beloved atlas as she traced her journey from England to India. She told them of the various ports of call and the people she had met on board. Besides Rose, she mentioned the lady who was translating Sanskrit shlokas into German and the man who owned coffee plantations in the Nilgiris. In between, Mariam sang for them the hymns she had learnt from the nuns at school.

It was such a perfect circle of friendship that Mariam had not seen love sneak in. Yet now that she had seen it, there was no unseeing it. Mariam's heart was hammering with fear, knocking on her ribcage with an intensity that could snap it into pieces.

Whom should she talk to? Madeline? Azeem? Both? What could she possibly say to them? Don't look at each other like that, don't feel what you're feeling, don't go there where you will get singed, burned, scarred for life, or killed even? A white girl cannot love a brown man except in her dreams. A brown man cannot love a white woman except at the cost of his life. Perhaps, they were unaware of the nature of their attraction to each other, and if she spoke at all, Mariam would be guilty of bringing to the surface something that could remain hidden forever, run its course out naturally.

Yet, it was not in love's nature to remain hidden. It wandered at will, unaware of its own transgressions. It did not know rules. Boundaries are drawn on earth, while love lives in the skies. Love crosses borders not knowing they exist, not realizing that the guards are watching closely, that its flights are destined to be short-lived.

It gets shot at. Either the love is killed, or the lovers.

Mariam was alive. It was her love for Clive that had died. She had shot it down and put a heavy tombstone upon it to safeguard herself. There had been Richard after that. Again, love had flamed briefly and died.

Love was a fool with a reckless belief in its own immortality. When faced with questions of caste, class and colour, it wasn't much of a hero. Sometimes, it just tucked its tail between its legs and slunk off.

Mariam paced the ground outside her room, unable to stay indoors. An indifferent moon cast elongated pine tree-shaped shadows on the walls. A scared hare darted across her path. A pair of wood owls went whoo-whoo-whoo-whoo from their perch in a tall cedar tree—it had a majestic trunk and branches that raised skywards like many arms in supplication.

The night brought Mariam no answers. She went inside hoping the morning would.

'LEARNING ENGLISH DOESN'T change the colour of our skin, Azeem,' said Mariam.

They were on thandi-sarak. The shaded gravel path was an oasis of quiet at that time of the afternoon. They sat on a mossy rock facing the lake. Azeem had a small pile of loose stones at his side, aiming them at the water, watching them skip over the lake's surface. The stones flew parallel, from one point to the next, before finally sinking in. However deftly he threw, the stone's final fate was the bottom of the lake.

Azeem knew that Mariam meant well. It must have taken her great courage to ask to meet him alone and share with him her life's disappointments. But it made him angry too. Did she really think he needed to be told something so obvious?

He could not deny that he felt strangely intoxicated and pleasantly heavy, a man transported outside of time and moving in a slow daze, when he was with Madeline. But he had no dreams for his life that included her. He had known from the start that she belonged inside a different world from his. He simply wanted to learn English. It was inevitable that she would return to England, only the gift of her language his to keep.

Already, the language was opening doors for him. He felt it in the ease with which he was able to approach officials in the various offices when he ran errands for Norman sahib, in the confidence he felt when he walked into town.

An opening of doors was not something he could have turned down without thought.

Azeem did not like closed doors. He did not believe his place was outside them. 'Would you have changed the colour of your skin, if you could, to keep Clive?' he asked Mariam.

Clive was the Anglo-Indian home tutor of the Pinkerton-Smith children. He was fair-skinned and light-eyed, with a thin moustache and a disarming smile. He was of mixed Irish and Indian blood. Before the shorter sea route to India had made it easier for large numbers of British women to descend to India in search of husbands, the East India Company had been comfortable with their officials marrying local women. The children and descendants of these marriages received a British-style education and formed the second rung of the Empire, holding important jobs in the railways, the various administrative services and in teaching.

Clive had struck Mariam as a serious, sincere and good man. From the start, he had been courteous to her, approaching her with a diffidence she had found endearing. They had become intimate slowly, thrown together often by the nature of their jobs. He had been so lovelorn in the way he looked at her, so full of solicitude in the two years that he courted her—held her in his arms, rained kisses on her face, buried his head in her breasts—that she never suspected even once that he was ashamed of being with her, that her colour or impoverished background bothered him.

His real feelings were revealed when Mrs Pinkerton-Smith, their employer, walked upon them kissing behind a tree in the back lawn. She summoned them to her room for an interview.

'We love each other, we wish to marry,' Mariam said to her shyly. 'Clive will be introducing me to his family soon.'

The two of them had discussed it often; it had just got delayed for one reason or another. Sometimes his father was travelling on work; on occasion, his mother was unwell. Once, he had introduced her to his sister in church as the governess to the Pinkerton-Smith children. The sister had cool blue eyes the colour of hydrangeas.

'So, congratulations are in order, Mr Norton?' asked Mrs Pinkerton-Smith, arching her eyebrows delicately upwards.

Clive did not look at Mariam as he apologized to their employer. He explained to her that Mariam was 'an untouchable', a poor Christian convert from the sweeper caste, and his family would never countenance such a marriage. He implied that he had been swept into something against his better sense. His mouth had curled in distaste as he said 'sweeper caste'.

A small, cold weight settled in the place where Mariam's heart had just been fluttering. The flaming red flush on her cheeks disappeared. Her face turned grey, her hands trembled in her lap.

'I did not see you stopping to think of her untouchability when you were ravishing her so passionately behind the neem tree, Mr Norton,' said Mrs Pinkerton-Smith sternly.

Colonel and Mrs Pinkerton-Smith always treated Mariam well. The children looked up to her, seeking her opinion on things that mattered to them. Her place in the household came with a certain dignity. She had come to this house as an eighteen-year-old, fresh from the convent. Mrs Pinkerton-Smith had been a kind mentor, encouraging her to wear long Western style dresses like her own daughters, praising her intelligence and hard work, trusting her to take over the day-to-day upbringing of the younger children. The eldest two daughters behaved like friends to Mariam.

A deep, cold and wet shame filled Mariam's being, flooding her from her curled toes to her clenched fists to her face that had broken into a cold sweat, her dark forehead beaded and shiny with droplets of perspiration. She had allowed herself to be seduced and demeaned. Her position had been compromised. She would be sent back to the convent, a girl in disgrace. A bitter taste filled her mouth. *Untouchable.* She felt tears well up inside. This had been her home for years now.

'Mr Norton, I am afraid, but I will have to ask you to leave,' Mrs Pinkerton-Smith frowned at him sternly. There was no mistaking her disapproval and distaste. 'You have misled the poor girl knowingly.'

Clive moved from one foot to another uneasily and slouched in front of their employer's obvious displeasure with him. Even so, it was Mariam who lost her job in the end. She knew the Pinkerton-Smiths had fought with each other on her account. Colonel Smith said it would not be fair to penalize Clive—an excellent tutor and a decent stand-by fourth player for his bridge game—for a laddish flirtation with the ayah. Surely, the girl had known she was aiming too high if she had believed that he would marry her!

Mrs Pinkerton-Smith told Mariam that the children were outgrowing the need for an ayah. She was discharged with excellent references.

Richard was only a minor footnote in the sad romantic history of Mariam Das. He was her next employer's younger sibling. He visited and stayed as a house guest frequently. She was drawn by his marked attention to her. The sheer proximity of a good-looking, persuasive man briefly clouded her thinking. However, she was no longer the gullible fool she had been with Clive. She could read the writing on the wall quite clearly. She realized that humiliation quite surely lay in wait for her on the path ahead. She decided to look for another position and leave as quickly as possible, much to her employer's annoyance.

Mercifully, Norman had been agreeable to hiring her based on the two recommendations she had—one from the nuns and the other from Mrs Pinkerton-Smith.

And here she was now sitting by the side of a brooding lake, surrounded by dark mountains, feeling the chill of her memories, pondering over Azeem's question. Would she have traded her skin, her parentage, for another skin tone, another ancestry, if it meant she could marry Clive?

'No, Azeem,' she said softly. 'If I can't be respected or loved for who I am, I don't want love. I am reconciled to my aloneness. I mistook Clive for a different person. I did not want the person he revealed himself to be. Love can blind you to reality. It makes you see possibilities in people which are only a projection of your own desires, not their truth. My days of sentimental foolishness are behind me. I am content to grow into an old maiden aunt who spoils her nieces and nephews,' she said. 'It is you I am concerned for.'

'Don't be,' said Azeem. 'I am not about to make any mistakes.'

'Don't you see, even if you don't make any mistakes, even if it is Madeline who does or says something importunate, the blame will come to you. You belong to the subservient race. It will be your head that will roll. I got away with a lost job and a wounded heart. You may be hurt in more serious ways,' said Mariam.

'I have no family, Mariam. No place I belong to. I am just Azeem, the syce. I do not even have a family name anymore. No one will care what becomes of me,' he said. 'I have no fear of dishonour or of death. At every critical juncture of my life, I have asked myself what I stand to lose. And the answer never changes. Someone like me has so little to lose.'

In truth, Azeem had just found out he had a heart. And he had lost it to an English girl who could never be his. But that was no one else's business. Not even Mariam's. It was only his to know and deal with.

Mariam sat watching the handsome profile of the boy seated next to her, his darkling eyes, his swept back wavy hair, his broad forehead, his sharp nose, his cleft chin. She could understand some of the longing she had seen in Madeline's eyes. She knew a little of his history now from their conversations under the pear tree. Their reading of Umrao Jaan's story together had brought them all closer, taken them past his feigned coolness. He had opened to Madeline's genuine interest in him. He had told them of his noble bloodline, the murder of his entire family, his years in the school for poor boys, his subsequent job at the library where he had learnt calligraphy and illustration.

'But you care all the same. You have plans to make something of your life, don't you? Isn't that why you left Rannpur? Isn't that why you have learnt to speak English?

You are not just going to blindly walk over a cliff when you can see a chasm looming ahead of you?' exclaimed Mariam.

'And how exactly do you propose I walk away from this chasm that looms ahead of me?' he asked with a short, unamused laugh. 'Should I stop coming to work? Get reported for insubordination? Should I risk losing my job? Or should I tell Norman sahib his daughter is looking at me with adoring eyes and I'm afraid of what might happen?'

'The only thing to do is to stop the English lessons. Azeem, you know enough to get by now. Whatever else you need to learn, you can learn in your own time. I shall talk to Madeline.'

'Do that,' he said. 'If you can convince her.' Madeline wasn't the most pliable of girls, to his understanding of her. She liked having her way in most things. They were kindred spirits in so many ways.

That evening, Mariam broached the subject with Madeline. They were returning from a walk in the hills together.

'Nonsense,' said Madeline. 'I don't believe Azeem can wish to discontinue our lessons. I will talk him out of whatever silliness has overtaken him. Besides, we absolutely must find out what happens to Amiran next!'

Amiran was now a famous courtesan known as Umrao Jaan. She had just run away from the establishment of the madam she worked for with the mysterious Faiz Ali, who showered her with gold coins and jewels and wished for her to live with him in his little town, away from Lucknow. But Faiz Ali, it turned out, was not the man she had thought him to be. He was a dangerous dacoit on the run, and the police were closing in on him.

'That was such cliff-hanger we left the story at this morning!' said Madeline as she walked into the lodge to join her parents for supper. 'Aren't our classes the best thing ever?'

'Oh Madeline! How do I make you understand?' Mariam whispered.

There was nothing else she could do. She would have to speak to Norman sahib in the morning.

AZEEM

Nainital

1906

THERE WAS THE sweet smell of fresh horse dung on a path carpeted with fallen oak leaves. Cool springs that sang of the sweetness of their water burst out of the rock walls forming one side of the mountain road they were riding on. These were dizzying, circular roads, spiralling upwards at a steep incline. Paddy fields emerged out in delicate steps hewn out of steep mountain faces, swaying a tender green with a new sprung crop. A blue kingfisher flashed across the green. Clouds, birds, butterflies, flying insects, everything seemed iridescent and brighter hued in the mountains.

Two men, four horses. They were headed on deputation from the Remount Depot, Saharanpur, to the Public Works Department's rest house at Ranibagh to present themselves to one Mr Norman Evans, the senior engineer. A bemused Raju watched as Azeem got off his horse and tethered it along with the other horse he was leading to a tree. He then knelt to the earth reverentially and kissed it.

He had gazed at these mountains from afar, all his life, as a small boy in Rannpur, as a young lad in Saharanpur. They had always called out to him, beckoned him with the promise of adventure and excitement. Now he was here. There was music in the air. A cuckoo bird was singing in a branch overhead. Elsewhere, a barbet was drumming away on a hollow tree trunk. Their separate notes merged in his ears, a sound of ineffable sweetness.

Azeem had a theory that many worlds spun in simultaneous suspension, bubbles of consciousness, each microcosm spinning on its own ethos, composed of its own aether, oblivious of the others.

What a person thought, believed and lived by was dictated by the time-space bubble they spun in. It influenced what they wore and ate, how they spoke, the work they considered worthy, the relationships they embraced, the morality they subscribed to. Most lives were lived inside of one bubble, untouched by the essence of any other. His father's life had been like that, as was true of the maulvi in his school. So, too, his friend Raju.

Azeem's own experience of life had been different. He had drifted from one bubble to the next, each phase of his life transient. He wore for survival the camouflage of whichever world he was thrown into, all the while belonging nowhere, never sure of how long he would live inside any particular illusion.

He was equally a nobleman's much indulged son, a poor orphan in a charitable school, a lowly clerk in a grand library, an accomplished horse groom at a breeding depot, a syce on deputation to a British engineer. He was all of these, he was none of these. Shunted from world to world, his sense of reality, he realized, was less solid than that of his fellow humans. He understood reality as an ever-changing thing, it could not hold on to a man's spirit any more than a man's spirit could hold on to a fixed certainty forever.

Yet when suddenly life changed one day, from sharing a room with Raju at the Public Works Department guesthouse to living on the grounds of Oak Park in Nainital, the transition was swifter than any Azeem had experienced so far. He felt dislocated out of all time-space coordinates, the change had been so without warning.

Of all the bubbles he had drifted into, the one he wished most fervently was not a dream he would wake up from was set in the lake-town nestled in the seven hills. It held him spellbound from his first vision of it—the whispery white clouds serenading an emerald lake, the tree-clad mountains guarding it shoulder to shoulder, their presence grave and magnificent. This space wore a fragrance of freedom; it carried the music of sweet laughter; it danced to some dreamy celestial song with stars as bright as diamonds in its skies. It was a town of gabled green and red tin roofs, giddy on its own promises of freshness and novelty. It was free of history, free of bloodshed, free of ancient griefs, free of heat, of dust, the wounds of too much living, too much human civilization. It was a town in love with living, and it wore its youthful heart on its sleeve.

It was as if a book illustration of a magic town for elves, angels and friendly djinns had sprung to life. Its air was pine-scented and invigorating. Its streets were clean. Its people were storybook people—British ladies and gentlemen, Indian rajas and ranis, and smiling, craggy faced Pahari men and women. Its buildings were villas, chalets, cottages and castles like ones he'd never seen before. Its flowers were everywhere, growing under rocks and out of mountain sides, along untended paths, beside the lake and in elaborately laid out gardens. Its birds were spectacular in their hues, some carrying the entire rainbow on their unabashed wings.

On the far side of the town, on The Flats, was a mosque, its mihrab pointing to Mecca, its minaret calling the faithful to prayer. He did not go inside the mosque often, but even seeing it from the outside gave him solace. This town of abundant churches and temples had also thought to make a place of worship for him. It said to him by its existence, 'You belong here as much as the others, feel at home.'

Nainital was a portal leading into a new life. And opening the door to it was a young girl with liquid golden-green eyes and a smile like a mountain meadow in spring.

WOMEN ARE WATER, Azeem thought to himself, as Madeline and Mariam entered his life. Madeline was free-spirited like the Gola river that flowed past Ranibagh guesthouse—a babbling brook, a seasonal freshwater stream, its gurgle and swift current irresistible, but its dominance short-lived. Madeline would disappear from the landscape of his existence as quickly as she had appeared; the memory of the rainbows that danced in her waters would be the only joy he'd know.

Mariam was still and serious like the lake at the small settlement of Bhimtal nearby. He did not know how deep her thoughts went. Sitting beside her was restful. She offered space for looking into one's own face, an invitation to introspect.

Women were water, and he did not know how his life had suddenly led him into the oasis of their company.

Was it some mirage he had conjured out of his own deprivation? Would he wake up and realize he had never actually escaped the desert of never-ending masculinity? Male faces, male voices, male bodies, male values and ideals.

Only blurred memories of womankind remained from his childhood. He had the faintest recollections of his mother, aunts, sisters and girl cousins. They were like a song whose words were forgotten, only a few snatches of the tune remained. In his father's home, the outer rooms as well as the area beyond their mansion and the wider world belonged to the menfolk. Women lived in the zenana, the inner rooms. When they stepped out, it was in full purdah, only their eyes revealed to an outsider's gaze. As a child, he flitted between the two worlds, mardana and zenana, but he also always knew which world was to be his finally.

In the arenas he had inhabited since, there was no place for women. The madrasa was for poor boys, everything about it male—the teacher, the cook, the general dogsbody who swept, cleaned and ran errands. Its pranks and punishments were all male in nature, brusque and boorish. Perhaps, even the parrots in the cages were male, selected for the brighter, bolder colours that the male of the species has to offer.

As a young clerk at the library in Rannpur, he worked again in an all-male environment. He only knew women from the smell of food being cooked, the sounds of dishes being washed, the sight of laundry hanging out to dry in the tightly packed neighbourhood in which he rented a room. Sometimes he knew women as voices, the overheard voices of neighbours—a girl humming to herself as she went about her chores, a mother calling to a child to come home after play in the evening, a wife chiding a drunken husband in the silence of the night, an old woman tossing and sighing on her bed with aches and pains.

The Remount Depot was a free world, its landscape open and generous, its air not cloistered. Women were not required to remain behind purdah. They walked along its paths unfettered. Yet, there were only a few women on the campus and none that he had any reason to know.

The first time a young British girl stared at him, he froze like a statue under her gaze for a few seconds. He did not think of himself as visible to women, any more than they were visible to him. And yet, there was Madeline, though he did not know her name, openly staring at him. He looked down at his boots, then turned his back to her and walked out of the brewery, leading the horse out. He felt his back turn warm, his neck flush. It was as if he had lived behind purdah all his life, and someone had just lifted the veil. Waves of shyness washed over him.

His next meeting with Madeline was in Nainital. He schooled his face to maintain a studied cool before he stepped forward to take Steel's reins from her. And there she was jabbering to him in Hindustani, laughing at his surprise. The morning she rode with him to Cheena Peak, he understood something crucial to her being. She was like his idol, Mirza Hadi Ruswa. He was so clever that he could not be held back by societal diktats. Rules were for ordinary people; the gifted, in any culture, were exempt.

Madeline. Umrao Jaan Ada.

English lessons under the pear tree, walks on cobbled streets, exhilarating rides to the tops of different peaks. Opaline lake. Azure skies. Maps, atlases, journeys. Calligraphy and drawings in ink. This was a 'tilism', a world conjured out of magic and illusions, out of spells and runes, out of hopes, wishes and dreams. An enchanted world—defying the laws of mankind, bending the forces of the physical world—had emerged mysteriously out of aether and taken them in its embrace. He was a willing prisoner of this realm.

He only wanted a talisman which could help him stay inside of it.

But magic would not be called magic if it didn't vanish as suddenly as it had appeared.

He had been bouncing stones on the lake's surface, when good, quiet, sensible Mariam had shaken him, shattering his dream world. She was giving words to something which existed only because it remained unnamed. To point a name at it was to point a gun and shoot it down.

It angered him.

Mariam was a part of the magic world, the veil behind which it breathed and lived. How could Mariam walk out of the magic and call it out? Mariam—who had become the signature of all things protective and kind in his life, an alter-mother-sister-friend-being, who made up for all the feminine absences in his world. He felt the betrayal like a lacerating wound.

And Madeline? There was no mistaking the look in her eyes. Subterfuge was not among the languages she knew or spoke. Or cared to learn. She looked at him with a clarity of being which said that she loved him. That the thing that flowed between them—the recognition that each felt more whole, more alive in the other's presence—was to be held sacred, not to be evaded or ignored.

Who was he to listen to? To Mariam who was urging him to break out of the spell, or to Madeline who was beckoning him further into its thrall?

MARIAM'S PLAN TO put a distance between Madeline and Azeem worked.

Azeem changed places with Raju. He worked for Riley, the junior engineer, and stayed at Ranibagh. Raju shifted to Nainital and worked for Norman sahib. It was not clear to Azeem what exactly had transpired, but the order came from Norman sahib, and he was relieved to obey it. He knew Mariam was behind it in some way. He did not care to know the details.

He had had time to reflect on Mariam's warning. The only possible outcome of his growing closeness to Madeline was scandal and uproar. Punishment and retribution. He did not wish to be the head that rolled. Upon retrospection, he did not wish for the bloodline of his ancestors to come to an untimely ignoble end with him. Quite simply, he wished to live.

Without Madeline, his days became empty, reeked of futility. The survey work was coming to an end. The workdays were not so long. He swam each morning in the Gola, its cold, crystal clear, rapidly gushing waters reminding him of Madeline, and simultaneously curing him of his desire to be with her. Every evening after work, he took Copper for a long ride, happy to be alone in the woods with his thoughts. At night, the jackals howled on distant slopes, their dismal cries echoing his feelings.

In the beginning he relished the freedom that came with the distance between them. He could say her name aloud if he wished. He could shout it out and hear the mountains echo it back. He could call out his own name, hear it reverberate across the slopes and pretend that it was Madeline calling to him. He could carve 'Madeline and Azeem' into a boulder in the river with his carving knife. He carved their names on trees deep inside the forests and was thrilled at the prospect of some stranger chancing upon them many years hence and becoming party to their secret. He recalled her ever-changing eyes, now golden, now brown, now green, and tried to capture that light-filled gaze on drawing paper with ink. Away from her, he was free to think of her in ways that he would have been scared of when she was near.

Raju brought him news of the Evans family when they met in the course of work. They all seemed to be busy with their lives—boating, riding, meeting friends and watching plays or matches. It hurt him to think that he had been forgotten with such ease, that there were no dark hollows beneath Madeline's eyes which spoke of his absence, no slowness in her steps that told tales of a heavy heart.

The rainy season passed. Autumn brought a chill that echoed the chill lurking in his heart. Norman sahib and his family would be leaving in a couple of weeks. He would never see Madeline again.

'Meet me at Khurpatal today after your survey work for the day is over,' said the note Madeline sent him through Raju.

She must have enquired and found out that Raju was working with him; they were taking some additional measurements needed for completing the survey work near Khurpatal. It was a lake, the shape of a horseshoe. They had ridden to it together once. They'd seen it from a distance many times, walking up the stone paved path to Land's End, standing near the railing at the top and looking at the lovely lake cupped in the scenic valley below. There were no bazaars on its slopes, no eateries, no boats for rowing, no pony rides for children. Only those who wished to be alone sought to go there.

When Azeem rode towards the lake, Madeline was already seated on the solitary bench by the lakeside. Her father's horse was tethered to a nearby tree. She looked older, wiser, more restrained; her hands folded on her lap as she watched him dismount. She was wearing a lime green dress with a powder blue lace bodice, and a matching lace bonnet from underneath which her hair tumbled out in waves to cover her shoulder and back.

'Oh Azeem, I have missed you so!' She leapt up from the bench and her arms were around his neck as she hugged him.

'Madeline!' He opened his mouth to rebuke her sternly, but what emerged was a whisper, and before he knew it, he was whispering her name again and again, holding her tightly to him.

They sat down on the bench together. She held his hand in hers.

'We are leaving for Jaunpur soon. Will you promise to come and meet me there?' she asked.

'Why?' he asked with a short, unamused laugh. 'Does your father need shooting practice?'

'Mariam has been haranguing me about how I am putting you in danger with my silly dreams about you and me. That is why I have been so good and have behaved well all these days. I have been helping Mamma with her cataloguing work at the library every day and accompanying Papa to all the matches and theatre he cares to see. And I never once spoke about you to anyone, not even to Mariam after that stern lecture from her,' she said.

'And?'

'Azeem, I hate the sly, scared creature I have become. I cannot bear to live like this. To pretend that you are nothing to me when you are all I can think of every minute. I want to spend my whole life with you. I have had enough time to think about it. I know this is what I want.'

The trees around the lake were glowing red, orange, and yellow. His heart was leaping up in matching flames. Her hazel eyes were tinged with gold flecks, her brown hair had tints of auburn, as if autumn was getting personal in its attention to her, its light transfiguring her body and face.

What she wanted was impossible. She was not made to be a syce's wife living on the Remount Depot stud farm. Besides, the first thing he would lose would be his job if their love for each other became known. He would be a man without a job or a home. It didn't make any sense.

'I do not think we can live together here in India. Or in England, for that matter. Both places would treat us terribly,' she broke into his thoughts. 'I see so much prejudice everywhere I look. I can't think of one person who would understand my feelings. Perhaps, my friend Rose if I could speak to her face to face. I have thought many times of confiding in Papa about my love for you but have held myself back each time. Much as I adore him, I know he will not understand any more than Mamma would. To tell them would be to complicate things in ways much worse than they already are for us.'

'Madeline, the only place where you and I can love each other freely is in our imagination. I have been happy these many days dreaming of you. Go back home now, go to Jaunpur, go to Oxford, go wherever your life takes you. Take these memories of our time together with you. I know you won't forget me any more than I can forget you, but this must end now before it even begins,' he said.

There was a chasm of race and class separating them. He would be a cad to encourage her to plunge into it.

She let go of his hand and rested her head on his shoulder. His arm reached around her and drew her closer, the scent of her filling him up, urging him to drown in this moment and never surface out of it. They might have no future, but this here was the present, and how perfect it seemed, this proximity, her breath mingling with his. He lifted her chin and kissed her on the lips. Once. Twice. And then again, and again, as she kissed him back fiercely. If they were to live on memories for the rest of their lives, then he must gather a few memories of her touch and taste to fill up his forever. He would never love anyone else like this.

She was stroking his cheek, tracing his jawline with a finger, drawing his head into her bosom. As the scent of her skin hit his nostrils, he groaned, a creature pushed beyond the limits of forbearance. The Madeline of his fevered night-time longings was in his arms, her softly undulating body pressing into his, her nails digging into his back as his lips explored her partially exposed breasts. He could not tell if the hammering in his ears was the sound of her heart or his. This had to stop before anyone saw them!

'Madeline. Not here. Not like this,' he said in a ragged whisper.

There was an abandoned pump house he had come across during the survey work. He explained to her the way to get there. She would meet him there early the next day, at the time she went out riding. She would not be missed.

There were no words in any language of the world to capture Azeem's next three trysts with Madeline. Clandestine meetings, stolen time, the knowledge that she would be leaving soon, the danger of being discovered in each other's embrace and separated forcibly—all of this added an edge to his longing. As she lay on his blanket—her breasts rising and falling like poetry, her skirts dishevelled, her delicate ankle and calf exposed to his worshipping eyes, her own eyes smoky with unslaked desire; as she ran her fingertips over his naked chest, he swore to himself that he would walk to the ends of the earth if required to make her his. For her, he would become dust, if that was what was asked of him.

'See … this is India. This is England,' she said, pointing out both places on the world map, encircling them in ink. 'See how small they are compared to the rest of the world. We can make a home for ourselves anywhere else if you believe that we belong together, as I do. Promise you will come to Jaunpur. We will find a way to run away someplace else. I do not ask anything of you except a promise to live your life with me. It shall truly be for better or worse. Not just an empty vow made in church.'

She left the atlas with him and took his copy of *Umrao Jaan Ada* as a keepsake. He promised to go to Jaunpur to meet her. They would plan their escape when they met there. They would find their own country of love, a nation of two people who wanted nothing more than to cede to each other—to be clasped, held, possessed, ravished, taken irrevocably, unmade and made anew—to become two inseparable parts of a whole new continent.

SERENA

New York

1990

'SO, THIS IS how it has ended,' Serena Walker sighed ruefully as she cleared the dark mahogany surface of the prized wooden desk she had inherited from her grandfather and let her gaze travel across her eighteenth-floor corner office in Manhattan for one last time. She stared for a few silent minutes at the framed photographs of her grandparents, Rose and Alfred A. Allye, wiped them gently with a soft tissue, and lowered them into the cardboard carton positioned beside her. These photographs had held pride of place on her work desk for the last twenty-five years. The spirit of her grandparents had been her guiding light, her North Star from the time she had joined AAA Publishing in the summer of 1965, a young editor straight out of college, charged with both vaulting ambition and high ideals.

Serena had not so much joined this job as begged, argued and pleaded with her Uncle Norman to create it for her. Thanks to her formidable powers of persuasion and negotiation, she had become the founding editor of Pinnacle Books, a new imprint in the AAA stable. At twenty-five years of age, she had a handpicked team of three staffers and a clear mission statement for her imprint. Pinnacle had a mandate to bring out the work of women writers on a diverse range of subjects. She knew it was something Granma Rose would agree with and encourage her to do had she been alive. Serena, having been with her grandmother in the last days of her illness, listening to and recording in her notebook the many stories from her life, was aware that equality and fairness an open-armed embracing of differences, were values that had been very dear to her.

'Where are the women in our literary titles? In our non-fiction list? This is 1965. You surely can't believe that women have nothing to share with the world other than romance and recipe books, that the serious subjects of our time are the sole domain of men?'

Norman Allye had taken odd bits from the physical features and mental strengths of both his parents, and they combined in a unique fashion such that he resembled neither of them. He was his own person from the start, and AAA publishing had grown across territories and imprints under his leadership. He had a keen mind, impeccable taste and a solid streak of conservativeness running through him, more an expansionist than a visionary. Serena had badgered her Uncle Norman again and again, publicly at family gatherings, discreetly over specially requested meetings at his office, in fact on every occasion that put them in the same room for over five minutes, her keen bright eyes and gesticulating hands speaking even louder than her words.

Norman had capitulated slowly but surely. He was unable to deny indefinitely his younger sister Sarah's eldest daughter the space she was demanding in the family firm. Pinnacle Books started with a modest budget and the immodest ambition to 'bring literature from the margins to the forefront by publishing high quality fiction and non-fiction focusing on feminism, civil rights, race relations, environment and American culture by diverse, hitherto underrepresented voices'. Its chief objective as far as Norman was concerned was to keep his way too intense niece busy and off his back.

'Heck! Yes! I know it's a privilege. I'm not denying it!'

She admitted this to her special group of girlfriends from Wellesley College when they gathered over a dinner her mother had hosted to celebrate her new job. 'But I really don't see any virtue in wringing my hands and agonizing over "why me?" Why should I underplay what I have been blessed with in life? I'm going to take it, run with it as far and fast as I can, and hopefully blaze a trail. Now's the chance to walk my talk, go find and commission the best female voices across America and produce books that matter. Enough of women being pigeonholed into the romance and children's fiction slots, with an occasional thriller as a sop. We're going to occupy some serious space in the literary firmament. Let's drink to that tonight, girls. And I count on your support in every which way.'

It was such a long time ago, yet she felt the thrill of raising and clinking their glasses to Pinnacle's birth. And they had stood by her, these friends from graduate school—across the years, from their varied professions, from different parts of the country and world—and had cheered her on. They had been her tribe for as long as she needed them.

Dora, her personal assistant of the last ten years, walked in with a large mug of black coffee for her—piping hot, bitter and strong, wisps of steam and aroma rising from it. It would scald her, Serena knew that, yet she took a sip without waiting for it to cool.

Just like yesterday evening's blazing argument with Dave Nicholls, CFO, AAA Publishing. Even as she had flung herself headlong into it, she had known that she was burning her bridges with the firm forever.

Yet, her rage had been real, and she was glad she had expressed it and was prepared to act on it. She still could not believe how casually the finance department had vetoed her appointment of Professor Abril Antonio to head a new division focused on Hispanic and Latina literature. This, after she had spent the better part of two years courting the Pulitzer Prize-winning professor from Barnard College—a name to reckon with in her field. In fact, the entire proposal for the new division was being put on hold for the moment.

'This is too sudden, Serena,' said Dora in a hushed tone as she was walking out, her face glum, reflecting concern perhaps for her own position in the wake of Serena's departure. Serena looked at her assistant's receding figure and noticed, not for the first time, her sensible attire—smart slacks, a knit top, pumps—and sighed to herself.

At least this flash resignation from AAA Publishing would give her a chance to wear something other than a business suit. After joining the family firm at twenty-five, eager to be taken seriously, she had resorted to power-dressing with a vengeance—immaculately tailored business suits in the finest fabrics, silk blouses, high stilettoes and the best accessories money could buy, her hair worn short and always in the latest style. A woman of pedigree, poise and power is what she projected herself as.

Casual. Comfortable. Cool. These words didn't belong to her sartorial lexicon. At least, until now.

'You old battle horse, you,' she said to herself with a twisted smile. She had plunged into publishing thinking of it as her glorious silver sword to wield dexterously and battle for gender parity. Reality had been an endless number of undignified skirmishes, face down in the mud, bruised elbows, clothes-torn-at-the-knees type of scuffles. Issues so small that individually they seemed unworthy of the fuss she was accused of making, but taken together they meant that her list, her authors were not being given the respect they deserved. The paper quality, the typeface, the font size, the choice of paperback covers over hardbacks, the non-serious, unimaginative cover designs—quite simply, the default option for women authors was all that was cheapest and least exclusive.

Yet, Serena had stood up and called it out as many times as it needed calling out.

'Steamroller Serena' was what she was nicknamed behind her back. 'Sharp Elbows'. And this was inside the company owned by her own family.

Outside, the battles were so subtle, so invisible that she often felt foolish and delusionary naming them, let alone fighting them. Distributors and stores did not order and stock Pinnacle's books. There was no demand for them, they explained in response to her repeated inquiries. They were not wrong. In the absence of reviews and coverage in the print media, she and her team did not know how to create awareness and demand. It seemed to her that a woman author had to be four times more talented than her male counterpart to be allocated one quarter the amount of media space. Despite Serena's best efforts at sweet-talking and cultivating every book-pages editor she knew, more often than not she had to be content with finding Pinnacle books mentioned passingly in 'Titles Received' or 'Other New Releases' or its authors spoken of frivolously in the society pages for their choice of clothes or romantic partners.

Despite the lackadaisical support from the literary establishment in the starting years, Pinnacle Books made its mark steadily over time, notched up the readers, reviews and recognition that Serena had so doggedly pursued, using every trick available, and inventing a few others along the way. The books slunk into public eye, where they rightfully belonged.

The clock on Serena's office wall chimed out the passage of an hour, the beginning of another. She swivelled her chair around to look at the wall behind her. It was decorated with awards and citations, the successes her imprint had garnered over the years. Two Pulitzers, a few National Book Award winners, the O. Henry award twice, and a host of other accolades for history, sociology and science writing.

Sitting in this office as she had for the last twenty-five years, it was easy to think of herself, her professional life, as a resounding success. But tomorrow—no longer cushioned in these hallowed precincts, surrounded by golden framed plaques—would bring a reality check. It was easy to exaggerate one's own importance buttressed by the signs of victories won, but had the world outside really changed despite her best efforts? Didn't the highest advances, the prized review slots, the most favoured shelves in stores still go to men of a certain colour and class, as much now in 1990 as in 1965 when she had joined the business? Had it been worth the heavy price she had paid?

It had cost her her marriage to Ben. Her son, Arthur.

'This constant rage you have, I can't live with it,' Ben had said to her. That constant rage she had—she'd been unable to live without it. It went with wanting to be a torchbearer, she had tried to explain to him. You *had* to be angry with the way things were, feel the burn of injustice if tackling it was your life's work.

She had met and married Ben when she was twenty-eight. They were divorced two weeks before her thirty-eighth birthday. Not quite a decade. It was not clear to her when exactly Ben had started to leave her. There had been no single moment of rupture, no dramatic falling out or growing apart. For a while they had been a viable family unit—two successful professionals, one an editor, the other an upcoming lawyer in a well-established legal firm in the city, sharing an enviable life together with a young son, two kittens and a nanny. She had thought the relationship was going just fine till Ben told her otherwise. Or perhaps, she had not thought about it at all. Her job left her with very little time to think of other things.

She took out a box from the bottom drawer of her desk. In it were the photographs that Ben dutifully sent her each year—one of Arthur on his successive birthdays and the other of their whole family—Ben, Sybil, Arthur, Ben and Sybil's children together with their two huskies—that accompanied the annual Christmas missive. They lived in a posh suburb just out of New York, but she had met Arthur only a few times in all these years. Ben had persuaded her that it would be better if Arthur could belong fully inside his new family and not be asked to divide his time and loyalties between two homes. Arthur had turned nineteen this September, an amiable looking young man with Ben's blue eyes and a tentative smile.

Had she missed them, her husband and her son? Not sufficiently, perhaps. Singledom had suited her by and large. On a rare, wine-doused evening when opera music played out melancholy arias from her gramophone, she felt abandoned. Her heart wailed and shook with the soprano's grief and sobbed to the mezzo-soprano's slow coming to terms with life's betrayals. But on most days, she was grateful that Ben had found himself a more suitable wife, and Arthur a nurturing mother.

There was the soft padding sound of her assistant's sensible shoes outside her door.

Dora knocked again, just as Serena was putting the last of her personal effects into the box. She looked troubled and restless.

'I can't believe this is happening, Serena. It feels so brutal that you should leave at a day's notice after you have taken decades to build this. It will kill Pinnacle. Was no compromise with the management possible?'

'Dora, it's in the nature of compromises that they are always possible. But I think I'm done. My best is over. I don't know about Pinnacle. It cannot get killed so easily, I'd like to believe. The management intends to stick with our more established authors and keep the backlist alive. That will help maintain that patina of a serious publishing imprint. But the future, I suspect, will belong increasingly to self-help books and ghost-written celebrity memoirs. Frankly, I don't have the stomach for either.'

'But Serena, you cannot give up the good fight just like that!' urged Dora.

'Not just *like that,* Dora. I've taken the decision after reading the writing on the wall and being smart enough to get the message without pretending that things could go my way. This job, this imprint, AAA has been my life. But that time has passed. I spent so many of my early years here fighting with Uncle Norman, and now I look back and realize that both he and I were on the same side. AAA was his life and blood too. We were family after all, with shared values, with a common vision for the firm that we had inherited from our founders, his parents and my grandparents. Now, only the AAA name remains and a few of us have some shares. I'll hold on to my stake for now, but it's time for me to move on, disinvest my being from the company.'

She stared at the five cartons on the floor, her life here packed into them.

'This plant is for you, Dora, if you will have it,' she said, pointing to the luxuriant monstera plant in front of her window. 'I'm sure you'll continue to thrive here; you're too smart for them to let you go.'

'Thank you. I shall treasure this beauty; it will remind me of you. Where do you go next, Serena?'

'I wish I knew,' she said with a laugh and a shrug of her shoulders. 'Hopefully someplace that calls for a different set of vices. I've done my share of workaholism and black coffee for this lifetime.'

Power-dressing too, the thought silently crossed her mind.

MADELINE

Jaunpur

1906–07

IT WAS MID-NOVEMBER, and the weather in Jaunpur was balmy. The winter sun was mellow in the day. The evenings were cold and bracing. Norman was pleased to be back at home with his regular set of friends. This was the best time of the year here, with hunting parties organized regularly in the neighbouring forests full of pheasants, hares and deer. There were tennis matches at the club. The nights were also merrier for parties and dances, billiards, carrom and bridge.

Martha, Norman liked to believe, was more relaxed now than she had been during her first spell in the town. She did not seem to find social conversation as tiresome as before. She appeared to have plenty of stories to share of her experiences in Nainital that were of interest to the other ladies. Martha and he had come to a clear understanding that he was to manage the household and staff with Mariam's help. Martha found domestic duties onerous; they left her feeling fatigued and disheartened.

Norman felt just a twinge of guilt, and much pleasure, in the new arrangement. Mariam was a skilled housekeeper. An inspired one too. It was obvious that she delighted in looking after and sprucing up the bungalow. He and Martha were hosting a large party at Christmas. Mariam's suggestions for the occasion were fresh as well as practical. He was confident about the party now that it was in Mariam's capable hands. She had been getting Abdul, the cook, to try different recipes from his repertoire each night as a lead-up to deciding the final menu.

Madeline was living life on two planes. She was determined to keep busy and active. She did not care to let anyone guess the emotional turbulence inside her. She accompanied her parents on various social engagements with good grace, dressing up as required in the many nice gowns the durzee had made for her from the pattern books given to him by Martha. She participated in drawing room conversations and regularly met people her own age for games of badminton or tennis in the club.

Madeline even accompanied her father on a hunting trip, though she found out she did not like hunting at all. Her sympathies lay with the poor animals. Riding out into the countryside was beautiful, but, if it all ended in the skinning and roasting of some hapless creature, she found she had no stomach for it. Fishing was a gentler pastime, and she did not mind accompanying her father for such trips by the river. Of course, fishing wasn't fair to the fish—but there it was. Her gut reacted differently to the two activities. It had its own mind, outside of logic.

She went riding each morning by the banks of the gently meandering Gomti. Astride a horse, the river breeze in her hair, she felt as if the reins of her existence were in her own hands. She could make her life jump over or sidestep any obstacle in the path.

However, later in the day, when she sat with the old librarian in the nawab's library, trying to master the Urdu script, she felt acutely aware of the different worlds she and Azeem had been born into, the vastly different trajectory their separate lives were positioned to move along.

She could not see what alternate universe they could leap into which would welcome them both equally. It made her melancholic when she dwelt upon it without coming up with satisfactory answers. She frequently took out Azeem's copy of *Umrao Jaan Ada* and lovingly turned the pages. 'One day you will hear the remainder of the story in his voice,' she promised herself.

Between Madeline and Mariam, there were now some differences, some emotional distance. They were no longer so trusting of each other, sharing every confidence. Madeline knew that Mariam had in some way been responsible for Azeem being banished from Nainital. She understood that Mariam had meant well, but she also resented the fact that Mariam had judged her based on her race rather than the person she had shown herself to be through her words and actions.

'Mariam, don't you see you are being prejudiced in your own way? To be prickly about your colour and build boundaries around yourself and Azeem to keep me out only because I'm English isn't fair, is it? You are not looking at the Madeline I am, the Madeline you know. Why are you conflating your experiences with others with your expectations of me? It is cruel. You cannot hold me responsible for all my countrymen, only for my own behaviour. Tell me of a single instance where I have wronged you or Azeem,' Madeline said. 'Or led you to believe that I am less than sincere in my intentions.'

Mariam grappled with Madeline's words inside her own head as she went about her busy workdays. She knew that Madeline was clear of heart. That her love for Azeem went deep. She did not think Madeline was dallying with Azeem in the manner that Clive had with Mariam. Yet, she could see nothing but danger ahead for Azeem if he were to come here at Madeline's bidding, as she had asked him to. Mariam hoped that better sense would prevail, that for his own sake he would bury his hopes of being with Madeline permanently and get on with the rest of his life. It would hurt, but in time he would forget her. Madeline, too, would see it all differently once she was back in England, living the life she was born to live. The pages of her existence would rapidly fill up with new friendships and an academic career. Azeem would fade into a fond memory, the merest flicker of a could-have-been. It was in love's nature to enrapture, but equally to pass. This was summer madness, which Mariam could not encourage with a good conscience.

Martha silently watched Mariam as she vigorously went about transforming the bungalow. Everything was being given a thorough airing and cleaning. Cut flowers from the garden adorned the previously empty vases in each room. The outdoor cane chairs were painted a luminous white, considerably enhancing the beauty of the front lawn.

Martha admitted to herself that she had mixed feelings about the place looking prettier and more hospitable. A large part of her was glad to be relieved of the burden of tasks she had no talent or enthusiasm for. However, she was recurrently troubled by the thought that apart from their shared devotion to Madeline, she and her husband now had so little in common. Norman would have been happier with a comely housewife than an intellectually inclined woman like herself. Their years apart had left them little shared ground to build a life upon together.

The faux Britishness of Nainital—its temperate climes, gothic architecture and many English boarding schools—had charmed her into a temporary truce with India. She had given Norman the impression that she was open to the possibility of staying on.

Returning to Jaunpur had brought back some of the old tensions. India was a large country, and Norman's job would require him to be posted in different places, most of them like Jaunpur, possibly none other like Nainital. She would much rather be back inside her old life in England. She waited for an opportune moment to tell Norman. It would have to wait till after Christmas. She did not wish to cast a shadow on his happiness before the party.

Meanwhile, she watched Mariam Das with bemusement. Pity the girl wasn't white. She would have made some Englishman here a very suitable bride, what with her cut flower arrangements, her inspired menus and her good-natured smile.

THE DAY OF the party arrived. It was a Christmas lunch. Norman felt gratified that everyone he had called had accepted the invitation. About a hundred guests, of all ages, were expected. They were mostly his compatriots from in and around town, but also the Nawab of Jaunpur and a few other prominent Indians Norman had come to know socially over the years. Some guests, like Riley, his junior engineer from Ranibagh, were from out of town and lodged at the club.

He was glad that he had thought to invite Riley at the last minute. It would be good to hear of the practical measures the department was considering, based on their report.

Mariam was flitting all over the bungalow. The front lawn was set up with round tables seating six each. The verandas by the front and two sides of the house, the drawing room, dining area and study were also open to guests. She hurried from one place to the next, checking that everything had been set up properly.

Long clay pitchers filled with the tall stems of Indian tuberoses and their delicate white florets lined the veranda walls, filling the area with a gently teasing perfume. Set at the center of each table outside was a small pot of poinsettias, brightly red and green in their Christmas hues. Ram Deen had worked indefatigably over the past week, specially taking the plants from the flower beds in the side garden and repotting them for the party in small white ceramic cups. Mariam had promised him a generous tip for his effort. Abdul had set up a temporary kitchen at the back of the bungalow, with outdoor brick ovens for doing the Christmas duck roasts. There was a large cauldron for the partridge curry, as well as skillets and cast-iron pans for making the mince cutlets with mashed potatoes and chicken croquettes—these were to be served as accompaniments. The salads, the trifle pudding and creamy caramel custard had been prepared ahead of time and lay in an icebox inside the kitchen. The silverware and crockery had been counted and entrusted to Gobind well ahead of time. Liveried waiters had been taken on lien from the club for the occasion. Mariam intended to retire behind the scenes as soon as the first guest arrived—but, for the moment, it was her party. She was enjoying it immensely.

Martha, much to her own chagrin, had woken up with a slight headache—mercifully, not a full-blown migraine as much as an annoying heaviness behind her eyes. All Norman had asked of her for this party was to be a smiling presence by his side to welcome his guests. She was dismayed that she might fail at even that.

Mariam had laid out Martha's dress for the party a little ahead of time, so that Mariam could attend to supervising the party arrangements. It was a handsome navy gown with just a touch of fine white lace and pearl buttons. The cook and butler were in the makeshift kitchen in the backyard. There was no one Martha could ask to bring her a cup of tea. It annoyed her terribly that she could not just walk into the kitchen and make herself a pot of tea as she would have at home in Middlesbrough. The British Raj was too darned fusty to live inside of permanently. Thank you, but no thank you, she muttered to no one in particular.

Madeline was in a state of suppressed excitement. Her ruse had worked. As she helped Norman send out the Christmas party invitations, her gentle dropping of Mr Riley's name and enquiries about how the Nainital work was faring after his departure from there had had the desired effect. Mr Riley had been invited to the party. It was up to Azeem to find a way of accompanying the junior engineer on his visit, using his ingenuity. Mr Riley would need someone to carry the files and survey maps. A few revisions had been requested by the town council.

Late last evening, they had received word that Mr Riley had reached. Early this morning, as she returned from her ride, she had seen Azeem. He was standing in the veranda handing over to Gobind two large cardboard boxes containing files and maps.

'Gobind, I need some water please!' she said, even as she hurriedly handed over the reins to the waiting groom.

'Meet me at the ruins near the Atala Mosque at 3.30 p.m.,' she told Azeem in an urgent whisper. She walked inside quickly. Now was not the time to linger and be found out.

By then, the formal sit-down lunch would be over. Post-lunch, music and revelry would be in full swing. She intended to slip away unnoticed. Hopefully, with a full basket of the best food from Abdul's kitchen. She had already packed a blanket to sit on, plates and glasses.

She even had a firm idea, at long last, about where they must escape to.

NORMAN KNEW HIMSELF to be a hopeless dreamer. When his friend Colonel Arthur MacLeigh introduced him to his son, Lt Adam MacLeigh, who was visiting his parents over Christmas on two weeks leave from his posting in Calcutta, Norman was struck by the thought that the handsome, blond, blue-eyed officer might make him a wonderful son-in-law someday.

Norman watched Adam through the course of the afternoon to see if he lived up to the favourable first impression. Of course, Madeline would always determine the course of her own life, but Norman was not averse to playing a well-meaning matchmaker. If he were to introduce them, and there were the beginnings of a romance between the two, it struck him as a cheery prospect. Nothing immediate, of course. He understood only too clearly that Madeline would be going back to attend college at Oxford in summer.

Madeline curtseyed, smiled, laughed through the party, determined to give her father no cause for disappointment. She knew how much he wanted the afternoon to go off well. Only when the guests were settled down for their post-lunch coffee and cigars did she consider it safe to leave. She rushed out from the back of the house, behind the makeshift outdoor kitchen, with a basket of food packed for Azeem. She was wearing a lavender and pink gown with ruffles and knew herself to be looking particularly winsome. She was excited at the thought of Azeem's surprise at seeing her dressed so fabulously.

It was a long walk to the ruins by the riverside, one that she could not possibly hope to take alone, dressed like this, without drawing unwelcome attention. A fair number of horse carriages stood parked outside the bungalow gates, waiting for the guests they had brought for the party. She persuaded a coachman to give her a ride up to a narrow walking path leading to the riverside.

'Thank you. Please go back and wait for your sahib. I have an urgent errand to run. I'll be dropped back by a friend,' she told the coachman, who looked hesitant to leave her there alone and return to his post.

Azeem stood leaning against a stone pillar of a Sharqi-era ruin, a small distance from the mosque. The afternoon light fell in a slant across his face. He had spent much of the day exploring Jaunpur on foot, as Riley sahib had left to attend the party at the Evans' bungalow by noon. The climb up to the fort was a rewarding one. From the top of the hillock, he could see the Gomti river and its magnificent bridge on one side and the entire city laid out on the other side, a labyrinth of narrow streets, walled compounds and single- and double-storeyed houses. Inside the fort complex, there was a mosque of exquisite beauty, its trellised walls glinting bronze and golden. A short distance away, a maze led one into a weathered stone building with an array of round domes of different sizes stacked side by side to form a roof of startlingly asymmetric beauty. Closer inspection showed it to be a bathing house for the queens, built in the Turkish hammam style. There were also the graves of those who had lost their lives in the uprising of 1857. Unlike the nawab of Azeem's birthplace, Rannpur, the Nawab of Jaunpur had sided with the mutineers and not the British. He had paid a heavy price for it. Jaunpur was now under British rule. Rannpur was still the nawab's fiefdom.

Azeem took a sharp intake of breath as he watched Madeline walk up through the arched doorway of an abandoned, dilapidated twelve-pillared hall, carrying in the crook of her arm a picnic basket. She looked like a fairytale princess. He blinked and shook his head in disbelief. He did not know when his own life had left the shores of the everyday and ordinary. It had begun to unfold like a story, full of adventure, intrigue and a beautiful damsel.

Azeem loved her deeply. Mirza Hadi Ruswa had loved a Christian girl too. His heart had broken when his Sophia left for Paris, never to return. Would Madeline leave him? Would he too take to writing mournful poetry like Mirza Hadi Ruswa?

Azeem found it difficult to believe that he was standing here waiting for Madeline, with no plan in his mind and no resources to make any plans. Quite simply, she had called, and he had come. There had been nothing else to do. One look at her now, and all his doubts felt vanquished. In her presence they were insubstantial, legless fears. With her by his side, the tragedy of his past, the limitations of his present, all vanished. He could do anything, go anywhere, become anyone.

'Azeem, here you are!'

She looked more beautiful than all his dreams of her. Those eyes, those lips, the hair in a cascade of honey brown ringlets. The arms reaching out to circle his neck.

She was here with him. He was holding her and kissing her, the thought that she might go away, never to return, adding to his ardour. Her eyes were shut, her face was rose pink, the flushed heat of her skin was making of his breath an uneven, ragged whisper, his heart a tambourine.

She laid out the blanket, and they sat with their legs stretched out on the sandstone floor, his back against the pillar, her head leaning into his chest, his arm wound around her waist. He had plucked a rose for her from the club lawns. It was tucked behind her ear now. In the broken dome of the twelve-pillared monument, a pair of pigeons had made a nest and were feeding their young. There were pigeons in the eaves and elsewhere, fluttering and calling out to each other. 'There are young lovers kissing amidst the ruins, thus life renews itself each time'—the pigeons were saying, perhaps.

'I have a plan for us,' Madeline said to Azeem.

He leaned his head over hers, willing her to speak. He had not eaten since the morning. The smell of food was distracting him. But more than food he needed to know what plan there could possibly be for them. His mind had yielded none in the time they had been apart.

He had with him only a hundred different words for being bereft and desolate.

'Wait,' she said. 'Eat something first.'

He watched her fill up his plate. She poured out sherry in a glass. It was against his faith, but he had never been very devout, rebelling against the enforced piety of the madrasa he had studied in. He was willing to eat and drink what she served. Not just today, but every day of his life—if there were some angel who could hear him and make the seemingly impossible possible, make her his forever.

'We have to find a way to get to New York City,' she said while he ate. 'Everyone has a fair chance there. It is the place for dreamers to realize their dreams. People from different parts of the world head to New York to find work. America is a whole new continent, hungry for people to build it. We will build a life there. So long as we are ready to work hard, we will be able to thrive.' She had read everything she could put her hands on in old newspapers and periodicals at the club. Millions of people from Italy, Portugal, Spain, Greece and other parts of the world like Turkey and China were making their way to Ellis Island. New York was opening its gates to as many as ten thousand people each day.

A big city like New York was like them, young and freedom-loving. Its sinews were strong, its spirit lively. It was not bent under the weight of history and tradition like their two countries—Britain and India. If they could get there, they could carve out a life. But it was on the other side of the world.

'Madeline, there are oceans to cross from here to there,' said Azeem. His life has been landbound up to now. He has never seen the sea except on an atlas, the expanses of blue on it overwhelmingly large in contrast to land.

'Remember, human beings have been seafarers for thousands of years, from the civilizations of ancient Egypt, Greece and Crete to modern times. Liners, like the one I travelled by, connect all parts of the world now. So long as we know where we're going, we'll find a way to get there,' she said.

Did nothing daunt her?

Azeem was not scared on his own account. He had seen death and devastation as a child, penury as a teenager, hard work as a young man. He had lived in many places, knowing none as a permanent home. He had always had a magical belief in his own abilities and luck. He had often been visited by the thought that his life lay elsewhere, hidden from view but waiting for him to show up. He was ready for adventure. The thought of America sent a thrill through his body, filled him with elation.

But Madeline had loving parents, had always been cherished and looked after, and had a shining future ahead of her in her own country. Could she leave it all for their uncertain life together? What if she regretted it later? What if they died enroute?

'I will do anything you tell me; go anywhere you ask me to. Nothing in my existence here compares even remotely with the joy of spending a lifetime with you. But do think before *you* make further plans. You have so much to lose. Your parents, your home, the prospect of going to college. Am I worth that much to you? Won't you look back and wonder why?'

Madeline watched Azeem gravely. It was not as if she was unaware of what she was turning her back to in choosing him. As she opened her hands to reach out for his love, her parents' love would fly away, perhaps forever out of her grasp.

Azeem's eyes were dark with emotion. She could see a pulse beating at his throat. She reached out and wove her fingers into the turbulence of his night-black hair. Her eyes narrowed in thought as she sought the words to answer him. She spoke, at last, with a soft sigh.

'Azeem, I was always terrible at arithmetic. My mind thinks in music. When I think of a life without you, my heart plays the most woeful dirges. Howls of despair begin to drown me. Everything feels dark and dismal. As soon as I think of us together, my heart bursts into joyous melody, it plays tunes of mounting ecstasy. I feel as if the sky has opened and showers of light are raining down upon me. I don't want to hurt Mamma and Papa, but I must choose my own dreams over theirs. This much I know. I was made to fly like a bird in open blue skies, not to lay down my head like a sacrificial lamb at the altar of other people's expectations.'

At last, Madeline and Azeem decided that when she left for England, he too would find a way to board the ship that left from Bombay. They would jump ship together at some opportune moment. Maybe in Port Said or Aden. And slowly make their way to America. Neither of them feared starvation. They were able-bodied and intelligent. If birds, squirrels, bees, bats, all of creation's creatures except humans, could feed themselves each day, surely they could too.

'I must go now, before I am missed,' Madeline said. 'I will send you the details of my passage once it is booked.'

They worked out a coded message so that it could not be understood by anyone else and there was no danger of the plan being outed by some intermediary delivering the message.

Norman and Riley had a meeting scheduled for the next morning. Riley and Azeem were to board an evening train the very next day. It was unlikely that Madeline and Azeem would be able to meet again in Jaunpur.

Madeline packed her basket. She was ready to go. The blanket was still spread on the floor.

'Just a few minutes more,' said Azeem. 'Please.'

She lay down on the blanket and pulled him to her, her lips meeting his in a fervent kiss. Just one kiss more, then she would leave.

Time slowed and stood suspended between one kiss and the next. The evening deepened. Outside the ancient ruins, the last rays of the sun paid obeisance to the river, and the waters of the river turned first ochre, then vermillion.

NORMAN HAD WORKED himself into a state of panic by 5.45 p.m. when he set off with a search party of three policemen to look for Madeline. His daughter had been kidnapped! He had been looking to introduce her to Lt Adam MacLeigh for the better part of the afternoon but could not spot her. He did not make much of it then as it was a busy party. Several small groups had formed and scattered across different parts of the bungalow and its grounds.

Martha had retired to her room a bit early, but only after seeing off most of the guests. She had a slight headache. It had disappeared for much of the day but had returned towards the early evening. Once everyone was gone, and Norman could not find Madeline anywhere, he went out in search of Mariam. She was supervising the washing, counting and putting away of the silverware along with Gobind.

'Do you know where Madeline might be?' he asked her.

Mariam looked back at him blankly. She had been preoccupied much of the afternoon. A party of that size took a lot of managing behind the scenes, to see that everything went smoothly. She couldn't recall when she had last seen Madeline. She left her work to help him look for her. Perhaps Madeline had stepped out to walk one of the other young ladies home and would be back soon. They decided to wait another twenty minutes.

As the minutes ticked by, Norman felt a mounting anxiety. By about 6.30 p.m. there would not be enough light to search properly, and soon after it would be pitch dark. And very cold. If he did not hurry, the chances of finding Madeline before she came to any harm would diminish. He asked the syce to bring his horse and went to his bedroom to pick up his pistol. Martha was in bed with a cooling bandage strip on her eyes. He thought the better of saying anything to her in that condition. There was a chance that he was overreacting and Madeline was fine.

Collecting the three local chaps on duty from the constabulary, he rode towards the riverbank. The old monuments there could be a hiding place for low-life characters. Also, those seeking to make a quick escape would head towards the bridge. Crime rates were mostly low in Jaunpur, but the kidnapping of young girls had occurred in the past. Dacoits from a neighbouring district, notorious for its crime rates, sometimes conducted their raids as far as Jaunpur or Varanasi. Winter months were the riskiest as night fell early and the cold weather kept most people indoors.

At the riverbank, the party of four men broke into two and scoured the place, running in and out of several spots, in a hurry to make the most of the last rays of sunlight. Norman ran up the steps of the pillared hall with a broken dome, followed by the Indian policeman in his party.

His eyes fell on the skirt of Madeline's lavender gown. A man's body covered most of Madeline from view, only an arm spread out on the floor was visible. His daughter was being ravaged by some scoundrel. He whipped out his pistol in fury and shot the man in the leg. He could not aim any higher without the risk of hurting Madeline. But the rascal should not run before Norman got him.

A hundred pigeons flew out, squawking and calling from the top of the broken dome, as the gunshot rang out in the silence of a cold, dark winter evening. They spread like a grey-blue bruise, a spreading smudge of pain streaking the evening sky.

The policeman who rushed in behind Norman saw a young man's leg gushing blood on a blanket. A young English girl in a diaphanous gown leapt out from under the man and screamed, 'Azeem! No!' and covered his body with her own to protect him from another shot.

Norman stared at the scene in front of him in growing confusion. What was Azeem doing here? Why was Madeline holding him like that? His eyes took in the scene. There was a blanket spread out on the floor, a picnic basket next to it. It was a lovers' tryst!

Madeline and Azeem?

Madeline and Azeem!

He felt a sickness at the pit of his stomach.

Mariam had lied to him!

The next half an hour unfolded in a strange nightmarish stupor. The other two policemen had found their way to them. Azeem's wound was bandaged in the light of the torches the police constables lit. The bleeding had stopped. It was not a deep wound. He had been hit on one side of his calf. He was handcuffed and taken to the lock-up.

Madeline's face was ashen, her hair disheveled, her expression distraught as the party made its way back into town.

'It's not fair!' she said, as she saw Azeem getting handcuffed. 'He has committed no crime. I came on my own to meet him, he did not force me in any way!'

'Madeline! Enough! We will talk about this privately once we are home,' said Norman sternly.

It was pitch dark now. A bat flew past them, low and ostensibly sightless.

Azeem was staring ahead, his face entirely without expression.

Once, Norman had liked the boy. Today his only thought was that he wished that their paths had never crossed. Outrage, betrayal, shock, anger and shame tussled for top place in the turmoil in his head. How could a mere syce have the temerity to seduce his daughter and take advantage of her?

Lt Adam MacLeigh's face came to his mind briefly. His mouth twisted in bitter regret. There would be gossip now about Madeline unless he managed to cover up news of this incident right away, as if this evening had never happened. He would need to go see the police commissioner tonight itself. He would need to ensure complete silence from the constables. He would also need to see Riley—lest he launch a search for his syce. Azeem had likely come to Jaunpur with him.

'See that his wound is attended to and keep him locked until further orders,' Norman told the constable in charge before heading home with Madeline.

'Papa, I love him. I wish to marry him,' said Madeline, the moment they were alone.

'Not another word from you today, Madeline!' he said. 'Not to anyone. Go straight to your room and go to bed. We'll speak tomorrow morning.'

Norman felt terrible as he bolted her in for the night. But already, she had abused his leniency beyond all imagination. He did not dare take any more risks.

He went to the back of the bungalow and knocked on Mariam's door.

She opened it tentatively. She was in her nightgown, her hair plaited in two dark braids. She looked tired and vulnerable. She, too, had misled him. His face tightened momentarily. He would have to leave their discussion till later.

'Please tell Martha I have gone out on some business and will be out till late, should she ask. Madeline is sleeping in her room. You are not to disturb her on any account. I hope that's clear,' he said and left abruptly.

Mariam nodded bleakly.

In the hours that he had been gone, Mariam had pieced together what may have happened. One of the waiters from the club had told her that Madeline had packed a picnic basket. A waiting coachman had dropped her near the riverbank. She was obviously going to meet someone. It could only be Azeem. He must have accompanied Mr Riley. How had Mariam failed to connect the dots?

What a day it had been.

IT WAS THE next evening before Norman had a chance to summon Mariam into his study and confront her with the lie she had told him. He had spent the most exacting twenty-four hours of his life and was in a foul mood. If Mariam had told him the truth from the outset, this entire fiasco could have been averted.

The police commissioner, although an acquaintance of so many years now that he could be described as a friend, had been dispassionate and stern in his assessment of the situation.

'Look here, my good fellow, we can't just shoot the boy and throw him into the Gomti for the crocodiles to take care of. He is an employee of the Remount Depot, on lien to your department, accompanying one of your officers on tour here. His sudden disappearance while on duty would raise many awkward questions even if my chaps hadn't witnessed yesterday evening's assignation with your daughter. Right now, I can get them to be quiet, hush up the matter. Indians have strong notions about family honour, and their sympathies will lie with you. But should the boy come to any harm, their loyalty will be with their own kind. The whole story would come out and leave us red in the face.'

'How do you suggest we handle the situation? You will agree that he cannot go unpunished for this!'

Norman's face betrayed his agitation. His mind was still struggling with the fact that his own syce had so blatantly transgressed the limits. Madeline may have encouraged him with her English lessons and her foolish notions, but he had no business meeting her clandestinely or following her this far. He almost wished he'd shot the fellow dead. They would have made up some story later to explain the situation. Alive, he was a nuisance.

Riley, who had been called in to the police commissioner's residence, tried apprising him of the situation. 'I am sorry, I had no idea,' he apologized. 'My office boy, Nigel, wanted to spend Christmas with the family. When Azeem volunteered to come in his stead, I accepted without a second thought. The lad has a fascination for travelling. I've seen him with his head in an atlas often.'

The meeting with the police commissioner ended with no definite course of action decided. Azeem was shifted from the police lock-up and housed in the quarter guards' barracks, his movements restricted. Norman and the police commissioner were to meet again the next day. Much to Norman's embarrassment, the commissioner had suggested that they take Colonel MacLeigh into their confidence. With his experience and connections in the army, he would help in handling the matter with the officer-in-charge at the Remount Depot.

The morning's meeting extended into evening before all aspects of the matter could be settled. Azeem's station commander at the Remount Depot, Major Wilby, was disconcertingly invested in the boy's well-being. He thought highly of Azeem's skills as a syce and vouched for his character. He telegrammed to insist his boy deserved a fair hearing before dismissal. Finally, MacLeigh had to contact Major Wilby's own senior in Lucknow. It was agreed that Azeem was to be posted a thousand miles away in the western province of Baluchistan as a soldier in the 130th Baluchi regiment.

The cold desert conditions of Baluchistan were punishing, needing fitness and endurance of a high order. If it weren't for the extreme physical hardship, the posting itself was a promotion for Azeem, from the rank of syce to soldier. For Norman, it was the most expedient way of tackling the problem, given that the syce had the backing of his reporting officer. Azeem was to be sent to Baluchistan over the next few days, under armed escort so that he did not try and escape.

Norman still needed to talk to Madeline and Martha. It was turning out to be a very bleak and unexpected Christmas. Martha had taken poorly after the party and was confined to her room. Madeline had orders from him to stay confined. Her meals would be sent to her. Norman intended to speak to his wife and daughter the next morning. For now, he chose to summon Mariam to his study.

She was standing before him with a resolute look on her face, her hands folded in front of her.

AS SHE STOOD facing Norman, Mariam felt an odd defiance welling up inside her. Mariam's morning had begun with a terrible scare. Gobind had returned from his morning run to fetch milk, vegetables and eggs with whispers of a rumour from the local market. There had been a shooting in the ruins by the river. An English girl had been found romancing an Indian man. No names were mentioned, but Mariam did not need to be told who it was.

A shooting! Azeem! Oh no!

It was like a stone had been thrown into a hornets' nest. Thought after stinging thought rushed at her. She reeled from their onslaught, tried to shelter herself from their attack.

A shooting? Azeem could be dead. Or mortally injured. Madeline! Foolish, foolish, foolish girl. Why had she called him here? Who had shot him? Mariam should have done something. What could she have done? Madeline would be able to tell her what happened. She must speak to Madeline immediately. Norman had forbidden her to speak to Madeline. The poor, poor child. Azeem injured or dying. Madeline locked up and forbidden to speak to anybody. It wasn't right.

The moment she saw Norman leave the house, Mariam made her way to Madeline's room. She did not care if she lost her job for disobeying her master. She had to find out what had happened. She would serve Martha's breakfast a little later. Martha would probably appreciate not being disturbed after the hectic party; she had been feeling poorly and had slept without having even a light supper.

Mariam appeared before Madeline with oatmeal porridge and morning tea.

'Mariam! I am so glad you came,' said Madeline, getting out of her chair and rushing to hug her. She placed her head on Mariam's bosom. She was still wearing her gown from the party. Her hair was disheveled, her eyes like live coals burning out of her face. Her bed had clearly not been slept in. She had probably spent the whole night pacing the floor. Luka, the tabby, sat on her windowsill looking at her with some concern.

'Papa said I am not to speak to anyone without his permission, but I have been up all night talking to Luka. It helped to just keep talking. I would have turned to a howling banshee if I absolutely could not speak at all,' said Madeline. 'My darling Azeem, how terrible that Papa should shoot him like that. Mariam, you must help me get him out of jail. We must make Papa understand.'

A small wave of relief passed through Mariam. Her body unclenched. She hadn't realized how tightly wound up she had been. Azeem was alive.

'Tell me what happened, Madeline,' said Mariam firmly.

'Azeem and I ...' Madeline began. Then she kept quiet. It was best that she told no one at all that they were planning to run away together to America. Nobody was to learn of that, not even Mariam. What no one knew, no one could try to prevent from happening.

'Yes, go on quickly please. Is Azeem okay?' said Mariam, impatient with Madeline's pausing and fumbling for words.

'Yes, yes. Oh, thank god for that. Papa fired at his leg. So that he wouldn't run, I suppose. It's a small wound and the policemen with Papa bandaged it immediately.

The problem is Papa thinks Azeem is to blame in some way. That is simply not true. It is unfair. Why should he be jailed for meeting me? I told Papa I love Azeem and wish to marry him, but he refused to talk to me. He just keeps telling me to be quiet. I'm eighteen years old. I know my own mind,' said Madeline.

Mariam felt a flash of anger at Madeline. She just refused to see that she had put Azeem in great danger. And that idiot Azeem, he had come here at Madeline's bidding. What on earth did these two think they were doing?

'Madeline, for pity's sake, I beg you please, stop saying such things. No one is going to let you marry Azeem. Not your father, not your mother, not the pope himself. Every time you take Azeem's name in front of anyone, you will just make sure that he is in greater trouble. If you really love him, the first thing you must learn to do, for his sake, is to keep quiet about loving him. It is easy for you. You will go back to England. He must survive here. The less enemies you make on his behalf, the better,' snapped Mariam.

Madeline sank into the chair in her room with a heavy movement. Luka bounced back into her lap. She stroked his head absent-mindedly. Something in Mariam's words had struck home.

'Mariam, I do believe you are right. Even though you do not understand me, or the depth of my feelings, you are right. I do put Azeem in greater jeopardy when I mention our intention to marry. I stand duly warned. Thank you. I shall be sly from now on. Papa and Mamma don't deserve my honesty if they have no desire to hear my truth,' said Madeline. Her face was mutinous, stormy with the emotions that crossed it.

Mariam wondered at the willfulness of the girl.

'Madeline, please don't do anything foolish. You are very young. Listen to your parents, even if you don't like what they have to say. You will perhaps understand them better when you are older. They want what is best for you,' said Mariam.

She left after saying that, hoping that Madeline would mull over her words, also somewhat doubtful that she would.

There was Martha to attend to and a lot of tidying up after yesterday's party. It already seemed a lifetime ago. She went in later, with a lunch tray, to Madeline's room.

'Have a hot bath and go to sleep for a few hours.' She tried to persuade the girl gently.

Madeline looked like a ghost. Pale and drawn.

The rest of the day passed in a rush.

Now Mariam stood before Norman. She was still resentful of the fact that he had shot at Azeem. Did he think that he had a right to shoot anyone he pleased? Is this what belonging to the ruling race meant? Did he think Azeem's life was his to play with? She had thought better of him.

'I had thought better of you, Mariam,' said Norman, interrupting her thoughts.

She looked up at him puzzled. What had she done? It was he who had shot Azeem.

And then it came back to her in a flash!

'You lied to me about Azeem and you,' he said sternly. 'Had you told me the truth, none of this might have happened.'

Mariam flushed. Having served its purpose, her lie had receded from her mind. She had requested Norman to replace Azeem with Raju as his syce in Nainital. She had said that she and Azeem were getting drawn towards each other, and she would appreciate his help in putting a distance between the two of them. She wanted to end the matter before it could go any further.

'I ...' she said.

'Yes, go on,' he said. 'Who did you want to protect? You thought Azeem would lose his job if I knew the truth? Is that it?'

'You have to believe me,' she said, her forehead furrowed, her palms moist. 'I did not know there was anything between them. I had not seen anything untoward to warn you about. I was just worried that they were being drawn towards one another. I thought by acting on my intuition, I could prevent something that could harm them both before it went any further. I still don't understand what happened.'

Norman examined her face intently. She seemed sincere. And everything she had told him earlier matched what she was saying now—except, she had substituted Madeline's name with her own.

'I wish you had seen fit to tell me the truth, Mariam,' he said. 'Trusted me a bit.'

'I am sorry if I failed you,' she said woodenly. 'I could not have reported Azeem based on a mere suspicion.'

If Norman wished for her to leave, she would have to do so immediately. The prospect of returning to the convent, to her parents and the nuns, so quickly again in need of another placement, was a bleak one. Her face was overcast with gloom.

'Are you telling me Madeline has never confessed her feelings for him to you? That you were completely unaware of them?' asked Norman.

'Madeline is young and impressionable. I expected that her feelings would pass as quickly as they had developed. I hoped she would return to England soon and forget all about Azeem—if she hadn't done so already, by coming away from Nainital. I did not see why Azeem should be punished for Madeline's feelings. For surely, he would have lost both his reputation and his job if I had discussed the matter with you. We are not rich people like you, sahib. We need our jobs to survive. We work hard to keep them. I have tried to explain this to Madeline many times, but she cannot see beyond her own wishes,' said Mariam.

The unfairness of the situation made Mariam feel bitter. Now Madeline's willfulness would cost both Azeem and Mariam their jobs. When Mariam was younger, she had believed devoutly in the goodness of white people, imagining them closest to Christ, for they had brought the lord to her. Her many years of service and her experiences with them had taught her that goodness was a personal, not a racial trait.

Norman was ruing the tempestuous nature of his own daughter, thinking how ungovernable Madeline's passions could be, when Mariam spoke up again.

'Please let me know when you would like me to leave,' she said.

'Leave? I have not asked you to leave, have I?' he replied, wondering at her belligerence.

'It has been my experience that no matter whose fault it is, the blame always falls on the servants,' she said.

If she were to lose her job, Mariam decided, she may as well speak plainly before she left. Norman might have paid her wages, but he had not bought her soul. Of course, old-timers like Gobind believed that if you had eaten someone's salt, you owed them your loyalty, no matter what. But Mariam was not like Gobind. The nuns had taught her different values, they had told her to stand up for truth and justice.

'Mariam, that is not true,' he said, annoyed at her accusation. 'You should know me better by now.'

'Why did you shoot Azeem then? Was your daughter not equally at fault?' she asked.

'For Christ's sake, I did not know it was Azeem! I saw a ruffian molesting my daughter. Had I not feared hurting Madeline, I would have killed him point-blank with a shot to his head. Spare a moment to think of my shock when I saw it was Azeem and found out that Madeline was at those ruins to meet him,' said Norman.

'And now?' asked Mariam. 'What is to become of him?'

'He is housed at the quarter guards' barracks for a few days. Then he is being sent to Baluchistan. He will retain his job, in fact get a promotion as a soldier. You will agree that distance needs to be put between Madeline and him.'

'How long do you propose to keep Madeline locked up in her room?' asked Mariam.

Norman emitted a deep, low sigh. He looked exhausted and at the end of his tether. 'Mariam, I need your help. I will speak to Martha tomorrow. It is just as well that she has been too poorly to show much curiosity. But I need to tell her. Together, she and I will talk sense into Madeline. Make her see that her behaviour has been foolish and completely out of line. You must keep an eye on Madeline. Be a friend to her, as you have always been. If she tells you anything that I should know, please share it with me immediately. And on no account is she to leave the house yet,' he said.

Mariam nodded and waited to be dismissed.

'I'm sorry I spoke harshly to you. I understand you were doing what you thought was best in the circumstances,' he said.

'Should I ask Abdul to serve your supper by 7.30 p.m.?' Mariam asked, as she walked out of the study. He watched her receding back, the neatly coiled bun at the nape of her neck.

'Yes, please.'

Another long day.

MARTHA WAS LOOKING wan and weak. She was seated on the sofa near the window in the study. The sun streamed in through the open window, bathing her in its warmth. It could get quite chilly in the last week of the year.

'My darling, how are you this morning? It is good to see you out of the bedroom. Is that porridge you are having?' asked Norman as he came into the study.

'I think I have caught some nasty bug, Norman. I feel queasy at the prospect of solid food and can't hold in anything for long. I have the runs. And chills too.'

She looked completely wretched.

'I'll call the doctor in to see you. Let me go send Gobind with a message requesting him to visit.'

As Norman walked out of the door, Martha stared at him bleakly. Though she did not feel up to a prolonged conversation, this was perhaps the right time to tell Norman of her desire to head back to England. If he could book them a passage in early March, they would be back in England at the start of spring.

Her promise of spending a year in India would have been honorably discharged. Almost. She was keen for Madeline to get acclimatized to being back in England before she set out for Oxford. It bothered Martha greatly that her daughter had become a stranger to her. Martha no longer understood what was going on in her head. Madeline seemed to have changed, though Martha could not put her finger on what it was that concerned her about Madeline's behaviour. She was as affectionate and exuberant as before, but beneath that veneer there was some mystery. Her eyes were faraway too often.

Norman stepped into the study again after sending Gobind to fetch the doctor. He studied Martha's face as she stared out of the window. He wondered if he should tell her about Madeline's misadventure right away or wait till after the doctor had visited. No … there could be no delay in Martha being told. She would certainly ask for Madeline now that she was out of her own bedroom.

'Martha,' he began.

'Norman,' she interrupted. 'Could you book us a passage back in March? I think it is time that Madeline and I headed home.'

She felt relieved to get that off her chest.

Norman looked at her silently, trying to read the expression on her face. Perhaps, she had already heard. Had Madeline visited her mother, unknown to him?

'So, you are aware?' he asked with a gentle frown. 'I would have liked to have told you myself, my dear.'

'Aware of what?' she asked, bristling with sudden foreboding. She had always feared something would go wrong.

'Er, nothing,' he said. He had misunderstood then. Maybe it was best to tell his wife later, not now.

'Norman, tell me what has happened,' Martha said sharply. She put down her porridge bowl on the tray and pushed it away. 'Is something the matter with Madeline? Where is she? It is unlike her not to ask after me knowing I'm unwell.'

There was nothing for it but to speak right away and hope for the best. It would be at least half an hour before the doctor arrived.

'There has been an unfortunate incident, my dear,' he began.

'Is Madeline hurt? Has she also fallen ill? Did she have an accident while riding?' Martha's face was tinged green with fear.

'She is alright and in her room. You are not to worry on that account,' said Norman. His eyes fell on the vase on the mantelpiece and its arrangement of gaily speckled maroon and white dahlia blooms. They felt strangely disconcerting at this time, their festive cheer at odds with the grim reality of the moment.

'Please tell me what has happened! Say what it is, I implore you,' said Martha.

'After the Christmas party, Madeline was nowhere to be found,' said Norman.

'She was kidnapped! No! But you said she is in her room!' said Martha.

'She had absconded to the riverside to meet Azeem. You remember the boy?' he said quietly.

'Azeem? Why on earth was he here?' she asked. Understanding dawned on her face even as she asked. She clutched her head in both hands as the room spun out of focus, its white walls, sunlit window, olive green curtains, bookshelves and flower arrangements all coming together in a blur of spinning colours.

'Please tell me you are not going to say what I think you are about to say,' she said weakly, her voice a hoarse whisper.

'She imagines herself to be in love with the boy. Fooled me into inviting Riley for the party so that Azeem could come here with him,' Norman said. 'Perhaps, we have given her too much liberty, raised her with too many new-fangled notions.'

A shooting pain went through Martha's head. She felt a mad rush of anger cloud her eyes momentarily.

'Really, Norman?' she said testily.

Madeline's upbringing was at fault ... and not his insistence that they come to this wretched country in the first place! From the moment she stepped on to the ship she knew she had made a terrible mistake. There was some sorcery in the air of the East which had cast its spell on Madeline, taking her further away from Martha each day. The bright and beautiful girl she had raised was now enamoured by a horse groom. Not even a prince or nobleman of breeding and education, but an unlettered syce with nothing to recommend him but his dratted good looks.

She felt an urge to scream and put a palm across her mouth. Sobs of frustration and despair racked through her body. She felt as if a hard stone had been thrown through the pane of her life—a life she had devoted years to building, a life that she had been so proud of, now lying shattered in fragments. Norman could not even see that it was all his fault.

He sat down beside her and put an arm around her shaking frame. He had rarely seen Martha so undone in all the years he had known her. She was a resolute woman, one not given to displaying her feelings easily.

'Take heart, my love. Together we will talk sense into Madeline,' he said. 'She is our own sweet child. It's just a difficult age.'

MARIAM WATCHED WITH sorrow as cheer deserted the Evans bungalow in Jaunpur and left all three members of the family estranged from each other.

The Christmas party had left in its wake a deep pall of gloom.

January dragged along like an impaired creature without a cane, slowly and painfully. The mornings were miserable, with a thick winter fog casting a grey pallor on everything. The nights were long, cold and dreary. The family gathered in the parlour each evening around the fireplace, with a coal fire set up and kindled by Gobind. But the warmth did not reach their hearts. Their eyes were bleak, the conversation sparse and strained.

Martha had been suffering from biliousness since the party. She experienced a general feeling of discomfort, distention and nausea after eating. Her attacks were generally preceded by a sensation of extreme cold on her feet and followed by bouts of peevishness. The doctor had prescribed calomel pills and soda water. She was to avoid meats, milk and alcohol, and eat light puddings, soups and vegetables. She did not make a good patient. However hard Abdul tried to cook her appetizing meals, she ate poorly and looked dispirited. Her head was often heavy, her expression dour.

Norman had aged since the shooting incident. Several days had passed before Azeem could finally be dispatched to Baluchistan. The strain of waiting for his departure and keeping Madeline under strict watch had worn Norman down.

In the days that Azeem was in Jaunpur, it had been impossible to contain Madeline's repeated pleading and arguments on his behalf. After he was deported, she fell into a despondent silence, unwilling to engage with anyone, especially her parents. She spent most of her time in her own room. Luka, the cat, remained the sole recipient of her affections, nestled on her lap or perched by her window. He once dragged in a mouse as an offering, hoping perhaps to draw her out of her sustained misery.

When their initial attempts at convincing Madeline of her foolishness failed, Norman and Martha ended up deeply resentful of each other. Norman implied more than once that Martha's suffragette associations and ideas about women taking their lives into their own keeping had influenced Madeline at an impressionable young age and made a rebel out of her. Adding to this aggravation were Madeline's own accusations. She insisted that her mother had failed to live up to the high ideals of equality and freedom that she had preached to her students.

Trapped between two faultfinders questioning the core ideals of her life, Martha felt extremely ill-used. How could her ideas be belittled in this manner by Norman and Madeline when they had been hurled into the chaos of another country, another continent that functioned with entirely different precepts and rules? Martha could not possibly have raised Madeline for a world whose existence she had had little idea of till a year ago. Taken out of its natural time and place, everything became questionable.

Martha maintained that Norman should have known better than to insist on their coming to India and exposing their young daughter to the dangers of an alien land, full of exotic influences. Now not only had Madeline lost her heart to a local boy but Martha herself had caught some strange bug which could well be the death of her.

Norman had always felt great pride in the life he had built for himself in India. While he had been happy to defer to Martha's wish to stay on in England for the sake of her lofty ambitions for Madeline's education, his patience had finally worn thin. He had lived more than his fair share of years alone, providing for a family without expecting anything in return. The admiration and willingness to adapt he had hoped to see in Martha had been almost completely absent over her visit to India. The sympathy he had felt for her illness started getting tinged with some rancour, a belief that she had brought it upon herself with her attitude to the country, rigid and unaccepting of its many gifts, blind to its beauty.

The rancour seeped into Norman's relationship with Madeline too. Norman had never envisaged being in such an adversarial relationship with his only and dearly beloved child. When Madeline refused to engage with him, labelled him as the worst kind of bigot, and accused him of racial prejudice, class discrimination and a misuse of authority, it broke his heart. Norman had never seen himself as an insufferable member of the ruling race in India. Some of his compatriots undoubtedly were high-handed and arrogant. Norman did not count himself in their number. He had always had Indians amongst his good friends and had deliberately sought out their company. His deep passion for Indian medieval architecture had made him plead the case for the protection and conservation of monuments with the highest authorities in the Raj. His junior engineers all held him in high esteem as a fair and just boss. Even his treatment of Azeem, all said and done, had ensured that the boy's career had not been permanently derailed. To have Madeline judge him so harshly left him not just resentful but aching and wounded.

Yet, try as he might, Norman could not see himself condoning his daughter's marriage with Azeem. And that, it seemed, was what Madeline still wanted.

FEBRUARY, MARIAM HOPED, would be kinder than January had been. The first clusters of verbena and phlox, so painstakingly planted by Ram Deen in November, had begun to raise their bright faces to the sun on either side of the path from the gate.

The fog had receded at last, and the days shone softly again. Mariam had asked Madeline if she would like to go out walking by the riverside, but Madeline had turned her down each time. It saddened Mariam to think that she had lost Madeline's friendship and trust. She wished she could do something for the family, make them feel closer to each other. The little attentions she paid to their food—a favourite soup or pudding served more frequently—and to the fresh arrangement of flowers in their rooms seemed to bring little cheer to them. Scarcely a nod in notice, if that. There was so little Mariam herself had to offer, given that she was feeling sallow and hopeless. Only her nightly reading of the Bible brought her some comfort.

One evening, as the family sat in the parlour, Mariam knocked tentatively and walked in. If her faith held her up, maybe it could help them too.

'May I sing something for you today?' she asked. 'I only know how to sing hymns, but Madeline used to like listening to them once.'

Martha stared moodily into the distance. Madeline looked up from the book she had been reading and gave Mariam a questioning look. Madeline knew Mariam well enough to be aware that it would have taken her all her courage to walk in and make this odd request. She wondered what Mariam's motivation was.

The awkward silence was finally broken by Norman. 'Yes, thank you. That will be a nice change. Please go ahead,' he said, politely.

Mariam had chosen what to sing after great thought. This hymn had seen her through moments of great personal turmoil and sorrow. It had been a balm to her grieving soul in times past.

She began tentatively:

'Abide with me: fast falls the eventide
the darkness deepens
Lord, with me abide ...'

Mariam's sincere, convent-trained voice filled the parlour. She sang with her eyes shut, her neck tilted up, the slightest hint of nervousness evident from the shaking of her hand where it rested on the armchair. Her voice rose higher with each successive stanza, ending in a long crescendo.

Hold Thou Thy cross before my closing eyes.
Shine through the gloom and point me to the skies.

Heaven's morning breaks, and earth's vain shadows flee;
In life, in death, O Lord, abide with me.

When Mariam came to a stop, she looked down at her feet in embarrassment. Perhaps she had been too forward. Just because the hymn had seen her through days when she had felt hollowed out and empty, it did not mean it would help the Evans in a similar manner.

A hush filled the room where her voice had been.

In the glow of the fire, Norman saw two tears roll down Martha's cheeks. Poor Martha, she was suffering. They were all suffering. Someone had to yield.

'Norman, please book our passage home,' whispered Martha hoarsely, as she caught him looking at her tears.

'Yes, my dear. It shall be as you wish.'

Norman had not wanted to make any bookings given the state of Martha's health. But it was just as well done now as later. She might recover at the prospect of returning where she belonged. However much as he may wish for it, she did not belong here.

Mariam got up to leave the parlour. Both Norman and Madeline's eyes trailed her to the door.

'How many more talents do you have hidden inside that phlegmatic demeanour, Mariam Das?' Norman thought to himself, as Mariam walked away softly, dressed in her plain, high-collared cotton gown, her dark hair knotted at the nape of her neck.

'Mariam,' said Madeline. 'Wait!'

Mariam turned to face her. Her cheeks were aflame with the discomfort of her sorry attempt at making the family feel better.

'I'll come walking with you tomorrow, after breakfast. If that's okay?' said Madeline. Mariam nodded gratefully. It had done something after all. A tenderness for Madeline filled her.

'Thank you, Mariam. That was very beautiful. And extremely thoughtful of you,' Martha said.

MADELINE AND MARIAM had been walking together almost every day since that evening in the parlour. Yet, their return to friendship was tentative. They often sat together in the evening in Madeline's room trying to find common ground, create some little space for agreement. Mariam sang hymns and psalms for Madeline at her request, and Madeline recounted for her stories from her favorite operas, breaking out every now and then into an aria, full of feeling.

They leaned on music to convey the nuances and depths of what each wished to tell the other. Conversation between them was not as unguarded or trusting as it had been before. They spoke of the past sometimes, remembering incidents from their days in Nainital but, by unspoken agreement, neither spoke of the future and how it might unfurl, what regrets each would carry forth when their time together ended.

Martha and Madeline's passage back to Southampton was booked from Bombay on 20 March, just a few weeks short of completing their year in India. Martha was still bilious, and the doctor had said he would not recommend a long sea voyage unless her health showed substantial improvement. But there was a doggedness to Martha, a determination to get well and be declared fit to go. She was convinced a change of air would do her good. She was also fixated on getting Madeline back to the safe environs of England—her belief firm that a healthy distance from India was just what Madeline needed to recover from her senseless infatuation.

With Martha and Madeline headed back to England, Mariam could foresee that her services would no longer be needed. She knew she should look for another position, but her heart was not in it. She did not want to be an ayah with yet another English family. It asked everything of one in terms of devotion and gave back only a pittance in return.

Yet, she also understood, and only too well, that she needed the money to send back to her parents and to save for her own future. She had to work. She was not trained for any other job. If she had worked longer here, stashed away a bit of her salary, she would have been able to train as a stenographer or a receptionist, and remove herself from a job that required living with a family, caring for them as her own, without having any claims on them.

'Mariam,' said Madeline, as they walked along the riverbank.

'Yes?' said Mariam.

'Will you walk with me to the ruins where Papa shot Azeem? I have not dared revisit the scene, yet revisit I must before I leave,' she said.

'Will it not be too painful for you, Madeline?' Mariam asked.

'No one can choose a life without pain, Mariam. We can only choose how to meet the pain. I would rather face it, my eyes open and looking, than flee, unaware of how the hurt will hit me again and again as I try to get away,' Madeline said.

Mariam reached out for her hand and squeezed it. They walked towards the monument. A rash of pigeons rose from the roof as they climbed up the four broad stone steps leading to the arched doorway.

Inside the twelve-pillared hall, with its broken dome and the smell of birds' droppings, Madeline stood reliving the afternoon with Azeem. Sunlight was playing on the sandstone floor, casting shadows of the arched columns, interspersed with the lace filigree pattern of the windows. Memories besieged Madeline—their whispers soft but urgent in their plea. Promises had been made that afternoon, a future planned. They were promises she would need to keep, a future she would have to find her way into, however impossible it seemed.

'This is where we were lying together, his body partly covering mine, his lips on mine, when Papa burst in and shot Azeem in the leg,' said Madeline at last. She looked young and vulnerable, her voice breaking with a sense of betrayal as she spoke.

'He did not know it was Azeem,' said Mariam, feeling an inexplicable urge to defend Norman. 'He thought you were being forced.'

'And afterward?' said Madeline, with an angry snort. 'After he knew it was Azeem and that I was not being forced, that I was here of my own accord to meet him? Did he behave like a fair and honourable man then? Or did he just abuse his position to banish Azeem to the back of beyond?'

Mariam was quiet. For the first time since the shooting incident, she had allowed herself to really think of Azeem. The Azeem who had sat with her on the bench under the pear tree at Oak Park with his copy of *Umrao Jaan Ada*, his voice measured and mellifluous as he read to them; the Azeem whose ink sketches and calligraphy danced on the margins of that well-thumbed book; the Azeem who had practised his English with Mariam after their lessons with Madeline to ensure that his grammar and diction were perfect, that he was making no errors; the Azeem whose horsemanship was splendid, almost magical, as he performed his gymnastic tricks with Raju at Snow View, the movements fluid and poetic against the majesty of the Himalayas; the Azeem who had sat beside her on thandi-sarak, chucking stones on the lake's surface, declaring that he knew better than to dream of a future with Madeline …

But he did not know better. He was now in exile in a distant cold desert.

Madeline watched the play of emotions on Mariam's face. Did she dare trust Mariam with her plans, did she dare to take the risk? For, if Mariam spoke of it to her parents, her hopes of making a getaway would be permanently squashed.

'Mariam, come sit with me outside on the steps, let's watch the river for a bit,' she said. She needed to be sure before she spoke.

A small peepal sapling was growing out of a crack in the wall of the ruin, its heart-shaped leaves green and fluttering with new life. Love was like that, Mariam thought to herself. What inhospitable terrain it took root in, how tenaciously it clung, how beautiful it looked as it defied pragmatism, as it took chances with life.

Madeline stared into the flowing waters of the Gomti. Time was going past swiftly. She could not keep sitting on the shore for fear of drowning. She would have to dive in; it was all or nothing. There was only a little over a month left for her departure from India. It was important to get the details of her ship and the travel dates to Azeem. He would need to get to Aden somehow, meet her there. Mariam was her only way of getting the message to him. She would have to take a chance.

'Mariam, that afternoon when Azeem and I met, we put together a plan to escape to America, build a new life there together. I need your help to get a message to him. Your brother works in the telegraph department, doesn't he?' she said, her eyes searching Mariam's for understanding.

'Your message will be seen by his seniors, will it not? He may get into yet more trouble, Madeline.'

'I will send it in a code we have agreed upon. No one else will be able to decipher it. Say you will do it, Mariam. Please,' said Madeline. 'You were our friend once. The only one I can hope understands our love, the only one I can ask for help. No one else will even begin to appreciate the strength of our feelings.'

Mariam looked towards the sapling growing out of the monument's wall. The monument was lifeless, a remnant of history, its time of power and glory past. Tender sap flowed in the veins of the sapling's green leaves. If some cruel hand did not pluck it out, the sapling could survive, even thrive. It could become in time a grand tree harbouring in its many branches whole civilizations—birds, bees, butterflies, squirrels, owls, countless other creatures. The monument was sad and full of dignity, it tugged at Mariam's heart with its melancholic pride. The sapling was life, begging for a chance.

Life.

'I will speak to my brother. I'll see what he can do to get your message to Azeem as quickly as possible,' said Mariam.

AZEEM

Baluchistan and Beyond

1906–07

AS HE WAS transported, under armed escort, from Jaunpur to Quetta, first by train, then by road, then by train again, Azeem found his grasp on reality turning elusive. He was hurtling too fast through successive bubbles of existence; the landscape, the food, the weather, the men escorting him all kept changing, one set yielding to the next before his mind fully registered their presence.

The prospect of Madeline's absence forever from his life, their rude, abrupt separation in the middle of a kiss in the most glorious, rapturous, hope-filled afternoon of his life had dislocated his heart, knocked it clean out of his chest. It throbbed now in the calf muscle where he was shot by Norman.

His ribcage had a gaping hole where Azeem's heart used to be. There were hollows beneath his smoldering eyes. His face was unshaven. His brows were taut with anger. His face was a play of light and shadow as he sat staring out of the barred windows of the train, chugging through the northern plains of India from east to west, its speed turning the landscape into white noise, the beauty blurred and drowned.

The guards nicknamed him Miyan Majnu after Laila's legendary lover, from the famous Persian folktale. As he changed hand from one set of guards to another, his legend grew. He was as handsome as a king, they said, the best horseman of his time. He was a dethroned prince from an independent northern fiefdom. He was an erudite scholar; he spoke six languages. A well-born English girl was desperately in love with him and had tried to kill herself to punish her parents for refusing to let her marry him. Truth and lies mixed and created around him a mystique, an aura of someone special, someone distinguished and refined by suffering into an otherworldly being. Someone to be talked about in hushed whispers.

Azeem was lost in his own thoughts, unaware of the conversations of his minders, of the stories they were telling each other over successive cups of hot tea in the morning and army ration rum at night.

If he was suddenly jolted into full consciousness, with a startling awareness of the world outside, it was as he embarked on the last stretch of the journey.

The passengers were moved out of the broad-gauge line at a small station called Hirok in the Bolan Pass of Balochistan. It was 1,400 meters above sea level, Azeem noted from the board at the railway station. The station itself was surrounded by dark, sombre, brooding mountains on all side. The Pashtun guards accompanying Azeem moved him to a narrow-gauge train that hurtled into a gorge, its walls dizzyingly steep. The train began a vertical climb that left Azeem in a spellbound daze and stopped at a station some 400 metres higher. As far as his eyes could see, there was snow. He had only seen snow-clad mountains from a distance before.

Azeem was transferred again to a broad-gauge line. The train made its way through a succession of tunnels and bridges to Khost, the last stop. As Azeem looked out of the window he wondered if this was the end of the world. Did it fall into nothingness from here? The cold chilled him to the bone.

The Baluchi regiment he was posted to was stationed between Quetta and Khost. The Prince of Wales had just been designated its colonel-in-chief, following his visit to India. There were men from all over the country stationed there, though more Pathans, Hazaras and Balochis were now being recruited. The regiment had distinguished itself in the Burma wars and more recently in suppressing the Boxer Rebellion in China.

The area was a hotbed of tension as Britain and imperialist Russia vied with each other for control over Central Asia. Azeem finally understood the inspiration behind the miles and miles of steel tracks laid out across steep chasms and gorges, and the tunnels and bridges that danced through a large, cold wasteland where nothing grew and only fierce, long-bearded tribesmen roamed. The railway had come here for military reasons, to transport men like him to their duty stations on the border.

There were no open hostilities on the front when he arrived there. Just a war against the brutal, blustering cold. The area was a semi-arid desert, there were no trees, nothing to shelter them from the howling wind. Hail pelted down upon the rooftops, exploding like gunshots. Flash floods were frequent as were landslides. One had to keep clearing the road so that essential rations and supplies could be delivered.

Camels, their faces stoic and older than the mountains, carried water, milk, potatoes, coal and logwood to the camp. In Azeem's head, camels were meant to live in undulating, never-ending stretches of golden desert sand. Yet, here they were, in this terrain of steep pastel cliffs and glistening white snow, carrying their daily load. Dry rations were kept in the stores, guarded by sepoys. There were few fresh vegetables, scarcely any meat.

The men of the regiment were issued gloves, gumboots and overcoats for outdoor use. The unit's uniform of red trousers, long rifle green shirts and turbans added colour to the dim interiors of the mess halls and canteens. The night belonged to oil lamps, rum, log fires and camaraderie.

Azeem sat at the edge of all the groups, all conversations. Punjabi, Urdu, Pashtun, Baluchi, Sindhi all tumbled and churned and became the sound of male bonding. There were songs, ribald jokes and bouts of arm-wrestling with bets laid.

It was a world devoid of women, its contours unyielding and harsh. There was no trace of femininity in sight. It was the world he had accepted unquestioningly till he had met Madeline. Now, thoughts of her haunted him constantly. He yearned for a whiff of her fragrance, a glimpse of her hazel eyes. He tried to recall the precise timbre of her voice, the tinkling melody of her laughter, the soft fabric of her dresses, the burn of her touch upon his skin.

He finally understood the true nature of exile. Exile was a world without women, without feminine grace, a vast uninterrupted expanse of maleness.

Exile was looking into the bleak mirror of life and finding no answering face inside.

THE OFFICER-IN-CHARGE OF the camp was an Anglo-Indian by the name of Captain Alfred Asghar Ali. The sepoys addressed him as 'Alfred sa'ab' and his British seniors in the headquarters called him 'Al'. His mother was an Englishwoman and his father a Muslim nobleman. When asked which faith he belonged to, Alfred was known to answer 'humanity'.

That he was a practicing member of his faith was clear from the concern he showed for the well-being of the men under him. Rations were distributed fairly, work dispersed equitably and in rotation, and there was no hint of favouritism in the ranks. The men idolized him with good reason. He was a tall strapping man with gentle eyes and a ready smile. Frequently kind, always just.

Alfred Asghar Ali had a practice of joining his men around the campfire on many nights. He did not participate in the singing, the games or the ribaldry. Instead, he singled out a sepoy and sat at a small distance from the main group to talk to him and enquire about his family, his home, his health.

He understood well how this brutal terrain—with harsh cliffs and steep gorges, with little vegetation and scarcely a few blades of grass, with extremely hot summers and freezing winters—could impact the mental health of men unused to such climes. Battle fitness was only half about physical training, the other half was a stable mind. He talked to the boys in rotation, offered comfort and courage when needed, and looked out for early warning signs that a man was heading for trouble, becoming depressed and suicidal, or manic and murderous.

Captain Ali singled out Azeem more often than some of the others. He knew the boy's history, the circumstances that had brought him here. Azeem's sombre, silent persona intrigued him. He was as rugged and brooding as the mountains that surrounded them. The captain searched his eyes for signs of suppressed rage or madness, something to suggest that the man might cause himself or anyone else harm. He saw nothing but a phlegmatic refusal to engage, a personality that had withdrawn inside a cocoon woven out of personal grief.

'Drink. It will keep you warm, help you loosen up,' he told Azeem as they sat together one evening by the fire. Azeem was looking especially drawn. Sadness added poetry to his fine features, a melancholia that spoke in muted tones. But it would not do to let him wallow in his sorrow endlessly.

Azeem nodded but didn't move.

'Go fetch me a tumbler of rum with hot water, and one for yourself too,' ordered Captain Ali.

Azeem got up, headed indoors to the mess, and returned carrying two pewter mugs containing rum.

They sat down in a silence more companionable for the presence of the warm mugs of amber liquor swirling inside. Around them was the animated conversation of men around the campfire, the fire casting a dance of shadows on the ground.

There was nothing to say. Words had deserted Azeem. His sense of exile was acute. But Azeem liked Captain Alfred Asghar Ali's face, with its subtly conveyed interest in him. He was grateful for it.

'May I have the job of looking after your horse?'

This was an infantry regiment. The sepoys didn't have horses. Only the captain had a beautiful greyish brown stallion for his use, and there were a few commonly held pack mules for transportation and sending post. Azeem missed being amongst horses. He missed their limpid dark eyes, their neighing and sighing, the comfort of their wordless allegiance.

'I'll put you on the job on the next rotation of duties. Bhura is a strong, mettlesome horse. He could do well with the care of an additional syce. You'll have my permission to take him out for his daily exercise,' said the captain.

The captain wished he had thought of it himself. He dwelt on the time after his father's death when the family's German Shepherd puppy had gently nosed out his hurt, healed him of his grief, brought him into feeling after a long spell of numbness. He hoped that Bhura could help where he himself was not making much headway, that the horse would thaw Azeem's frozen heart.

When Azeem had a chance to ride out in the rugged countryside, he felt more resolute, less defeated by life. His eyes started mapping possible escape routes, filing away scraps of information on the lay of the land, the hamlets and the landmarks in the vicinity. Even though it was only an imaginary exercise, his mind was stronger for it, his heart less afflicted.

It was mid-February when Madeline's telegram made its way to the camp and was given to him. His hand trembled as he stared at its brief, coded message. She had not forgotten, not given up on their plan. Now it was his turn to show his mettle. He had no time to lose if he was to meet her in Aden by the end of the following month. He had to reach there before her to meet her by the docks. He had to plan for their immediate escape, so she was not found and taken back on the ship. Did he dare to steal Bhura, did he dare to ride him across thousands of miles, here to there? It was his best bet to cross the mountainous passes. When he reached Baghdad, he could sell off the horse and use the money to make his way southwards till he reached Aden.

He began to map out his proximate route on Madeline's trusted atlas. It was still with him, the talisman that he had carried at the bottom of his overnight bag when he went to Jaunpur to see her.

Given the sensitivity of the region, nothing that came into the camp went further without being scrutinized by the camp in-charge. Captain Ali was puzzled by the message that Azeem received. It talked about Umrao Jaan Ada running away from Faiz Ali and joining Nawab Sultan at the end of March. The captain had never heard of Mirza Ruswa or his popular Urdu novel. His own education had been in English. His favourite author was Thomas Hardy. *Jude the Obscure* was his most beloved book. Perhaps Faiz Ali and Nawab Sultan were relatives of Azeem, but the missive alluded to a date. He decided to keep a strict watch on the boy.

He found that Azeem was purloining dry rations, water canteens, coal and matches. He was obviously planning a journey.

That night, Alfred Asghar Ali called the boy to the side to talk to him. 'Tell me about the English girl you loved,' he said.

The boy looked at him with mutinous eyes, his shoulders stiffening, the face bristling with a quick succession of emotions—anger, sorrow, confusion.

'Sometimes it helps to talk to another human being. You have nothing to fear from me,' said the captain, placing a gentle hand on Azeem's tightly rigid shoulders.

Azeem stared at him bleakly for a few moments and then began to talk to him of Madeline and of Nainital.

Alfred had spent his schooldays at St Joseph's Academy in Nainital as a hosteler. When Azeem told him his story, he could see it unfold before his eyes. He could see Norman Evans, the Public Works Department engineer, at his rest house in Ranibagh. He could visualize Martha Evans at the library on Mall Road and walking up the Ayarpatta hill past the Governor's House to meet the nuns at All Saints'. He could imagine the bench under the pear tree at Oak Park, he could see Madeline and Azeem riding to Cheena Peak, exploring Land's End and Snow View on horseback. He formed a picture of them holding hands at the solitary bench at Khurpatal. He could see Mariam the ayah, he could feel her heartbreak at the hands of an Anglo-Indian tutor called Clive, a weak boy who had the nerve to desire a girl from a different community but not the courage to marry her. He could visualize Mariam sitting with Azeem on thandi-sarak trying to steer him away from the kind of heartbreak she had suffered.

Alfred Asghar Ali felt he belonged inside of this story, had a role to play in it. If the boy was to make a getaway, he would need travel papers. Otherwise, he would be held at one of the many sneakily hidden check-posts beyond the Bolan Pass in the Afghanistan or the Iranian parts of Baluchistan and brought back to camp. As an officer of the British army, Captain Ali had a travel permit. Hostilities were at a low, he did not foresee a mission across the border for a few months at least.

When Azeem was declared an absconder from the regiment two days later and a look-out notice was issued at the border posts for him, no one knew that he travelled as Captain Alfred Asghar Ali, with valid travel papers. He was charged with the theft of his commanding officer's horse, dry rations and fourteen pounds in cash from the coal purchase account he had been handling.

The captain did not intend to report the loss of his papers just then. Perhaps he would report them damaged or destroyed in a flash flood or a fire a few months later and get a new set issued.

AZEEM STOLE OUT of the camp in chill pre-dawn darkness. He had already smuggled supplies out a day earlier and had hidden them on the road ahead. The moon was down, the stars paling, a hint of light breaking in the east as he unobtrusively took Bhura and rode towards Kolpur, using the railway tracks to navigate his way out till Chaman and into Afghanistan.

The road through the pass was on the bed of a mountain torrent, particularly dangerous with snow melting at this time of the year. It was composed of loose shingly gravel on which the horse could slip and be hurt.

Azeem rode through rocky chasms, the dark hills closing in on the road at times, the path steep and perilous. He remained cautious, keen not to attract any attention from robbers, border guards or fate.

The terrain beyond belonged to fierce Marri Baloch tribesmen. Silent, grim and oftentimes armed with rifles, they watched him from the distance as he approached human habitation. The men were hawk-eyed, eagle-beaked, with jet black hair and moustaches curling up to thin, menacing points. Their loose-fitting attire in shades of camel and beige merged into the coffee-coloured hills they inhabited. They waved him on after they were satisfied that he was no threat, merely a solitary, unarmed traveller riding west with valid identity papers.

In contrast to the Marri Baloch men, the Pashtuns he met on the road to Kandahar were boisterous, garrulous people. He was reminded of his childhood in distant Rannpur as he sat down on a rug with a group of caravanners and ate out of a large communal vessel. Hoary old men with flowing beards and winged eyebrows called him a madman when they found out he was riding to Baghdad. They threw back their heads to laugh at him and poked him in the ribs with long, bony fingers, asking him if he was for real. They dug into their wooden crates and offered him the choicest pomegranates and apples to carry. They gave him big lumps of brown sugar to feed the horse. They took him to a stream to refill his water canteens. Last, they warned him of the danger on the road ahead, of getting caught in the crossfire between two warring factions.

On the road from Kandahar to Persia, Azeem almost lost his life. He had lit a small fire at the back of a narrow cave, among the rocks, to cook himself a meal. There was no wind, and the stars were just emerging. He rolled out his blanket and fell off to sleep. The horse was inside the cave with him. As he dozed, the wind rose and filled the mountainside with a moaning sound. The horse began to whinny and stamp. Azeem woke at the sound and saw the entrance to the cave filled with dark, menacing shadows. Aiming rifles at him were five turbaned Pathan men, their faces scowling, their eyes murderous.

The smoke rising from the fire he had lit had alerted them to his presence. Azeem held his hands up high to show that he was unarmed and wanted peace. The horse looked as if it might try to bolt in fear. Panic filled Azeem; it felt like the situation was out of his control. If he reached out to steady the horse, the men would misunderstand his movement and shoot him. If he didn't, he would be left without any means of getting away.

Suddenly one of the men pointing the rifle at Azeem emitted a gut-wrenching howl and fell to the floor. Blood gushed out of him. He had been attacked by another group of men, seven or eight of them, carrying daggers. The rival faction had also seen the smoke from the fire.

In the ensuing melee, as the warring tribes settled old scores, Azeem gathered the bag with his travel papers and a water canteen and led the horse out. He hurried to make his escape.

'Oh, Madeline!' he whispered to himself as he tried to put as much distance as was humanly possible between himself and the blood-drenched cave. Somewhere behind him a gunshot rang out and ricocheted over the mountains. It exploded again and again in waves.

In Persia, the terrain was gentler—a vast panorama of rounded foothills, silver streams, emerald grass and small trees. The sky above was cerulean, and a few hawks wheeled, swooped down and rose sharply again.

Azeem travelled faster now, anxious to get to Aden in time. He bought food in the villages along the way and preferred to sleep in the open to avoid questions. The walls, domes and minarets of ancient ruins in the distant horizon seemed wraithlike.

In Baghdad, Azeem sold off the horse, even though he was reluctant to part with Bhura. The animal had been his comfort and strength over the preceding days. But the desert journey ahead would be lethal for the horse, who had already done too much too fast and was worn to the bone. As was Azeem.

However, he could not stop. There wasn't enough time.

He bought a passage on a camel caravan to Riyadh. They traversed the mud plains of Mesopotamia, the swollen muddy waters of the Tigris on one side and of the Euphrates on the other. The camels moved surprisingly fast across the endless brown flats. They passed villages of brown mud houses, brown donkeys, brown people, brown clothes. Everything seemed fashioned out of the same clay.

In the desert, the camel caravans journeyed by moonlight to minimize exposure to the heat. No matter the hour of travel, everything shimmered. At night, the sand shone under the stars, and by day, dust-storms, filled with a hazy heat, took Azeem along the road to Riyadh. A bewildering desolation filled his head.

At last, Azeem reached Aden, after seven weeks of relentless travel from the snow-capped mountains of Baluchistan to the scorching red cliffs at the tip of Arabia. He waited at the docks, gathering news of the steamer ship due in from Bombay.

'Come, Madeline, come,' he whispered.

She had called him. He was here. She must come now.

HE HAD READ about Aden from the travels of Ibn Battuta. Some six hundred years later, this port in Yemen on the Indian Ocean was as inhospitable as the fourteenth century traveller had described it being—a bleak, waterless, baking hot peninsula, angry and ugly, surrounded by scorching red cliffs, with no vegetation. There were reservoirs cut out of the rocks to store rainwater. Aden lay halfway between Bombay and Suez. Shipping lanes branched out in all directions. By the piers, there were sky-high stacks of coal. Steamships stopped for a few hours to refuel their coal, and travellers were allowed ashore to buy trinkets and postcards to send to family and friends.

Azeem stood, hidden from view, staring at the gangway, willing Madeline to alight from the ship. He had been waiting for the last three days, his anxiety mounting as there were rumours of sea storms in the Indian Ocean. What if something happened to her en route? The perils he had survived, the hostile precipices he had ridden through in the dead of the night, the chaos he had navigated after being caught between warring tribes, all of this would be to no avail should she not turn up. In fact, his whole life would be devoid of meaning, stranded here in the middle of nowhere.

A small group of passengers began to alight.

Was she there?

He spotted her.

She was walking with a slow, awkward gait.

But she had come, she was here!

As the passengers were escorted beyond the dockyards, he could hear her talking loudly.

'It is such a pity, captain, that we cannot make a trip to the reservoirs right away. I am so curious to see the Queen of Sheba's water tanks.'

Her voice was high-pitched. She was hoping it would carry to Azeem if he were in the vicinity.

'Where did you say we are going now? To the shops at Steamer Point? I hope to buy a whole stack of postcards for my Mamma. She was meant to be on this voyage, but her jaundice took a turn for the worse and the doctor forbade her from travelling.'

She was alone! Had she been ill too? There was something strange about the way she was walking, too laboured.

She managed to finally detach herself from her group in the bustling downtown bazaars of Crater.

And Azeem revealed himself, stepping out from the shadows and into the open street. Madeline's face lit up. He signalled to her to follow him into a side alley.

'You are here!' they said to each other simultaneously.

They stared, enraptured, tracing with their eyes the changes their time apart had etched on their faces. Each was older, somewhat worn down by the experiences and stresses of the time since that fateful Christmas. Travel-worn and tired too.

They dared not touch each other. An Oriental man and a white woman in a side alley of a busy bazaar in Aden were enough to draw unwanted attention even as they stood a discreet distance apart, merely talking in muted voices. They must move fast. Before Madeline's group missed her.

Azeem traced his way to a small room he had rented in the older Arab quarter of the port. Madeline followed at a distance. She was almost fainting with the heat. She was wearing multiple layers of clothing as she could not have carried a change of clothes without arousing suspicion. Her handbag was heavy with packets of biscuits, tin cans of tuna, baked beans and soups that she had been secreting away from the start of the voyage. Now Azeem had an explanation for the awkward heaviness of her gait.

Leaving her in the room, he rushed to buy for them both Arab tunics and headscarves. If they merged with the local populace, they would be able to pass undetected through the crowds. It was good that Madeline had carried food. The less they interacted with people in Aden, the less likelihood they had of being traced.

They made their way to the yards at Ma'alla and caught a dhow to Egypt. To onlookers, here was an Arab tradesman and his young wife, covered in a black cloak from head to toe.

Madeline and Azeem stayed in Alexandria for over a fortnight. They worked their way through the city's underbelly, searching for a means of getting another set of travel documents, so they could get to Lisbon, and from there cross the Atlantic on a steamer to New York. Madeline's name and description could already be on a watch-out list. They dared not take the risk of her travelling as herself.

In the teeming bazaars of Alexandria, one early morning, Azeem heard a man singing 'Ek Onkar Satnam' to himself. Punjabi was a language many men of the 130th Balochi Regiment spoke. The chant was familiar to Azeem from Sunday mornings in the camp when the Sikhs in the battalion gathered to pray. The turbaned man whom the voice belonged to turned out to be an unlikely settler in Egypt. Subedar Jarnail Singh was an ex-army man who had fought on behalf of the British in the Boer Wars in South Africa. Wounded and dispirited by war, he had taken advantage of his missing-in-action status to begin a new life in this port city.

Jarnail Singh made a living selling dried figs and apricots. He woke up early each morning from his makeshift shelter near the Citadel of Qaitbay and walked to the main market nearby. He bought a sack each of figs and apricots at wholesale rates and a large bundle of leaf bowls. He settled down on the pavement outside the bazaar and proceeded with quiet concentration to apportion the contents of the two sacks into the small bowls. He placed them, filled with small servings of figs and apricots, in neat stacks in two baskets, placed one basket on either shoulder and then proceeded to walk through the streets of Alexandria calling out, 'Figs-figs, apricots-apricots, only for you,' in a deep, strong voice. His daily route took him into the smaller souks and lanes, past all the four main mosques and finally to the dockyard and the beaches.

He returned home with tired muscles, his baskets empty and his pockets full. He kept his earnings in his old tin army trunk that lay carelessly on one side of the awning he sheltered under. Jarnail Singh had picked up his trade a few months after he washed up on the shores of Alexandria, with a war-weary soul and a catatonic gaze unable to forget the bloodshed he had seen. An aged dry fruit seller had hired him to walk behind him carrying the baskets of figs and apricots, as the load was heavy and the seller well past his prime. When the old fig-seller died, he had carried on plying the same trade, along the same well-worn route through the city. He said that he thought of it as a service to god, bringing his sweet, nourishing wares to those who needed them. It calmed his body and mind, brought peace to his spirit.

'I have been puzzled. Why has god been showering an old man like me with such largesse? I have no expenses to speak of and no desires left to fulfil in this life,' he told Azeem. 'Now, I know his plan. It is meant for you and your bride.'

With Subedar Jarnail Singh's help, they got a set of false travel documents. The agent they approached was satisfied with the documents Azeem was carrying. The Alfred in his name, the stamp of the British India army on his identity documents would serve him well. Azeem retained Alfred Asghar Ali's name. For Madeline, he created an offer of employment as a governess for a New York-based family. Madeline took her friend Rose Eliot's name. She felt Rose would be happy to have her use it for the purposes of a romantic escapade of this order. Despite their protestations, the old subedar insisted they take his entire savings. He had no use for the money. It would give him great happiness to think that it would buy them a passage to New York and some resources to set up Azeem in a trade.

'When the old fig-seller died, he left behind a mattress full of silver and copper coins in the ruins of the citadel. You will give his life and mine meaning, bring our souls joy, if you allow us to participate in creating your new life in the new world you are journeying to. Take it, take our blessings, prosper as love such as yours deserves to.'

It was Lisbon where Madeline and Azeem—now Alfred and Rose—stopped before moving on to New York. The city was vast and sprawled across seven mountain terraces; many centuries of history existed simultaneously in its folds. Multicoloured houses with balconies, old, weathered cathedrals and bustling markets full of fish, fresh fruits and vegetables were everywhere, and amidst it all, a recently built tramline carrying people over the vast distances in the city. Fisherwomen in long black skirts and baskets on their heads walked narrow streets, melancholic music flowed out of cafes, and quaint, crescent-shaped boats with black hulls and pink sails lined the harbour.

Quartered in a small room in the old Alfama neighbourhood, Madeline and Azeem waited to secure their passage to New York. From the small, overhanging balcony of their room, they could see the red tiled roofs of the city spread out below them, and in the distance, the vast Tejo river as it made its final journey into the embrace of the Atlantic. Now that they were in Europe, they finally felt safe. They could discard the garb of the Arab trader and his wife that they had worn since Madeline had landed in Aden. She was not sad to bid goodbye to the long black tunic and the netted veil covering her head and face, though it had served its purpose well. There was a strange thrill to buying smart new Western clothes for their new life together and scouring the city for the best bargains for dresses, shirts, pantaloons, shoes and hats.

Walking up and down the steep, winding, cobblestone streets with Madeline, Azeem felt unreal, like a person out of a storybook, not the flesh and blood creature who had walked about in his shoes a year ago. They were in a city founded and named after Ulysses, the hero of Homer's *Odysseus*. Here, Ulysses had stood, on the brink of the known world; soon, he would venture westwards, sailing across the Atlantic and into the unknown.

One night, as Azeem read out aloud the last few pages from *Umrao Jaan Ada* to Madeline, her head resting on his lap, the star-filled Lisbon sky twinkling outside their window, he mused if the difference between people and stories was so great after all.

'We're all walking tales, aren't we?' he said to her, his index finger twirling around an errant lock of her hair spilling out of the loose knot she had tied with a red ribbon.

'What do you mean?' she asked, emerging reluctantly from the dream state his reading voice had taken her into; her mind had been lost in the poetry and music of Umrao Jaan's life.

'Ulysses, Umrao Jaan, you and me, everyone who is born and walks this earth is an unfolding story. Some stories are written and recited and recalled over the centuries, some are known only for a time to the few people in their immediate surroundings.'

'It's an utterly charming idea!' she exclaimed, her eyes suddenly awake again, alive to his thoughts. 'Our world is a coming together of millions of narratives. Every time a human being is born, a wholly new story is born—for our lives are our stories. But Azeem, who then is the storyteller?'

'God? Time? No, wait, perhaps we are, each of us, both the story and the storyteller. Life happens to us all in unfolding moments and events. But without words to describe happenings, there can be no narrative. Our lives become our stories in the words we use to tell them to ourselves and to others. There would have been hundreds of courtesans in Lucknow at one time, but there was only one Umrao Jaan. She picked the words that became the story of her life.'

'I like the thought. You and I are just embarking on the story of *our* lives. Let us promise that we will make it the best we can. There will be challenges and difficulties, hardships and struggles, for no life is without those. But we will choose our words, set the tone of our tale. Let us agree to make it a fable of adventure and romance. Let us ensure it comes with a happily ever after.'

Madeline decided they should book their passage to America as separate individuals and not a couple travelling together. It was very likely that the Bombay steamer's captain had filed a missing person's report for Madeline Evans with the harbour police at Aden. Her aunt and uncle, who were to receive her at Southampton, could well have filed another one there. If news of Azeem's desertion from the Balochi Regiment reached Norman, the family would piece the story together and there would be look-out notices for a runaway couple.

'I think it would be good if we travelled first class, since we now have the means to do so. Let us give our story a dream start. You can pretend to be a prince of some sort. It wouldn't hurt, really, to be a rich Indian prince with business interests in America. And I could be a lowly English governess in impoverished circumstances, making her way to America to work with a wealthy family. I shall be a perfect Cinderella to your dashing prince, a damsel imminently in need of rescue from a life of drudgery. Everyone loves seaboard romances. Those in the vicinity will be glad to help it blossom. We will enact a great, moving courtship drama for them. If we're lucky, there might even be a clergyman aboard to marry us,' said Madeline.

'For you, I'll become anything,' he laughed. 'Even a prince.'

For just a moment, his face clouded over with the thought of a boy called Azeem who would cease to exist. Then he drew Madeline into his arms, and it did not seem like such a terrible thing.

Prince Alfred Asghar Ali was ready to woo his English Rose.

SERENA

Los Angeles

2015

SERENA STREEP FELT a huge discontent simmer through her being. Her partner Alex had left the morning papers, along with her coffee, by her bedside and ducked in for a quick shower, before leaving for the day's shoot. Alex, fifteen years her junior, had recently hurtled into mega-stardom courtesy his role as a brooding, dysfunctional detective in an HBO series, while her own career was finally heading into a pale, whispery sunset. She was content with this reversal of roles.

She turned to the society pages with an inward groan. She knew that LA's supplements would recount her seventy-fifth birthday party. There was a picture of her, covering almost a quarter of the broadsheet. She stood at the centre of the large, extravagantly lit hall, resplendent in her long, black dress, stylishly slit to the thigh, and impossibly high heels, a champagne flute in one hand, the other flung out in animated conversation, a ring flashing on each finger. Surrounding her were throngs of people, listening with great attention, their eyes shining with interest.

'Iconic actress, singer, songwriter, businesswoman and humanitarian turns seventy-five,' the supplement read. 'Before moving to the West Coast in her fiftieth year, Ms Streep had an illustrious career spanning twenty-five years as an editor at Alfred A. Allye, a publishing house then largely owned by her family. A bitter disagreement with the senior management led to a parting of ways. The publishing world's loss became the entertainment world's gain as Ms Streep (then Ms Walker) moved from NY to LA to star in a film by director Stanley

Streep. The actor–director duo got married during the filming of *Agatha Einstein, Singer*—detailing the life of an embittered fifty-year-old divorcee whose prodigious singing talent was belatedly uncovered through *America's Got Talent*. Ms Streep separated from her husband in 1994 amid rumours of Stanley Streep's involvement with actress Rosemary Carter Moore. Ms Streep is currently in a relationship with *Doors of Perception* actor Alex Huxley, who is also partner and co-owner of their film production house, Selex Cinema.'

Who was this much acclaimed woman they wrote about and how exactly was she connected to the Serena who lived inside her head, forever young, always needing to prove herself? And why did they insist on raking up her connections with people and worlds that were nothing to her now? 'The past hasn't really passed if it bothers you still.' That was Alex's take on the matter. How had she got such a wise young beau? She'd lucked out with him, as with most other things in the latter part of her life. He'd been forty-five when they had first moved in together—then, as now, the more stable of the two, and much calmer.

'Serena, give yourself a chance to put it all behind you. Call her today. There's no Oscar for playing the best ostrich ever,' Alex called out to her as he let himself out of their home in Hidden Hills. She was free for the day. As good a time as any other to brood about her life and get overtaken by moodiness.

As good a time as any to take her head out of the sand.

She decided to go for a quick shower, instead of her usual extended and indolent soak in the bathtub, luxuriating in salts and aromatic creams, against a backdrop of soft classical music. She followed this up with mindfully creaming her body with various lotions and carefully brushing her long hair which she wore silver and straight. She had more time now than in her heyday for self-care regimens and herbal teas, and while she did not believe in striving to look younger, she did wish to wear her age with as much beauty and grace as she could muster.

Forgoing her lingering breakfast, she headed for the library and settled into the chaise lounge. She opened the envelope containing Sybil's letter and stared at it with a bemused expression. She had read her ex-husband Ben's wife's letter many times since it had arrived a couple of weeks ago. It wasn't clear to her why the letter should confuse and upset her as much as it had. It was not that she had been entirely unaware of the existence of her granddaughter. Sybil had continued to send Serena the family's annual Christmas–New Year newsletter after Ben's death. The family had grown, as families do. Arthur had become a lawyer like his father. He was married and had two children. She was happy for them, happy for the courtesy of being included in their list of family and friends. It was all entirely cordial but distant and had suited her perfectly.

This out-of-turn letter on a September morning, with its strange request, had left her feeling oddly bruised. A world that had washed its hands of her, told her it was best if they remained politely acquainted rather than intimately related, was now seeking to embrace her, draw her into a familial hug. Arthur's daughter, Tara, was enrolled as a freshman at the Theatre, Film and Television school at UCLA.

'Tara is eighteen, an intelligent and very intense young girl. She has idolized you greatly since the age of twelve. I think both her choice of course and college has everything to do with her admiration for you. She would really like to meet her "real" grandmother. I am sending you her phone number, and I hope you will find it in your heart to connect with and spend some time with her. She is a lovely young girl, and her need to reach out to you runs very deep. I hope you will accept her request. I know a rejection from you will hurt her terribly.'

'Alex!' she wailed when she first received the letter. 'I don't do "grandmother!"' Or mother. Or aunt. Or wife. She was largely a failure when it came to real world relationships. She had steadfastly refused to marry Alex though they had been together fifteen years now. Live-in partner was the best she could manage. And that too because Alex was most non-interfering, a little Zen monk of a human possibly from the moment he was born. His tolerance and generosity of spirit towards fellow human beings still left her in awe after all these years.

Alex was right. It would be beyond churlish to ignore Sybil's letter and not reach out to the girl. She felt the same flutter of nervousness in her ribcage that she had in her early days in Hollywood when she had been a stranger in this world, an odd debutante, an actress of mature years with not much prior experience, trying to behave as if she fitted in, belonged inside all the glitz and glamour. If it hadn't been for Stan's ardent romancing and championing of her, she would not have lasted in LA beyond a couple of weeks.

She picked up her mobile phone and dialled Tara's number. Calling at 11 a.m. on a weekday was perhaps not the best time to reach a young college student, but waiting till the evening was a sure-fire way of putting it off for yet another day. Expectedly, she hit Tara's voicemail.

'Hello Tara, this is Serena Streep. Your grandmother Sybil tells me that you are now studying in LA and would like to meet me. Please call me back when you can, so we can firm up when and where.'

Tara called back in the evening, her voice sweetly breathless. Serena had meant to take her out to a café in town but inexplicably wound up inviting her home on the weekend instead.

'That's my girl!' said Alex, kissing her on the forehead—which was his special mark of approval—when she told him. 'I'll stay upstairs, out of the way, but you can always call me down if you need rescuing.'

Tara showed up on Saturday morning, punctual to the minute. Except for her large, red-framed glasses, she could have been Serena's younger self walking in through the living room and into the sun-filled study. The same flowing honey-gold tresses, the same hazel eyes, the same long-legged, slender frame. She was simply dressed in blue jeans and a white kimono-style shirt, ankle high boots and a matching bag.

As she poured Tara a cup of coffee in her study, Serena felt her curiosity getting the better of her.

'Did you want to meet me because I'm a famous actor or because I'm your grandmother?'

Tara looked uncomfortable for a moment, the expression on her face uncertain and guarded. 'I don't know what answer you would prefer, but in my head the two come together—you've been my grandmother, the famous actor, since I first watched *Agatha Einstein, Singer.* I loved everything about the film, the songs especially. I read somewhere that you wrote and sang your own songs for the film. Is that true?'

'Yes, I suppose. They were written way before the film was made though. Stan had this film idea that he wanted us to do together.'

She had been at loose ends after leaving Pinnacle—and then, suddenly, there was her childhood school friend and long-ago sweetheart Stanley Streep knocking on her door at midnight with roses and a film offer. He was in New York, he had got her number from a common friend from their time together in Nashville, he was calling to ask if he could come over on his way to the airport. He planned to take the flight back to LA that very day, but now that he fortuitously had her number, he urgently wanted to discuss with her a film idea he had been contemplating for many years. They had been a couple in the late '50s and early '60s, a part of the Civil Rights Movement together, penning and singing songs of protest like many others of their generation. Stanley wanted to use their music from that time, in a film starring her as a beleaguered divorcee with a golden voice. *Agatha Einstein, Singer.*

'I must have been eleven or twelve,' Tara continued. 'There was a DVD in our family movie collection. Then

I found all your other films there as well and watched them one by one, getting progressively more smitten by you, by the idea of you and the fact that we are so closely related. You were stupendous in *Martha, Myself.* And oh my god, *Ordinary Evenings!* What a film!'

'All my DVDs are part of your family collection?' Serena asked softly, strangely touched and surprised.

'My father had them all,' said Tara with something of a frown momentarily shadowing her face. Her eyes narrowed behind the large red frames of her glasses.

'When my mother told me you were Daddy's mother, I was very excited at first. Then disappointed and angry that you had not kept in touch with him at all. There was no trace of you anywhere in his life. No letters, no gifts, no memories to share. I asked him why, and he said he had been very young when you had divorced, and Grandfather Ben had said it was better this way and he had done as his father wanted. Grandpa was already dead when I found out, so I could not interrogate him.'

'I … I … perhaps I was to blame, Tara. I wasn't much of a mother. Sybil was so perfect in every way that it just seemed right to withdraw my claims, get on with doing the things I was good at.'

Life had been good to Serena for the most part, everything had fallen easily into her lap. A loving family, the best education, a made-to-order dream job, a successful and handsome lawyer husband.

And then baby Arthur had come as a resounding challenge to her belief in herself and her abilities. From Day Twenty to the rest of her four-month maternity leave, he and his colic had declared a relentless war on her nerves and sanity. The baby was all flailing arms and legs and cries that shattered the quiet of the entire apartment block they lived in for hours on end. The harder she tried to soothe him, the louder he yelled. And then, to her utter chagrin, the moment Ben's mother who lived a few blocks away arrived and took him in her arms, he fell asleep, an angelic smile on his lips. Nothing in her life had made her feel so inadequate as that first experience of motherhood. She clearly lacked some natural instinct that other women had. It had been a relief to leave the baby with a competent nanny and return to the infinitely more responsive environment of Pinnacle Books.

'I don't understand it. How could you just withdraw like that? Didn't you feel any compulsion to know your son better?'

'Tara, I don't know what answer you'd like to hear from me. But this is how it happened. Your father seems to have done fine without me. And I went on with living my life. Perhaps, I should have done things differently. But I could only do them as I knew how to at that time. We'll all have to live with that, won't we?'

An awkward silence filled the room.

'I'm sorry. I did not mean to offend you,' said Tara, after many tense moments had passed. 'I forgot my manners. I hope I haven't completely blown my chance of getting to know you better.'

'Let me get you some cookies. Our housekeeper has a secret pecan nut and peanut butter recipe that she safeguards fiercely. They are very good.'

'These are utterly fabulous!' said Tara, when the plate arrived, polishing off three cookies in quick succession.

'Let me go call Alex. He'd love to meet you, I'm sure,' said Serena.

Alex arrived, full of cheer. Serena felt waves of affection flood her being. Some were born with the gift of being easy on the nerves, comfortable in all situations.

As Tara and he started talking to each other, animatedly shifting from one subject to the next, from the courses Tara had selected that term to Alex's many years of waiting tables before getting his first blink-and-you-miss-it part, to their favourite Serena Streep movies, Serena found herself relaxing. It was lovely to observe Tara. She was intense and articulate, not lacking in opinions and views, not shy to share them.

'So? Are you okay?' asked Alex, after they saw Tara off to the door. 'She's an entirely charming girl. Why did you need rescuing?'

'My mistake. I began all wrong, dived straight into the deep end, and she was quick to follow. It wasn't the smartest thing to do. I had to call you to help us keep the conversation afloat. I'm so glad you were there. You were perfect. Cool and casual.'

'Always glad to be your hero, darling. Will you be seeing her again?'

'I am glad we did this. I think I would like to see more of her.'

'That makes two of you then. She absolutely adores you.'

'She startled me. Asked me how I could have been so absent from my son's life. I got defensive. And now it feels like déjà vu. I remembered my younger self and how much grief I had given my dear old uncle Norm, constantly backing him into a corner and looking at him righteously.'

Alex laughed, 'I feel for the guy!'

'I'M GOING TO call you Therapist Tara from now,' said Serena with a laugh. 'I feel so healed and strangely put together after talking to you.'

'I'll send the bill by email. You can pay me in pecan nut cookies,' Tara laughed.

They met frequently now, as often as Tara's busy schedule at college permitted. Often, Serena drove across, picked her up from college, took her out for a meal and dropped her back. The time when the city traffic put Serena into a foul mood was long forgotten; not even a trace memory of that once major irritant in her life remained. She looked forward to the drive now, the classical music from her car stereo filling her up, the thought of seeing Tara bringing a laugh to her heart, a smile to her face.

Talking to Tara had the strange effect of making Serena feel more reconciled with her life's trajectory, even the failures and heartbreaks. As if telling Tara about her life made the disparate pieces fall into place, all the jagged and uneven bits fitting into each other to create a larger picture that was whole and complete, breathtakingly beautiful even.

'How did you do it!' exclaimed Tara. 'One day you were a reputed editor in a publishing house in New York and the next day you simply packed your life up in a single suitcase and moved across the country to make a fresh start as an actor in a place no one knew you. Were you not terrified?'

'I think I was more terrified of staying on in New York with its constant reminders of everything I had lost—my job, my marriage, my son, my friends, one by one, due to my own preoccupation with work. I was unhinged from my moorings and had lost my sense of who I was and understanding of what truly mattered to me and what didn't. When Stanley landed up at my door well past midnight with his crazy idea, I felt like a criminal on death row suddenly sent word of a last-minute pardon. He and I had lost touch decades ago, and out of the blue, there was my first real sweetheart, a successful Hollywood director in his own right, offering me a part written with me in mind. There was this stash of songs I'd written and performed in local clubs and in street marches in the early '60s in Nashville. He hadn't forgotten my singing voice, the songs, us. It felt like love and a new chance at life were being offered to me.'

A troubled silence fell at the café table as Tara recalled what she had read about the bitter parting between the two within eighteen months of their marriage. Tara stretched out a tentative hand to cover Serena's, squeezing her palm gently for a moment. It had happened twenty years ago, and yet the person in front of her showed tiny flecks of hurt in her eyes.

'Don't look at me like that, poppet,' Serena laughed. 'It doesn't matter now. Back then I felt like a big fool. I hated the humiliation and the scandal. I had given Stanley

Streep a second chance to break my heart, and he broke it without a thought. The irony of it is that both times he left me for women who were just like me. Estella Vaz, whom he cheated with that first time, was a singer too, part of our bunch of songsters and protesters. Rosemary Carter Moore you know of, of course. He just liked the highs of romancing someone better than the steadfastness of possessing them.'

'Let me get this,' said Tara, as their meal concluded. She walked to the counter and cleared the bill for their lunch. 'It's such glorious weather, let's take a walk in the park down the street.'

It was the perfect time to be outdoors. The jacaranda trees were flush with flowers—the warm weather this year perfect for a second blossoming over fall. The city looked ethereal, the pavements and park grounds carpeted with fallen violet and deep blue blossoms. The skies a cloud of dark blue flowers, as though a gathering of Disney princesses were tossing their curly tresses.

They walked in silence as the paved pathway curved along the perimeter of the park. The sound of the traffic turned dull, its harshness absorbed by the greenery. Close, there were mourning doves, co-aahing in the bushes, and red-tailed hawks screaming and calling out to each other in the upper branches of the trees. Picnickers were chattering on blankets laid out by the water body. A group of college students played with a bright yellow frisbee on the greens, their shouts of excitement rising from time to time. Where had she read that silence was not an absence of noise but a quality of mind, Serena wondered. Tara, with her wide, wise eyes brought her closer to the quiet she sought.

'When your grandfather left me for Sybil it did not hurt so much as Stan's betrayals,' she offered.

'Is it because you loved Stanley Streep more?'

Serena halted in her tracks and turned to look at Tara, trying to understand her question.

Was there such a thing as more or less love? Wasn't love quite simply love, the tumultuous surging of hormones beneath the surface of the skin? Sometimes the tumult passed quickly, at other times it transmuted, the frenzy turning to calm.

'I think it was because Sybil was so different from me ... I understood Ben's leaving me better. I didn't take it as a complete betrayal. It seemed like our marriage *truly* hadn't worked for him. It felt honest to end it before it became bitter,' Serena replied.

'And Alex?'

Serena threw back her head and laughed. The afternoon sun washed over her, lighting up her face softly. Silver hair, golden skin, the deep rose of the silk fabric of her kaftan-style dress against her neck, a set of perfect white teeth. She looked at Tara with an expression of absolute glee.

'I'm so lucky to have him! And I'm not asking, "Why me?" We've been together fifteen years. Longer than either of my two marriages.'

'You don't like the idea of marriage anymore?'

'You know what the problem with marriage is, Tara? It doesn't wholly belong to the two people marrying each other. It's an institution owned by society. It comes with vows that are given to the couple, expectations that are hardwired into them across generations. It carries with it too much historical baggage. There is no fresh ground for a new marriage to stand on, the entire territory has been mapped out, claimed, bombed, excavated … a labyrinth underneath the surface.'

'I wouldn't know,' said Tara mildly. She was looking pensively into the distance, where the mallards were swimming along the water's edge, the mottled brown and orange colours of the brown-beaked females a perfect foil for the green heads, white collars and yellow beaks of the males. 'Surely, there is something to marriage, some purpose, some beauty?'

'Oh, but of course. You must learn to ignore me in my more jaded moments. I realized a very long time ago that the same life could seem blessed or wretched to me depending on which side of the bed I woke up from. The exact same event could be read as a success or a failure in my mind based on my mood. I do understand now that my marriages to both Ben and Stan were essential to the unfolding of my life. Without Ben in the past, there would have been no Tara today. Without Stan, no Alex, because I would not have been here, an actress.'

Tara smiled.

'Now, I'd better head back home. Alex said he'd be back early-ish.'

'Have you given any further thought to coming to New York for Christmas?'

'I … it's very kind of Sybil to invite me … but…' A strange, inchoate fear and longing stopped Serena mid-sentence. Her son. His wife. Her other grandchildren. Was it even possible to try and belong within a normal, wholesome family after being an outlier for so long?

Tara waited patiently for Serena to continue.

'We'll discuss it over Thanksgiving. Alex is so looking forward to having you over for the break, and there is something I would like to show you then. Something very precious. Things I got from my grandparents when I was your age.'

'COME, LET ME show you what I've been saving up for the last,' said Serena. Thanksgiving was over, the all too brief break was about to end soon. Tara would be heading back to campus the next day.

Serena glided towards the library, beckoning Tara to follow.

Tara entered and found her eyes taking in once again the beauty of the sun-filled room with its high-domed ceiling, its skylight and beautiful plant collection. The plants were arranged like living statues across the tiled floor and its many deep windows. This space was more a study than a library—there were only two tall floor-to-ceiling bookcases against the wall at the end of the room. Diagonally opposite, near the entrance, was a beautiful wood and glass display case. Serena was standing in front of this, waiting for Tara.

'See!' she stretched her arm out to point towards the show cabinet. An amethyst ring shone on her index finger, matching the teardrop-shaped amethyst crystals in her earlobes and her soft lilac pants. Set proudly in the cabinet were collectors' editions of the 'Tales from Around the World' series, carrying the line, *Life is a story we tell ourselves,* and the logo of a man and woman riding into the mountains. Lying next to them were two very rare books of even greater antiquity—an atlas and a copy of *Umrao Jaan Ada.* She had had a book conservator restore them and set them out in the display unit along with the vinyl recordings of Azeem's story in Alfred's voice. The tale of how the old English school atlas and the Urdu novel came to be with her was one she had shared with Tara during this vacation, having declared their time together as Family History Week. She watched silently now as her granddaughter carefully lifted and turned the pages, peering at it with gentle concentration before exhaling deeply.

'Wow!' said Tara, running her hand reverentially over the volume. 'Is it okay if I spend the rest of the day in this room?'

'Of course,' Serena replied. 'This drawer here has the jotters I told you about, with notes I had taken as I sat beside Granma Rose in hospital. Be here for as long as you wish. I'll bring you a tray for supper in case you remain ensconced here for a while.'

Tara was sitting in a pool of lamplight, studying the handwritten notes, when Serena came in with a supper tray for her. She set it down gently on the table. Tara looked up startled as the aroma of the housekeeper's signature seafood chowder and meat pie rose to her nostrils. She took in Serena's presence—the glowing translucence of her ageing skin, the shimmering silver of her hair, the poise and mesmerizing beauty of her body.

'Was your grandmother as beautiful as mine?' she asked Serena.

'Beautiful, am I now?' Serena laughed. 'We both have her colouring and her eyes. I wish she had lived longer. Maybe, then, I might have written the book she wanted me to. I sometimes feel I let her down. I did make a feeble attempt or two to write of her life … but it came to nothing. Her story confused me back then, disturbed me deep inside.'

'How so?' asked Tara. 'Sit down, won't you, while I dig into the chowder? I'm famished.'

'Remember, the 1960s asked us to raise flags of protest, to fight for dignity, to protest against racial injustice. But my grandparents were not vocal people in these matters. They kept their heads low and joined the mainstream, passing through life as unobtrusively as they could. It also rattled me a great deal … their silence. And that their silence worked in my favour. I grew up a rich, white girl in 1960s America—my mixed heritage forgotten.'

'Your grandfather …'

'There was no trace of Azeem in the grandfather I knew. There were only faint vestigial traces of foreignness left in him. He was an all-American man in every aspect of his life. It troubled me that Alfred A. Allye had acquiesced so totally in the erasure of his origins. It was only after I started working at Pinnacle that I came to understand my grandparents better. I understood that though they let go of their past, they did reclaim the lost parts of themselves in the books they published, the work they did together, the space they created for different voices to be heard.'

Serena and Tara sat quietly side by side. The sight of Tara enjoying a meal made Serena feel the kind of deep, grandmotherly love she had once thought herself incapable of. She was glad she would be going to New York for Christmas.

'Thank you for telling me Madeline and Azeem's story,' Tara said, placing her hand on Serena's and letting it rest there. 'I feel as if I'm a different person for knowing it, as if my idea of myself has expanded and become borderless. This girl I know as Tara feels infinite suddenly, flowing from the beginning of time to the end. We are not ever simply ourselves, are we? So many bloodlines and lineages combine in us, so many tales of love, adventure, hope, survival and courage flow in our veins. Our story is unique, born of all the biographies time has written before we were even born.'

TARA

Los Angeles

2025

WHEN TARA WALKER stepped on stage amidst resounding applause to receive the Academy Award for best director for *Once Upon a Summer*, she created history by being the youngest and only the fourth female director in the nearly hundred years of the award's existence. When she walked on to the stage once again a few minutes later to collect the Oscar for leading actress for her portrayal of Madeline Evans in the film, she leapt with exultation and wept tears of joy.

'I dedicate this award to my very fabulous grandmother, the late Serena Streep, and to her grandmother, Rose Allye, the pioneering publisher whose story inspired this film. The women of my family have never hesitated to question the status quo, this I can proudly stand here and declare. This award is for Rose and Serena. Also, for Martha Evans, Mariam Das and Madeline Evans—without their courage of conviction, I would not exist or be standing here today.'

Author's Note

I CAME ACROSS the story of Madeline and Azeem on the Nainital Nostalgia group on Facebook in a post by Tariq Quraishi, an exceptionally gifted raconteur and a veritable storehouse of stories related to Nainital and its surrounding areas. There was something about it that captured my imagination, and I kept revisiting it in my mind, repeatedly drawn to the idea of writing a story capturing the romance of those times and the beauty of Nainital. Like many other people of my time, I was fortunate to spend my summer vacations in Nainital with my family as a child. I knew I was not alone in my yearning for that lost summer hill station of our past. Its magic lives on in the hearts of many.

I contacted Tariq bhai and asked if I could write a story using his post as inspiration. He confirmed to me that the characters of Norman, Martha, their exceptionally gifted daughter Madeline, the syce Azeem and the maid Mariam did indeed exist. Their story has been recorded in the memoirs of Sir Yusuf, Nawab of Jaunpur. Norman and Martha separated after their daughter's elopement, blaming each other for the event. In 1910, Martha received a letter from Madeline postmarked New York, informing Martha of her marriage to Azeem and of the birth of a son they named Norman, in honour of her father.

This is as far as the known story goes.

Acknowledgements

I AM GRATEFUL TO Padmini Smetacek, Saikat Majumdar and Smriti Vohra for their attention to and engagement with earlier versions of this book; Smita Khanna of Jacaranda Literary Agency for championing the manuscript; Dharini Bhaskar, my editor at HarperCollins India, for her faith in the book.

About the Author

Manjul Bajaj grew up in Lucknow. She graduated in economics from Delhi University and then did a master's degree in rural management and another in environmental science. She worked in the field of environment and rural development before she became a writer. She is the author of *Come, Before Evening Falls* (2010), *Another Man's Wife* (2012), *In Search of Heer* (2019), *The Book of Bullah* (2024) and *The Songs of Meera* (forthcoming). She has also written two books for children—*Elbie's Quest* (2013) and *Nargisa's Adventures* (2016). Manjul's work has been shortlisted for various literary prizes over the years. She currently lives in Goa with her husband, her two sons having flown the nest.